Welcome to the not-so-simple life

Meet Divine Matthews-Hardison
in Jacquelin Thomas's previous novel

SIMPLY DIVINE

"Jacquelin Thomas has created entertaining characters that you care about, in a page-turning story that's sure to touch lives."
—ReShonda Tate Billingsley, *Essence* bestselling author
of *Nothing But Drama*

"*Simply Divine* is down to earth and heavenly minded all at the same time. . . . It made me laugh and tear up. . . . Refreshing! Great job, Jacquelin!"
—Nicole C. Mullen, Grammy-nominated and
Dove Award–winning vocalist

More acclaim for the wonderful faith-based fiction of bestselling
author JACQUELIN THOMAS

"Touching and refreshing . . . a solid contribution to quality Christian fiction titles written by and for African Americans."
—*Publishers Weekly*

"Bravo! . . . Sizzles with the glamour of the entertainment industry and real people who struggle to find that precious balance between their drive for success and God's plan for their lives."
—Victoria Christopher Murray

"A fast-paced, engrossing love story . . . [with] Christian principles."
—*School Library Journal*

"Entertaining."
—*Booklist*

Divine Confidential is also available as an eBook

ALSO BY JACQUELIN THOMAS

Simply Divine

divine **confidential**

Jacquelin Thomas

POCKET BOOKS

New York   London   Toronto   Sydney

POCKET BOOKS, a division of Simon & Schuster, Inc.
1230 Avenue of the Americas, New York, NY 10020

ISBN-13: 978-1-4165-2719-0
ISBN-10:   1-4165-2719-2

This Pocket Books trade paperback edition February 2007

10   9   8   7   6   5   4   3   2   1

Manufactured in the United States of America

For information regarding special discounts for bulk purchases,
please contact Simon & Schuster Special sales at 1-800-456-6798
or business@simonandschuster.com.

For my nieces
Courtney, Camille & Larika

acknowledgments

As always, I have to thank my Heavenly Father for my gift of writing. With Him, all things are possible.

I have to thank my family for constantly being so supportive and putting up with the long hours of writing. I love you all.

I'd like to thank the National Center for Missing & Exploited Children and the Cyber Tipline for the mountains of information you shared to aid me in the writing of this novel.

Thanks to the many readers who read and fell in love with *Simply Divine*. It is because of you that I enjoy what I do and I am forever grateful for your support.

chapter 1

I spot Uncle Reed and Aunt Phoebe immediately, they were standing near the street entrance of the baggage claim in Atlanta. I walk over to them saying, "All right, the diva is here. Divine Matthews-Hardison is back."

I remove the strap of my loaded-down Gucci backpack from my shoulder, praying that I'm not left with a bruise because I intend on wearing my new halter top tomorrow that Mom bought me in Martinique. She's finally loosening up enough to let me wear halters. I'm fifteen and starting tenth grade soon. I had to tell her to get a clue—I'm growing up.

"You won't believe *what* I had to sit beside on the plane. He was like, so totally gross." Tossing my hair over my shoulders, I huff, "They let anybody buy a first-class ticket these days."

I stiffen, momentarily distracted by my aunt's neon-green shirt and matching pants that don't quite reach her ankles. They're wide-legged pants at that. My aunt stands almost six feet tall and—glowing in this outfit the way she is—people can't help but notice her. Here I am looking all fly and she's dressed like . . . I'm like totally embarrassed.

"Aunt Phoebe, you can't be going around here wearing stuff like this," I fuss. "I can't believe you actually wore this out of the house." Stealing a peek at my uncle, I ask, "Uncle Reed, why'd you let her come with you to Atlanta looking like that? I see we need to do some serious shopping to get you a new wardrobe. And just so you know, Aunt Phoebe, neon colors are out."

"It's good to see you too, Divine," Aunt Phoebe says with a chuckle.

It's then that I realize I've temporarily forgotten my manners. "Oh, I'm sorry!" I wrap my arms around my aunt, giving her a hug. "You know I can't have you looking any kind of way. You have an image to keep, Aunt Phoebe. You're *my* aunt."

I embrace Uncle Reed next. "Sorry for being rude." I put on a big smile and say, "I'm back . . ."

A flash of humor crosses his face. "So, how was Martinique, Miss Diva?"

At the mention of the island where I spent the last couple of weeks, a grin spreads across my face. "Oooh, Uncle Reed, I had a great time. Mom and I didn't do anything but hang out on the beaches, eat a bunch of good food and shop."

"Child, I'm so glad you're here," Aunt Phoebe interjects. "Alyssa's been worrying me to death about when you were coming back."

"I told her that it would be a couple of weeks before school started." School starts August fifteenth, approximately ten days from today.

I pick up my Gucci backpack and continue, "I have a couple of suitcases. Mom said I didn't need to bring much more than that. I don't know who she's trying to fool. She carries this much luggage for a overnight trip."

"You still got a lot of clothes in the closet back at the house. A whole closet full. I don't even know if I've ever seen you in the same thing twice."

Running my fingers through my hair, I tell her, "Aunt Phoebe, you know how I am. I'm a trendsetter. Besides, a girl can never have enough clothes."

She cracks up with laughter.

"C'mon, let's get your luggage," Uncle Reed says, his eyes bright with humor.

"Let's get them quick," I say. "Because we need to stop at the first mall we find. Aunt Phoebe definitely needs a new outfit."

"Never you mind, Miss Diva. I'm comfortable in what I got on. Besides, I just came out here to get you. If your plane had come on time, I probably wouldn't have gotten out of the car."

Looping my arm through my aunt's, I say, "Aunt Phoebe, you know I love you so I hope you don't take this the wrong way, but please, never ever wear this outfit again. It's so done."

Fingering her collar, Aunt Phoebe responds, "Oh, I was actually thinking about wearing it to the back-to-school dance. You know I'm going to be one of the chaperones."

Tilting my head back, I peer up at her face to see if I can tell whether she's joking or not. I can't, so I say, "I'm staying home that night."

Laughing, we follow Uncle Reed over to the slowly revolving conveyor belt, laden with a mixture of suitcases and garment bags ranging from super cheap to top of the line. We stand there, our eyes searching for my new Hartmann luggage, a gift from my mom.

Ten minutes later, with suitcases in hand, we make our way to the parking deck to Uncle Reed's car. I keep telling him and Aunt

Phoebe that they need to upgrade to a Mercedes S600 sedan. My friend Mimi's dad just got one and it's tight.

As usual, Aunt Phoebe and Uncle Reed think they're down with the people or something by driving that boring black Cadillac. I have to admit it's cooler than the Nissan Quest Aunt Phoebe drives, even though the Nissan has all the tight stuff like DVD screens and a navigational system in it. Vans are just not cool. She should get an SUV.

Despite my relatives' poor taste in cars and clothing, I can hardly contain my excitement over being back with them. It's so obvious that they really need me.

I spent the first part of my summer at home in Pacific Palisades, California, with my mom up until a couple of weeks ago. Mom decided we should do some serious bonding, so we escaped to Martinique, French West Indies, before it was time for me to return to Atlanta.

During the drive from the Atlanta airport to Temple, I reflect back on how upset I was when, in true Hollywood style, Mom was sentenced to a court-ordered rehab program for abusing drugs and alcohol and sent me to Georgia to live with relatives I'd never met.

I was so totally against leaving sunny California for some hick town in the middle of nowhere. I was only fourteen then, but I've matured a lot since turning fifteen.

I still love California but it really doesn't feel much like home anymore. Not like Temple does. Maybe it's because my mom, R & B artist Kara Matthews, is away most of the time; since becoming one of Hollywood's most sought-after actresses, she spends more time starring in movies than singing in the recording studio.

Mom still owes Sony one more album. But after that, she plans to focus on acting. We decided that the best place for me right now is with Uncle Reed and Aunt Phoebe. I don't mind because my boo, Madison Hartford, lives in Temple. It was really hard not seeing him over summer break but we were determined to make our relationship work no matter what. We kept in contact via email and phone calls.

Alyssa was looking out for me too. She made sure that Madison didn't get stupid and cheat on me. As far as she knows, he's been a good boy. *That's my boo. He's so crazy about me.*

I pull out my compact mirror to check my makeup. I can't be caught looking whack. After all, I'm still a celebrity. I touch up my lips with my favorite lip gloss, Dior Addict Euphoric Beige. When I look up, Uncle Reed is pulling into the driveway.

"Oh my gosh!" I exclaim. "The house . . . it looks so different." Gone was the small, aluminum, matchbox-looking house that used to sit on this land. In its place is a sprawling ranch-style home with red brick covering the front and sides. "Wow. You even have a two-car garage. This is nice."

"We've had a lot of work done to it," Aunt Phoebe tells me. "We have all this land out here. We decided to make the house bigger."

I rush out of the car. "I can't wait to see what it looks like on the inside." I slip out of my jeweled thong sandals to feel the crisp, green grass tickling my bare feet.

It feels so good to be home.

My cousin Alyssa runs out of the house, screaming, "You're back! You're finally back. . . . Girl, I have so much to tell you."

We hug each other, jump up and down and then hug some more. We're both very excited about starting our sophmore year in high school.

"I told you that I was coming back."

"I thought you might change your mind. Divine, I'm so glad you're back. We have something to show you," Alyssa sings. "I can't wait until you see it."

"You must be talking about my room."

"Yeah. Divine, wait 'til you see it. I just know you're gonna love it."

We rush inside and down the hallway.

"I have my own bedroom! Praise the Lord," I scream. "*Yes.* Yes." I am beyond thrilled to have my own room and a full-size bed, but I'm ecstatic that Aunt Phoebe didn't decorate my room in that Pepto-Bismol pink she's so crazy about.

"Calm down, Hollywood . . . I mean, Divine. You act like you've never had nothing before." Alyssa has apparently developed a case of short-term memory. She was acting as hyped up as me not more than two minutes ago.

"You don't know how much this means to me," I tell her. "Don't get me wrong—it wasn't too bad sharing a room with you." I stop for a moment. "Okay, I'm lying. I *hated* sharing a room with you. I love you, Alyssa, but I just need my own space."

"Hey, it wasn't no prize for me either having you for a room-mate. You kept hogging up all the closet space. Even after Mama got you that armoire."

"Well, now you don't have to worry about it anymore. I have my own room and my own closet. A walk-in closet at that. Yes." I run my fingers along the scalloped edge of my new dresser. "I love it."

"I have a walk-in closet too." Alyssa takes me by the hand, leading me back toward the front of the house. "You'll see my room later. First you need to see Mama and Daddy's room. They have a sitting room now. And a big Jacuzzi."

I glance over at my uncle, who looks like a big teddy bear. "And why do you and Aunt Phoebe need such a big tub?"

"None of your business," he replies smoothly before giving Aunt Phoebe a wink.

"Gross," I mutter. The last thing I want in my mind is an image of my Amazon-looking aunt and uncle being all hugged up or worse, being all lovey-dovey. "You two are way too old to be . . . you know."

Uncle Reed and Aunt Phoebe laugh, but Alyssa looks about as grossed out as I do.

"The only folks in this house that should be doing anything is us. *We're married.*"

"TMI, Aunt Phoebe. TMI."

"What in the world is TMI?"

"Too much information, Mama," Alyssa explains with a laugh. Aunt Phoebe can be so lame at times.

Chuckling, I announce, "I think I'll go put away my stuff."

After a quick look at Alyssa's room, she helps me carry my luggage to my new bedroom. I still can't believe it. I actually have my own room.

"Where's Chance?" I ask. "I haven't seen that boy in a minute. I would've thought he'd at least hang around long enough to say hello."

"Pleeze . . . he's got Trina on the brain."

"I guess there's no point in me calling her then."

Alyssa agrees. "Especially not while she's with Chance. All they ever want to do is be alone. They don't even want me hanging with them anymore."

"Well, I'm back now. We can hang out together."

"Good. Penny's dating this boy named James, so she put me down too. I hardly ever hear from her these days."

"What?" I can't believe Penny's acting that way. My friend Mimi sometimes acts like that when she's going with a boy. But after I don't speak to her for a few days, she usually comes around.

"Yep. My own cousin put me down for a boy."

"What about Stacy? You still talk to her?" I question.

Alyssa nods. "Stacy and I still hang out from time to time but

we don't do it a lot. She's been dealing with some drama with her
mama and grandmamma."

"I'll give her a call tomorrow."

"She'll be glad to hear from you. She told me that you called
her from California."

I nod. "Yeah, I did. Right before we left for Martinique. We
didn't talk long because she was on her way out the door. What's up
with her mom and granny?"

"Her grandmama had a stroke and she's living with them right
now. She and Stacy's mama don't get along too well. Stacy says they
fuss and fight all day long."

Alyssa keeps me company in my bedroom while I unpack my
clothes. She even helps me put them away.

"Girl, Stephen is such a good boyfriend. He sends me emails
every day. He's always talking about how much he loves me."

"Don't let Aunt Phoebe get to them," I warn her. "Get a Web-
based email address like Yahoo or something. You know she checks
your Charter Broadband account."

"I already have one. Only Stephen has the address, but I'll give
it to you too. It's sweetlyssa at yahoo dot com."

I chuckle. "That's so corny."

"Stephen likes it. That's all that matters."

"Whatever," I mutter as I open a suitcase. "I bought you something."

Alyssa's eyes light up in excitement. "What?"

"You'll have to wait and see. It's a surprise."

"C'mon, where is it?"

"I'm getting to it. Just chill for a moment." I laugh at the expression on my cousin's face. I love irritating her like this.

"Okay, here it is." I toss a gift-wrapped package to her. "You're
not going to get your other gift until your birthday."

Pouting, Alyssa complains, "That's almost a month away, Divine."

"Well, you'll just have to wait another four weeks." Pointing to the gift-wrapped present in her arms, I say, "C'mon . . . open it."

"Oh my goodness," she screams. "A pair of Gucci shoes."

"I knew you'd love them. Mom bought Chance a pair of those Nikes he really wanted."

"I love my shoes." Alyssa slips them on her feet and starts dancing around the room. "These are so tight. Divine, thanks so much. You were really looking out for me."

Grinning, I sit down watching my cousin strut around in her designer shoes—her very first pair. Maybe now I can keep her big feet out of mine.

PUTTING AWAY MY clothes and talking nonstop has made us hungry. Alyssa and I stroll to the kitchen, laughing and whispering.

I notice that Aunt Phoebe had her entire kitchen remodeled. The ugly white cabinets have been replaced with custom-designed, honey-maple ones topped with double crown molding. "This looks so nice," I say.

"Mama loves her kitchen. She stays on me and Chance about keeping it clean, so you better watch out."

We hear the front door open and close. Shortly after, Chance strolls through the dining area.

"Chance, Divine's back," Alyssa announces when her brother walks into the kitchen.

He glances over at me. "Oh, hey girl."

I eye my cousin. I didn't expect Chance to jump up and down with joy, but I thought he'd at least sound a little more cheerful about my return.

"You okay? You look upset," I ask out of pure nosiness.

"I'm fine. Just got a lot on my mind. I'll talk to y'all later." He leaves us and heads to his room.

"What's wrong with him?" I ask Alyssa.

She shrugs. "I'on know. He was okay when he left here earlier. He and Trina must've had a fight, but they'll be fine tomorrow. They always do that."

Checking my watch, I note the time. "I need to call my boo and let him know that I'm back."

"He already called. Girl, all Madison did was walk around here looking pitiful."

"I missed him too. We emailed each other almost every day."

I excuse myself and rush off to my bedroom to call Madison. I'm so ready to see him, but I know Aunt Phoebe and Uncle Reed aren't going to let that happen. They're still stuck on that stupid rule of no dating or company until Alyssa and I turn sixteen.

Alyssa's the lucky one because her birthday is in four weeks and mine is still four months away—an eternity.

Pushing the depressing thought out of my mind, I focus on what's really important right now: talking to the love of my life.

"Madison, hi. It's me."

"Hey, boo." Just hearing his voice sends my spirit soaring up to the clouds. I can't help myself. I just start grinning from ear to ear.

"Where you at?"

"Uncle Reed's house. I got in today."

"Girl, I'm glad you're back. I didn't know if your mom was gonna talk you into staying in Cali."

"No. I told you she wouldn't. She's hardly ever home. Plus, she's thinking about selling the house in California and moving permanently to Atlanta."

"Are you gonna move up there when she does?"

"No. Mom knows I don't want to change schools. I only have two more years after this. Don't worry, boo. I'm not going anywhere."

"I'm glad. I don't want to lose you, Divine. I'm crazy about you."

"I feel the same way," I gush. Mentally, I tell myself to maintain my cool. I like Madison a lot but I don't want him to know exactly how much. I don't want him getting a big head.

Just when our conversation starts getting good, Madison's stupid sister picks up the phone, demanding, "When y'all getting off? I need to make a call."

"Hang up, Marcia," Madison yells.

I'm crazy about Madison but I can't stand his sisters. Especially Marcia. She is such a ghetto chick, which I find interesting since they don't live in a ghetto—they live on a farm with cows, chickens and I think there might even be a goat or something over there.

"Why won't your mom let you have a cell phone?"

"She says I don't need one."

I totally disagree. I need to be able to talk to my man whenever I want and it's hard with those crazy sisters of his always wanting to use the phone.

"Why don't you ask your dad?" I suggest.

"He ain't gonna do nothing."

Madison tries to change the subject, but I'm not ready to let this go. He shouldn't just take no for an answer. Play one parent against the other—at least try. "Have you even asked him?"

"I'm telling you, my pop is not gonna do a thing. He don't care about nothing but hisself, his animals and this land. He don't care nothing about cell phones—no kind of phone."

Marcia picks up a second time. "Get off the phone, Madison. I need to call my boyfriend."

"Hang up. I mean it."

I've had enough. "Madison, I'll call you back later."

He sighs loudly. "Okay. Let me let this stupid girl use the telephone."

Three hours after we hang up, I call back, checking to see if Marcia is done so Madison and I can finish our conversation.

"Look, Divine. Me and my boyfriend hafta work out some

thangs. We gon' be on here for a while, so you need to just try and catch up with my brother tomorrow."

Before I can respond, she clicks off. Oooh, I can't stand her. She's so rude! I'm dying to call back and tell her off but I figure it's not in my best interests to make my boyfriend's sister angry.

I get on my computer and send Madison an email, telling him to call me when his ol' hateful sister gets off the phone. If she gets off at a decent hour, that is. My aunt and uncle have strict rules about stuff like phone calls after a certain hour.

I lay back on my bed thinking about how much my life has changed since moving in with my relatives. Mom and Jerome never really gave me a phone curfew or anything. I even had my own private line in our house.

They didn't monitor my emails either—not like Aunt Phoebe does. She doesn't know about my Hotmail account, though.

It's not like it's a big deal anyway. I'm not doing anything sneaky. I've changed a lot in my way of thinking since I first came to Temple. Alyssa used to get on my nerves like crazy but we're cool now. She's like my best friend.

Aunt Phoebe and Uncle Reed aren't anything like my parents, but I don't hold it against them. I like being here with them because I know they love me and they care what happens to me. My parents care for me too. I know they do—they just got caught up in some madness for a while. My mom's really trying to get her life together—at least, that's what she keeps telling me.

I feel like I've changed a lot since becoming a Christian a few months ago, but then there are days when I think I'm the same Divine I've always been. The way I see it, there's not much that can be done to improve upon perfection. Still, I'm trying to be the best person I know God would want me to be.

chapter 2

I'm not in bed a solid two hours before I find myself getting back up. I'm hungry and if I don't eat something, I'm never going to get any sleep with the way my stomach's growling.

I climb out of bed and slip my robe over a pair of brand-new Victoria's Secret pajamas. Grabbing my flashlight, I leave my bedroom on a mission to the kitchen to raid the refrigerator.

In the quiet of the night, I hear something that strangely sounds like someone crying. I slow down a bit in the hallway, trying to determine where the sound is coming from.

I decide that it's nobody but my overly emotional cousin. Alyssa cries over everything.

I'm standing right outside Chance's door when I realize the sobbing is coming from inside *his* bedroom. I stand with my ear pressed to his door wondering if I should intrude. He and Trina must have had a serious fight.

I knock lightly on the door.

"Y-Yeah?"

I ease the door open, sticking my head inside. "It's just me."

"You need something, Divine?" Chance questions.

I can see the outline of his body in the dark room. He wipes his face with the back of his hand before leaning to turn on the bedside lamp.

Stepping all the way into the room, I answer, "I just wanted to make sure you're okay." Gesturing toward the door, I add, "I could hear you from out there. You sounded really upset." I don't mention the fact that he's in here crying like a girl. It occurs to me that I've never seen Chance upset enough to cry.

"I'm fine."

Why is this boy lying to me? I wonder. Okay, I really don't have a choice now. I have to call him out. "Chance, you're in here crying, so don't even try to front because I know something's wrong."

He doesn't respond. Probably too ashamed.

"This is about Trina, isn't it? Whatever is going on between you two, it'll be okay. C'mon, Chance. You know she's crazy about you."

"I know."

"And you're crazy about her. Just keep the lines of communication open and be honest about your feelings. Trina's so in love with you. She's not going anywhere." Look out, Dr. Phil. Move aside for Divine, the Doctor of Love.

Chance wipes his eyes. "It's late. What are you doing up?"

"I'm starving, so I was going to the kitchen to fix myself a sandwich. Want one?" Chance is the one person who usually makes these midnight food runs with me.

He shook his head. "Not tonight. I just need time to think."

Hoping to reassure him, I say, "Chance, I don't know what's

going on with you but I'm here if you need me. Anytime you want to talk. Okay?"

"I know. Thanks."

I pause at the door. "You sure you don't want to raid the refrigerator with me? I'll even let you have the last of the chocolate milk."

But not even the temptation of a cold glass of chocolate milk can sway him. "Not tonight."

I have no choice but to leave Chance to whatever is bothering him.

In the kitchen I pull out bread, mayo and mustard along with a packet of thinly sliced deli ham and a couple of slices of cheese.

Aunt Phoebe nearly scares me to death when she creeps into the kitchen.

"I thought I heard somebody in here."

"My heart almost stopped," I say. "Aunt Phoebe, you scared me."

"Oh, honey, I'm sorry. I heard footsteps, so I came out here to see what in the world was going on in my house this time of night."

"I see you still walking around with that bat." Aunt Phoebe keeps a bat in the house and one in her van.

"I'm keeping it too. Just in case I need to lay somebody out. If they crazy enough to break in here, I bet they won't break in nobody else's house when I get through with them."

I chuckle. "I'm sure glad you didn't come in here swinging."

"Me too." Her face twisted in a frown, Aunt Phoebe points to the sandwich. "I told you that you'd be hungry later. Girl, you better start eating real portions. Stop all that itty bitty bite-size stuff. You already skinny as a rail. I know you want to be a fashion model, but you got to live to do that. I don't know anybody using dead models." Leaning on the kitchen counter, she adds, "You better start eating."

"I do eat, Aunt Phoebe. I eat a lot."

"Humph," she grunts. "You take a bite of this, a bite of that. That's not eating. That's tasting."

"You want one?" I ask, pointing to the ham and cheese sandwich I just made.

Aunt Phoebe shakes her head. "That ham will sit on my chest all night long. Your uncle won't get an ounce of sleep if I ate that."

I eat my sandwich while Aunt Phoebe talks. I love listening to the stories about her and my mom when they were growing up. Me and Alyssa don't have anything on them. They were wild. Not in a bad way, but they were sneaky. We're not that brave.

When I'm done, Aunt Phoebe tells me, "You go on back to bed, sugar. It's late. I'll clean up in here *this* time."

I plant a kiss on her cheek. "Thanks, Aunt Phoebe."

On the way back to my room, I pause outside Chance's room. I don't hear anything. He's probably asleep by now. What happened between him and Trina to upset him like that?

AUNT PHOEBE TAKES us to the mall a couple of days later to finish our school shopping. The thought of having to deal with homework, reports and tests in less than eight days kind of puts a damper on things for me, but knowing that I can steal a few moments with Madison between classes makes me feel better.

"There is something big going on between Trina and Chance," Alyssa whispers. "He's been acting so strange. He didn't even want to come to the mall with us."

"I think they had a really bad fight. He—" I stop short of telling Alyssa about Chance crying in his room when Aunt Phoebe comes toward us, carrying one of the ugliest outfits I've ever seen. I can't believe a department store of this caliber would carry something that looks like that.

"Alyssa, what do you think of this pantsuit?"

Eyeing the outfit up and down, she frowns and asks, "For me or for you?"

"For you."

Screwing up her face, Alyssa shakes her head. "Mama, that suit is ugly. I don't want that. Why can't we go down to Express? I like their clothes. I want to dress more like Divine."

"Hey, don't pull me into this." I avoid being in the line of fire quickly. I'm not about to have Aunt Phoebe mad at me.

"The clothes I buy for you are nice. They don't go out of style."

"But I want a few pieces that are fashionable too." Picking up a purple top, Alyssa says, "Like this. This is tight."

I check it out. "It's cute."

Aunt Phoebe takes it out of Alyssa's hand. "It's nice," she admits. "But I think the neckline is a little too low."

"Mama, I'll wear a camisole under it," Alyssa promises. "I really want to buy this shirt."

Aunt Phoebe considered it a moment before saying, "Okay, I'll get it. But I better see something underneath."

"And these pants . . ." Alyssa holds up a pair of low-cut jeans. "Now I love these."

Shaking her head, Aunt Phoebe sighs. "You either want shirts cut up to here or pants cut down to there . . ."

I start easing away when Aunt Phoebe begins her sermon on the evils of fashion. She wasn't born with the designer gene, so she doesn't have good taste when it comes to clothes.

She and Alyssa are still going at it, so I walk over to the shoe department. I can't leave a store without strolling through rows and rows of shoes. Shoes are a girl's best friend.

"Hey, girl . . ."

I turn around to face Madison, my man. "Hey, boo." He looks so cute in a pair of Sean John camouflage shorts and a black

T-shirt. Madison's dark hair is now in shoulder-length braids pulled back into a ponytail. Aunt Phoebe says he should get a haircut, but I don't agree. I like everything about him—his long eyelashes, big brown eyes and that lopsided grin of his.

"I was wondering when I'd get to see you." His gaze travels over my face then down my body slowly.

Madison bends down like he's about to kiss me. I hastily take a step backward and steal a peek over my shoulder. "Aunt Phoebe is here with me and Alyssa," I tell him since he can't seem to take a hint. "Don't let her see you. She—"

"It's too late," he interrupts. "She's coming this way."

I'm about to die of a heart attack while Madison just acts so cool and calm. My man isn't afraid of anything—not even the tall Amazon woman that is my Aunt Phoebe.

"Madison Hartford, how are you?"

Why is she calling out his whole name like that? I wonder. I just hope Aunt Phoebe's not going to embarrass me out here in front of all these people.

"I'm fine, Mrs. Matthews."

Aunt Phoebe takes a look in my direction.

"I didn't set this up. I swear."

"Honey, I'm not accusing you of anything. I believe you. You didn't know until after we left Carrollton Mall that we were coming here."

I let out an audible sigh of relief. I thought for sure I was in trouble.

"Is your mother here?"

I glance over at Aunt Phoebe, horrified. I can't believe she's being so nosy. She's totally embarrassing me right now.

"Mom's over in the jewelry department." Madison laughs. "She wanted to get some new earrings."

My heart is hammering foolishly at the sound of his voice.

Madison's just standing there watching me and I'm wondering if he can hear it, if he ever feels this way.

Smiling, Aunt Phoebe says, "I think I'll go over and say hello. Don't you stray off, Divine."

I release another sigh of relief when my aunt walks off, leaving us alone.

Madison grins as he eyes me from head to toe, like he's really loving my low-waist jeans and the Old Navy top I'm wearing. "Girl, you looking so fine."

His words bring a smile to my lips. Madison knows just what to say to me.

"Hey . . . you think your aunt and uncle will finally let me come over to see you now? She and my mom been talking more and more."

I shrug. "I don't know. Maybe. I'll be sixteen in December. I ought to be able to have company." My insides jangle with excitement and in my nervous state, I play with the buckle of the shoe I'm holding. Madison's unexpected appearance sends a dizzying current racing through me.

"I hope so. I wanna spend some time with you. Away from school. We need some *alone* time. You think about what I asked you?"

I glance over my shoulder to make sure we're not being overheard. Madison's been trying to talk me into sneaking out at night. "I can't do that. My aunt and uncle would kill me—not to mention what my mom would do," I murmur in response. "Madison, I'm going to have a talk with them to see if I can get them to change their mind. I plan on talking to my mom too."

I give Alyssa a cross-eyed look when she walks up, joining me and Madison. I don't want to be rude, but right now I want to be with my boyfriend. It's not like we have much time together at all. I send her a sharp glance, hoping she gets the hint.

"What's wrong with you?"

I could've kicked Alyssa for asking me that. Rolling my eyes, I whisper, "Nothing."

Alyssa starts talking to Madison about Stephen, which irritates me to no end. Looking over my shoulder, I say, "I think Aunt Phoebe is looking for you."

"No, she's not. She's over in the hosiery department, getting stockings for Sunday."

"Maybe you should join her," I suggest pointedly.

Alyssa opens her mouth to respond but finally the light comes on inside her head, prompting her to say, "Oooh—my bad . . . you two want to be alone. Sorry."

Shaking my head, I say, "That girl can't take a hint for nothing," when she leaves.

Madison laughs.

Our expressions grow serious as we stare into each other's eyes. Madison leans forward and I lean in, longing to do what I've wanted since running into him.

Just as we are about to steal a kiss, Alyssa walks up. "Mama told me to come get you."

I groan loudly.

"I'll talk to you later, girl." Madison flashes a grin as Alyssa leads me away.

"He was about to kiss me. Do you know how long it's been since I felt his lips on mine?"

"Divine, you didn't want my mama walking up on y'all doing that. She was gonna come but I told her I'd come get you. Girl, she would've gone off right here in this store."

"Madison wants to be able to come see me at the house."

"You know how my parents feel about that."

"Maybe we can try and get them to change their minds. You're going to be sixteen soon and my birthday is only three months after that. We're not bad or anything, *and* we keep our grades up. Let's ask them to reconsider."

Alyssa thought about it for a moment. "I guess we can try. Just don't get your hopes up, Divine. Mama doesn't change her mind too often about stuff like this."

She and I wait until we get home before broaching the subject with Aunt Phoebe.

"Alyssa and I were talking and we would like for you and Uncle Reed to reconsider your rule about boys coming over."

"I'll tell you what," Aunt Phoebe says. "You and Alyssa present your case to us this evening and we'll see what happens."

"Thanks."

"I'm not promising anything."

When we're alone I ask Alyssa, "Do you think they'll change their minds?"

She shrugs. "They might. You can never tell with Mama. At least she's willing to listen to us, though."

"It's going to be so perfect with Stephen and Madison coming over. It'll almost be like we're dating."

Alyssa grabbed me by the elbow. "I told you, don't get your hopes up, Divine. They might still say no."

"I'm thinking positive. When we get through telling them everything they want to hear, Aunt Phoebe and Uncle Reed will have no choice but to give us their blessing."

"Aunt Phoebe, Alyssa's birthday is less than four weeks away and mine is three months after that. We're almost sixteen," I tell her even though she knows all this already. "Like, it's practically next week."

My aunt gives me a sidelong glance.

Okay, I'm stretching it a bit with this argument so I decide to take another tack. I switch over to the facts. "Most girls are already dating by the time they're in the tenth grade. All we're asking is that you and Uncle Reed consider letting Stephen and Madison come over to the house. We're not talking every day. Just once in a while." I steal a glance over at Alyssa, who's nodding in agreement. "I think we've proven to you and Uncle Reed that we are responsible and that we can be trusted."

Aunt Phoebe seems to be considering our words. After a moment, she tells us, "We'll pray over this and allow God to move on our hearts. Give us a few days and we'll talk again."

Why are they praying to God about something like this? I wonder. God has too many other things to worry about—I'm sure He don't want my uncle and aunt praying to Him about my attempts at a social life. I look up and whisper, "Sorry, God. I have nothing to do with this. I *know* how busy you are."

"Divine, you say something?"

I shake my head. "Aunt Phoebe, we really want you and Uncle Reed to give us a chance. We're not stupid. Alyssa and I know the rules and we're not going to blow this."

"Why do you two want to spend so much time with these boys?" Uncle Reed questions.

I look over at Alyssa, who responds. "We like Stephen and Madison. There's nothing wrong with that."

"There isn't," Uncle Reed acknowledges. "But right now, the last thing y'all need to focus on is boys. Y'all don't need any distractions."

"I think our grades show that we're not easily distracted," I contribute. "You know we've been talking to them for over a year and our grades haven't gone down once."

"We'll discuss it," Aunt Phoebe states. "Then we'll talk again. You've given us a lot to think on."

"Thank you," Alyssa and I say in unison. I grab Alyssa's hand and we head to my room.

"Girl, I think we did it," I whisper. "I think we changed their minds."

Alyssa shrugs. "I don't know. It's hard to say with Mama."

"Be quiet, Alyssa. You sure are negative. I sure hope when you turn sixteen it'll make you a little more optimistic."

chapter 3

"*Only* two more days left of summer vacation." I sigh as I slip off my Prada leather thong sandals, making myself comfortable on the carpeted floor in Penny's den. Aunt Phoebe and Penny's mom are sisters, so she's like, my cousin.

Uncle Reed and Aunt Phoebe left yesterday for Birmingham, Alabama, to attend a one-day conference, so Alyssa, Chance and I spent the night with Penny and her family. My aunt and uncle are coming back sometime tonight because Uncle Reed has to preach tomorrow morning.

Chance was outside playing ball with his cousins while me and Alyssa searched through stacks of DVDs, looking for something to watch.

"In a way though I'm glad to be going to school," I blurt. "But that's only because I'm taking driver's ed this semester. I can't wait to get behind the wheel of a car."

"I'm taking it too," Alyssa announces. "Daddy said he's not gon' try to teach us to drive. He said he doesn't have the patience." She opens up a can of soda and takes a long sip. "I can't wait to get my driver's license. I'll never be home."

"What are you planning on driving?" I ask. "Aunt Phoebe says we'll have to buy our own cars."

"I'ma get a job and buy one."

Penny hands a bowl of popcorn fresh from the microwave down to me before taking a seat on the sofa. "I've been driving since I was thirteen," she tells us. "It's not a big deal. I passed the test on the first try and got my license about a week ago."

I'm amazed. "You've been driving for that long?"

"Uh-huh. Uncle Harold used to let her practice driving that old truck they got sitting in the backyard."

"That rusty old thing?" Turning my nose upward, I release a small laugh. "That thing is ugly. I wouldn't be caught dead in something like that."

"Girl, it for sure beats walking," Penny replies with a laugh. "Willie Joe getting ready to fix that truck up. Wait 'til you see it after he paints it. He gon' put some rims on it too."

I shrug. "I'm not the kind of girl who rides in *trucks*. It's totally not me at all."

Alyssa and Penny break out into laughter.

"What's so funny?"

"I'm imagining you all dressed up and looking Hollywood while you walking down the street in your designer high heels, trying to catch a cab. Remember that time when you first moved here?"

"Humph. I'd never get anywhere around here waiting on a taxi. They take all day to run you around the corner."

"Pass the popcorn, Divine."

From my position on the floor, I glance over my shoulder to where Penny's sprawled out on the leather sofa. "I didn't hear the magic word."

"Pleeze."

"That's better." I turn around to hand the bowl of popcorn to her. "Did Alyssa tell you that Stephen and Madison might get to come over to the house to hang out with us sometime? It's almost a done deal."

Penny looks at Alyssa. "Wow. I can't believe it. Aunt Phoebe is stubborn about stuff like that. She was trying to tell my mama that I shouldn't be dating right now. I'm so glad mama didn't listen to her."

"Mama might still say no," Alyssa feels the need to interject. I can't understand why she's being so negative lately. Must be her hormones—maybe they're on strike or something.

"Well, I'm thinking positive," I tell them. "There's no real reason for Aunt Phoebe or Uncle Reed to deny us. We're basically good kids. And our grades are good."

"You don't know Mama, Divine. She can start buggin' over nothing."

My cousin's getting on my nerves with her pessimistic attitude. "C'mon, Alyssa. Can you at least try to think positive for once in your life?"

"I'm just being real." She reaches over, sticking her fingers into the bowl of popcorn. Clenching my mouth tight, I move my soda to keep her from knocking it over.

"The movie's about to start," Penny announces. "Ssssh."

Our conversation comes to a halt while we watch some boring movie Penny and Alyssa picked out. I make a mental note to make sure I pick the movie the next time we get together. I'm more into action-adventure films, while both Alyssa and Penny enjoy romantic comedies.

After the movie, Penny announces, "Mama made some fried chicken, collard greens, corn bread and—"

I cut her off by asking, "Did your mom make her macaroni and cheese?" I love Miss Shirley's mac-and-cheese casserole.

While waiting for dinner to be served, I make a quick call to Madison, but he's not home. At least that's what Marcia tells me. I'm not sure I believe her.

I put away my cell phone while hoping that Marcia will trip over her own big feet. I just don't like that girl.

"That was quick," Penny observes.

"He wasn't home. At least that's what his hateful sister said. Probably out playing ball with his friends."

"I tried to call James and he wasn't home either," Penny announces. "I've been calling him all day but he's not returning any of my calls. I don't know what I did."

"Probably nothing," I assure her. "Boys just trip like that sometime." I pick up one of the floor pillows and prop it behind my back. I have to sit on the floor when we're at Penny's house because her sofa isn't real comfortable.

"I don't know. We were hanging pretty tight until . . ." Penny's voice dies at the sight of her older brother.

Willie Joe steps over me, his gigantic foot landing flat on my sandal. "Boy, watch where you stepping," I yell. "These shoes cost over four hundred dollars."

I resist the urge to throw the bowl of popcorn at him. Willie Joe's had something against me ever since I turned down his offer to be my boyfriend. His mother and Aunt Phoebe are sisters, so I feel like he's practically related to me. Not to mention the fact that he looks like a big gorilla. He's nothing but a bunch of muscles, which is why he's one of the most popular football players in school.

He bends and picks up one of the sandals. "These lil' skimpy things here cost what? Girl, you need to go back and get your money." He chuckles. "You got robbed. I wonder how much I could get for them at a pawnshop?"

"Stop being such a jerk," Penny yells. "Get out of here."

"Shut up," he growls.

After he finds whatever he's looking for, Willie Joe winks at me and leaves. He's barely out of sight before Alyssa asks, "Penny, what were you going to say?"

"James and I . . . y'all know we were hanging pretty tight for a while."

"Yeah, I know. You put me down for him."

I chuckle. Apparently Alyssa's still a little steamed about Penny's absence during most of the summer.

Penny chews on her bottom lip for a moment before responding, leaving me to ponder what she's about to say.

"I didn't put you down. I was just spending time with my boyfriend. Anyway, James kept telling me how much he loved me." She glances over her shoulder toward the doorway to see if anyone was nearby. Lowering her voice, she whispers, "We got close."

"Are you saying that you and James did it?" I ask in a whisper. "You had sex?"

Penny doesn't respond.

"Well?" Alyssa prompts. *"Did you?"*

I'm just about ready to die of shock when she nods. "I thought he really loved me. He kept saying that he did. He said making love would make us closer."

I'm speechless.

"Did you use protection?" Alyssa inquires. "I hope you did."

"I'm not stupid. I went to the clinic and got some birth control pills. And he used a condom."

"So when did this happen?"

I glance over at Alyssa, trying to gauge her facial expression. She and Penny have always been close. I'm sure she's feeling a little hurt that her own cousin didn't share this information with her before now. I think I'd probably feel the same way. But then again, Alyssa's a better person than I am when it comes to things like that. She's not petty.

"A couple of weeks ago. Things were fine until we did it. I haven't really talked to him since."

"He's gotten what he wanted," I state. "What a jerk."

Penny's eyes are bright, like she's about to start crying. "I didn't want to believe it but I guess you're right, Divine. James just used me for sex. The thing about it is . . . I didn't even feel right about doing it in the first place."

"Did he force you?" Alyssa wants to know. She looks like she's about ready to go beat up somebody.

Penny shakes her head. "I mean . . . I wanted to do it at first, but then I felt bad afterwards."

"You probably felt guilty," I tell her.

Alyssa announces, "That was the Holy Spirit convicting your heart. Penny, I wish you'd come to me. We could've talked about it. You know, I never really liked James. Something about him was just not right."

"I thought you were just jealous of my relationship with him," Penny said.

"Nope. That definitely wasn't it. I just never really trusted him."

"Penny, it's good you found out now. I know it hurts you, but you don't need someone like James in your life," I state.

"Divine, you're right. I just hate that I gave him my virginity. Now I don't have anything to give my husband on our wedding night."

"Maybe if you never do it again he'll never know. It'll be like you're still a virgin." What would they do without me?

Alyssa and I both embrace Penny, hoping to give her comfort. We contain our surprise at her revelation until we get back home later that evening.

"Girl, I didn't expect to hear something like that coming out of Penny's mouth! I know you told me she was hanging tight with James, but I didn't think it was like that."

"I didn't know either. I thought Penny was still a virgin." Alyssa looks me up and down. "Any confessions you need to make? I'm getting ready to pray for Penny's soul. Do I need to add you to the list?"

"You sound like Aunt Phoebe. But no, I'm cool. I'm still the big V and proud of it."

"That's dogged out how James is treating my cousin. I can't stand him."

"It sure is," I agree. "But that's what Aunt Phoebe and my mom says happen all the time. Boys take what they want and then leave you."

"I wonder if Aunt Shirley knows Penny's on birth control."

"I don't think so. I think Miss Shirley would have a fit about that. She and Aunt Phoebe both say that parents putting their kids on birth control are giving them permission to have sex."

"Stacy's mom put her on the pill because she said that she didn't want Stacy bringing babies into the house."

"Is Stacy having sex?"

Shrugging, Alyssa responds, "Not that I know of, but then again—she probably wouldn't tell me if she was. I don't think I'd be telling my business like that."

Alyssa and I can't even have a boy come visit us at home and our friends are out there getting their groove on. If Aunt Phoebe and Uncle Reed ever find out about this, we won't have a prayer of a social life until we're thirty.

ALYSSA AND I were the first ones dressed and ready for church on Sunday morning. We sat down at the breakfast nook chatting while waiting for everyone else to get ready.

Checking my watch, I say, "Your parents must have been real tired last night. I've never known them to sleep so late."

Shrugging, Alyssa responds, "Driving from Birmingham was tiring, I guess."

I can't stop myself from pondering aloud, "I thought it was only a couple of hours away from here."

"More like three."

We can hear Uncle Reed's voice as he rounds the corner, entering the kitchen. He glances over at us in surprise. "I can't believe it. You two are dressed and ready? *Before me?*"

I laugh. "I bet you're thinking Jesus is coming back today, huh?"

He chuckles. "Have you two eaten breakfast?"

"I had a piece of toast," I respond while Alyssa answers, "I ate a bowl of oatmeal."

Aunt Phoebe is just as shocked to see us when she joins Uncle Reed in the kitchen. She's still wearing her robe, but her hair and makeup are done.

"I thought I was gon' have to wake y'all up. The house was so quiet, I didn't think anybody was up yet." She places four slices of bread in the toaster, then makes two cups of instant coffee.

"Chance might still be sleeping," Alyssa tells her. "I knocked on his door when I got up, but I haven't seen him."

Aunt Phoebe walks over to the doorway and yells out, "Chance. I hope you up and in there getting ready for church. You supposed to be riding with your daddy this morning. Hurry up."

Chance walks out of his room. He greets my aunt and uncle sitting next to us. Alyssa and I watch him silently as he puts on his tie. From the grim expression on his face, I can tell that he's still in a funky mood. Come to think of it, Trina sounded strange when I called her yesterday too. Even Alyssa thinks there's something really weird going on between them.

Leaning back in the chair, I close my eyes. I'm still a little sleepy because I didn't go straight to bed after getting home. Uncle Reed and Aunt Phoebe didn't get back from Birmingham until after nine. And when we finally left Penny's house, it was almost midnight.

"Looks like somebody didn't get enough sleep last night," Aunt Phoebe says.

I open my eyes, a tiny smile on my face. "I'm all right. Just resting my eyes while I wait for you and Uncle Reed to get ready."

"Just make sure you're not resting your eyes when I'm up in the pulpit this morning," Uncle Reed comments with a laugh.

I chuckle. "I won't." Silently, I add, as long as you're not boring. I don't like his Revelation sermons—mostly because I don't get them and they're kind of scary. I enjoy when Uncle Reed applies what's in the Bible to our lives today. It gives me a better understanding. Without his teachings, the Bible would be boring to me.

I glance upward. *Please don't take that personally, God. I'm not trying to be mean—just truthful.*

Half an hour later, we head out to the car. Uncle Reed and Chance left fifteen minutes earlier.

I weigh Aunt Phoebe with a critical squint. She's wearing a huge orange hat with orange and black feathers. It's no secret that my aunt loves feathers of *all* colors and *all* sizes. The orange and black suit isn't bad-looking. I just don't care for stripes. I figure she should've saved this outfit for Halloween.

"No orange and black shoes," I murmur when I notice her orange and black handbag.

"Oh, they had some," Aunt Phoebe responds. "I just didn't like them."

"Mama and Daddy are trying to match up these days," Alyssa announces with her eyes full of humor. "Did you notice the orange and black tie he had on?"

Her words draw my attention away from the scenery outside the car. "Uncle Reed has on an orange and black tie?"

Alyssa nods. "Yeah. It's striped."

"What's wrong with that?" Aunt Phoebe asks, turning to face us.

"Nobody matches like that anymore," I feel compelled to tell them. "That's so over."

"A lot of pastors and their first ladies are doing it," Aunt Phoebe counters. "One of the vendors at the conference had quite a few his-and-her suits. You shoulda seen them."

"Is that where you bought that suit?" I ask.

She nods. "We bought a couple of outfits."

Alyssa and I exchange amused looks.

"Maybe it's something new in your world," I say.

We arrive at the church and get settled because service is scheduled to start soon.

After the choir sings and the scripture is read, Aunt Phoebe walks up to the front of the church to make the announcements.

I squirm in my seat because I'm sleepy and beginning to feel bored. I can't wait for service to be over. As soon as we get home, I'm taking a nap.

Since school starts on Tuesday, Uncle Reed makes it the focus of his sermon.

"It's that time of the year again," he begins. "I don't know who's more excited—the parents or the children—about going back to school. I think everyone in my household is ready for the doors of Temple High to open." He chuckles.

I'm definitely not ready for summer to end but I am looking forward to going back to school.

"We all have to go back to school from time to time. Even in the day of the disciples." Uncle Reed pauses a second to let his words sink in. "Jesus was their teacher."

Uncle Reed went on to explain why Jesus used parables. "Matthew, chapter 13, verse 11 says that 'The knowledge of the secrets of the kingdom of heaven has been given to you, but not to them.' Verse 12 says, 'Whoever has will be given more, and he will have an abundance. Whoever does not have, even what he has will be taken from him.' Verse 13 explains it clearly to us. 'This is why I speak to them in parables: Though seeing, they do not see; though hearing, they do not hear or understand.'"

I like reading the parables in the Bible—they're about the only things I really understand. Alyssa understands a bit more than I do, but it's because she's been studying the Bible a lot longer than I have.

I make notes throughout Uncle Reed's sermon—it helps to keep me awake.

After the service, Aunt Phoebe and her crew give us backpacks filled with school supplies. I take mine while offering a smile of gratitude but I *won't* be taking this backpack anywhere. Mom bought me a Prada one, which I love.

I could've done flips around the church banquet hall when they came up short one backpack. I quickly offered to give up mine.

"We'll get you another one," Aunt Phoebe promises. "That was a really nice thing you did."

"Mom already bought me one for school, so I'm cool. Don't worry about getting a backpack for me." Please don't 'cause I'd never use it.

Aunt Phoebe has this look in her eyes as if she knows exactly what I'm thinking. She embraces me, saying, "Lord, I don't know what I'ma do with you, girl."

"Aunt Phoebe, I'm a fashion icon at school. Somebody has to set the trends around here. You know I'm telling the truth."

My aunt laughs. "C'mon, let's get your cousins and go home. I want to have dinner finished by the time your uncle comes home from his meeting. He didn't have much time to eat breakfast this morning."

Uncle Reed can really be a bear when he's hungry, so I say, "I'll go get Alyssa."

Chance is already outside waiting near the car when we walk out of the church. He is his usual sulky self. I'm crazy about my boo, but if this is what being in love does to you, I'm not so sure I want any part of it.

Aunt Phoebe asks, "Boy, what is wrong with you? You been moping around a lot lately."

Alyssa and I turn our attention to Chance, who mumbles, "Ain't nothing wrong with me. Just got some stuff on my mind."

This is getting ridiculous. I've got to find out what's going on between Chance and Trina.

"TRINA, WAIT UP," I shout as soon as Alyssa and I step onto the campus the first day of school. I notice that she has dark circles under her eyes, like she hadn't slept well or something. I make a mental note to suggest concealer. Girlfriend definitely don't need to be walking around here looking like that.

"Hey y'all," she greets us softly. Although she's trying to hide it, Trina looks about as upset as Chance. I guess that's why me and Alyssa haven't really heard from her. She and Chance are fighting so she probably thinks that Alyssa and I will side with him. *She's right*. Trina's my girl but Chance is family.

"You doing okay?"

"Why you asking?" Trina responds with a hint of attitude.

Alyssa gives me this look of bewilderment, prompting me to ask, "What's up, Trina? Are you upset with me or something?"

"No, why would you think that?"

"Well, you seem like you have an attitude. I notice that you and Chance are both running around like you've lost your best friend."

"I might have," Trina mutters. Before Alyssa or I can ask any more questions, she says, "We just need to work out some things. It's private. You know?"

I'm a little offended by her words. "We're not trying to be up in your business or nothing. But we're not blind."

"We'll work it out."

I cross my arms and pointedly look away. "Whatever."

"I'll see y'all later. I need to pick up a book in the library before class."

Trina walks off, leaving us in a cloud of confusion.

"That was so weird," I mutter. "I don't think Trina likes me anymore."

"I don't think that's it at all. I think she and Chance are having some serious problems."

"Well, she don't need to give me attitude. I didn't do a thing to her." I am too through with Trina. How can she treat me like this? We're supposed to be friends.

After third period, Trina comes toward me saying, "Divine, can we talk?"

I stop walking.

"Hey, I'm sorry about earlier. I just want you to know that I'm not mad at you or anything."

"You must have talked to Alyssa," I say.

She nods. "Why would you think that I'd be mad at you?"

"I don't know. You were acting so funny with me this morning. I figured you thought that I'd done something."

"It's not even like that, Divine. We're cool." She gives me a hug. "Sorry for being so rude. You're my girl."

"I'm glad we're okay."

"We are," Trina confirmed. "It's Chance and I that are having issues. I guess this thing between us is really stressing us out."

"I understand."

"I'm . . . I just need to figure out some stuff."

"Trina, Chance loves you."

Her lower lip trembles as she raises her gaze to meet mine. "I hope so because I really love him."

"I'm not trying to be up in your business, but if you need to talk—I'm here for you." Deep down, it's driving me crazy not knowing what's going on between them.

Later, during lunch, I see them across the room of the cafeteria, huddled together and, from the looks of it, deep in conversation.

"What is going on between them?" I wonder aloud. I have a strong feeling that whatever it is—it's serious. Very serious.

By the time *Law & Order* has reached the halfway point, I've already figured out who the culprit is, but with Chance and Trina I can't figure out a thing—and it's driving me crazy. I hate not being in the know. It just doesn't work for me.

chapter 4

$\mathcal{A}$*fter* only two days of school, I've already been given homework, two class projects and a test to prepare for—they don't waste time here at all. It's all good, though. I'm excited about being in the tenth grade.

My friends back home are most likely having the times of their lives because school doesn't start for another two weeks in California. Instead of doing my chores, I call Mimi because I'm feeling a little homesick.

I hang up when I get her voice mail, and then call my other best friend, Rhyann.

"I still can't believe you went back to Georgia for school," Rhyann tells me as soon as she answers the phone. "I thought you were going to stay here with us. Your cousins are cool and all, but

me and Mimi . . . we want you back here in California. Girl, this is
where you belong."

"This feels more like home to me," I confess.

"I can't believe you want to stay down there. I just don't get it."

It doesn't matter to me whether Rhyann gets it or not. This is
all about me. "Can we talk about something else? Like that guy you
were telling me about . . . Troy or something. Are you still talking
to him?"

"Girl, that's old news. I stopped talking to Troy a couple of
days after you left for Martinique. He was a dog. Dog with a capital
'D.'"

"What happened?" I ask, although I'm not really interested.
I've been trying to figure out a way to bring Madison into the conversation. I love talking about my boo.

"He was trying to talk to Mimi on the side. Like she not gonna
tell me."

I laugh. "Talk about stupid. He didn't know that Mimi's your
girl?"

"Oh he knew . . . Troy knew we were friends. He just didn't
care. It's all good, though—I already met somebody else anyway."

I switch my cell phone from my right ear to my left. We've been
on the phone for over thirty minutes and my arm's getting tired.
"You sure don't waste any time."

She laughs. "Girl, you one to talk. I know why you don't want
to come back here for school. You just want to be down there with
Farmer John."

"His name is Madison, not Farmer John."

"He's cute, Dec, but really . . . is he all that?"

"Yeah, he is," I respond, my eyes straying to his photo in the
small frame on my dresser. "I'm crazy about him. He feels the same
way I do."

"How do you know it's not about you being rich? I'm so sure this Madison person hasn't met many rich people. It's not like he lives out here."

"Rhyann, you're not exactly one of the rich and famous yourself," I point out. I'm trying hard to keep my irritation at bay.

"So what? I know plenty of rich people. I knew them before I met you and Mimi—even before I started going to Stony Hills Preparatory School."

I break into laughter. "Like who?"

"Lots of people."

"You're not counting all of the people on the posters pinned on your wall, are you? Just having them hanging around in your bedroom don't count, Rhyann."

She howls with laughter. "You so wrong for that, Dee."

"You're the one always going around talking about all these posters in your room and how the guys in them seemed to follow you around."

"Whatever . . ." Rhyann mutters with a chuckle. "Anyway, let me tell you about my new friend. His name is Hunter and we met online."

I laugh. "I still can't believe you've resorted to meeting people over the internet. Rhyann, you must be so desperate."

"*I am not.* I get lots of play. Dee, I wasn't looking for a boy on the internet. We just kind of ran into each other."

Rhyann's lying to herself, I decide. I haven't forgotten about the time she answered ads in the classifieds, trying to find a boyfriend. Then there was the time she set out to meet boys in college. On the weekends, she would ride the bus to USC and just hang out, pretending to be a college student.

"So, how did you run into Hunter?" I ask.

"In this poetry writing workshop I was taking online. Hunter sounds cool and his poetry is nice."

"Have you seen him in person yet?"

"No . . . I'm taking my time to get to know him. So far, though, it's going good."

"Then you are thinking about meeting him in person?"

"After my brothers check him out first," Rhyann responds. "He supposedly does spoken word all over Los Angeles."

"Let me know how it goes. I'm not much for the internet dating game."

"I wasn't either. Like I told you though, this just kind of happened. It wasn't planned at all."

"Just don't go thinking this is the guy you're going to marry," I advise. "You know how you are, Rhyann. You think you're going to marry every guy you meet."

"Like you're not dreaming of being Mrs. Farmer John. I bet you want your own barn too."

"His name is Madison. You know that."

"*He lives on a farm, Dee.* A farm. You live in a mansion. You've traveled the world. Your parents are famous. Really, Dee, what can this boy give you?"

I consider Rhyann's words. "Hmmmm, he's fine. He's cuter than most boys I've met so far. He's a great kisser, but then again—he's the first boy I've ever kissed. Anyway, Madison treats me good. The most he does is try to get me to skip school or sneak out of the house. He says he just wants to be with me."

"Girl, you know he wants sex, don't you?"

"I know. He keeps saying that he wants to prove his love to me—I told him that he doesn't have to do it that way. He can just tell me. Rhyann, I'm not giving up nothing. I'm a member of the big V club and I intend to stay a virgin."

"How does he feel about it?"

I shrug. "It doesn't matter how Madison feels. He knows I'm not doing that. Like I said, he's a good guy. He's not trying to disrespect or beat on me like Rochelle's sister's boyfriend does. Remember her?" I ask, referring to one of my former classmates at Stony Hills Prep. "Although I'd have to give that boy a whupping if he tried."

Rhyann laughs. "Girl, now you sound country."

"Southern is what I prefer," I reply. "Rhyann, there's nothing wrong with people who live in farm towns. Just like there's nothing wrong with people who live in places like where you live."

"C'mon, girl, you can say it. The projects."

"Rhyann—" I begin but she cuts me off by saying, "Dee, I'm not mad. Girl, I know where I live. It's a good thing I'm a genius. That's why I have a scholarship to Stony Hills Prep."

"You've told that lie so much you believe it." I laugh. "You're going to Stony Hills because they wanted more diversity in the students. That's why you have a full scholarship."

"And I'm a genius."

"You're smart but I wouldn't call you a genius. It's not like Mensa International is knocking on your door."

"Who?"

"Mensa," I repeat. "It's an organization for people with IQs in the top two percent of the country."

"Maybe I should check them out, huh? I'm not only brilliant . . . I'm fine."

I laugh. "I don't know about you."

"Girl, I make you and Mimi look even cuter when I'm around. Don't hate . . ."

"Actually, I'm pretty cute on my own. Look at my parents. Mom is hot and well . . . Jerome was the man back in his day."

"Your dad is still the man. Old dude is fine . . ."

"Like, that's so totally gross—you talking about Jerome like that."

"You look a lot like your dad."

I take her assessment with a grain of salt. Rhyann actually believes she and Beyoncé look alike but she is so way off base on that one. The only thing they have in common is a dyed blonde weave. Why she decided to go with that color, I have no idea. It doesn't look bad on her—just makes her look older.

Aunt Phoebe knocks on my open door. "You need to finish your laundry, sugar. There are other people in this house waiting to use the washer and dryer."

"Yes ma'am," I say to my aunt. To Rhyann, I say, "I'll give you a call sometime tomorrow. I have to get off the phone."

"Peace . . ."

I hang up.

Tossing the phone on my bed, I release a long sigh. I hate laundry day.

I carry the plastic basket filled with my clothing down the hall to the laundry room.

Alyssa comes up behind me. "What are you doing?"

"Laundry . . . duh."

"Washing clothes sure puts you in a nasty mood."

"I hate doing laundry," I respond while tossing my whites into the machine. "I can't stand it."

"It's not like you're doing it by hand. Just think . . . what if we didn't have any washing machines? What would you do?"

"I'd cut off my hands or I'd walk around smelling like a funk factory."

"You wouldn't have to worry about having friends, that's for sure."

I glance over at my cousin. "Are you trying to say I smell? I don't stink," I state. I take a whiff of the clothing in my hands and say, "And neither do my cloth—" I can't finish my sentence because I'm overtaken by a sudden coughing attack.

Alyssa doubles over in loud peals of laughter.

To pay her back for laughing, I throw a pair of dirty socks at her, which she successfully dodges. She throws them back.

"I could've been dying while you're standing here laughing at me."

"Hey, don't get mad at me. Those are your clothes trying to take you out," Alyssa teases. "You better hurry up and wash them before they try a second attempt on your life."

"You're stupid," I mutter before breaking into laughter.

With the first load in the machine, Alyssa and I head back to my room. I tell her about my conversation with Rhyann. "She's met some boy on the internet now."

"She's not thinking about meeting him in person, is she?" Alyssa questions.

"Not until her brothers check him out first."

"I guess that's smart."

"I think meeting a boy on the internet is stupid. Nobody should be that desperate."

"I just read a book about this girl who met a boy on the internet. It turns out that he lived two blocks away from her. He had a crush on her but was too shy to let her know in person."

"You and your romance novels," I mutter. "I suppose they live happily ever after."

"They fell in love. He was the type of boy she'd always been looking for—she just didn't know it by the way he looked. She went for the athletes and this guy was a computer geek."

"I don't think I want to meet a boy off the internet. He'd have to be something pretty special to get my attention that way."

"Rhyann is so pretty. She doesn't have to run after guys so much," Alyssa states.

"She loves the chase, I think. Rhyann likes to try and make guys fall in love with her. Then when they do, she isn't interested in them anymore. The girl is a playa."

"She's funny."

I agree.

Alyssa and I make girl talk until it's time for me to take my clothes out of the washing machine and drop in a second load.

While I finish up my laundry, Alyssa and Aunt Phoebe bake mint chocolate chip cookies. I smell them just as I put my last load of clothing into the dryer.

Since the laundry is almost done, I decide I can use a little cookie break.

My cell rings—it's Madison.

Warm mint chocolate chip cookies weigh heavily on my mind, so I decide to let the call roll to voice mail. I'm crazy about my boo, but after an exhausting evening of doing laundry, it's all about the cookies and a tall glass of ice-cold milk.

SATURDAY AFTERNOON, AUNT Phoebe allows Chance to use her van to drive us to TeenTalk, a social segment of our youth ministry program at church.

The assistant pastor, Michael Summers, will be our facilitator this month. I for one am thankful because Uncle Reed isn't coming for this session—he usually tries to be funny but can't really pull it off. He's lame to the point that it's embarrassing.

I notice that Chance is extremely quiet on the drive over.

"What's up with you, boy?" I ask. "You've been acting funny ever since I got back."

"What I'm going through has nothing to do with you."

"Oh, I *know* that," I shoot back.

Chance is really in a mood and I can't figure out why. Alyssa and I called Trina a couple of times, but she didn't say much either. In fact, she didn't even bring up Chance's name at all—something totally out of character for her. The girl usually doesn't want to talk about anything else.

I drop the issue for now but I vow to get to the bottom of this mystery. I'm way too nosy to just let it go.

Penny arrives within minutes of us. We gather in the banquet hall along with the other teens for light refreshments before locating a row of seats so that we can sit together.

Pastor Summers is always prompt and begins immediately. "Today, we're going to talk about something that's pressing on the minds of teens and adults. Sex."

Alyssa and I glance at one another while Penny shifts uncomfortably in her seat.

"Popular songs speak of the thrills of casual sex," he states. "Television rolls out sexual innuendos one after another. The internet beckons Web surfers to all types of erotic destinations and fashion boasts midriff-baring designs."

My ears perk up at the mention of fashion.

"Y'all have to deal with this at a time when hormonal surges and emerging feelings are making life confusing enough. But what happens when faith gets thrown into the mix? How does being a Christian affect your perceptions and responses in this sex-drenched society?"

The room is so quiet; you could hear a pin drop. Out of the corner of my eye, I see Chance squirming in his seat, which leads me to wonder if he needs to make a bathroom run.

"A lot of Christian teens are having sex and suffering painful, sometimes devastating consequences," Pastor Summers continues.

If he only knew . . .

I steal a glance over at Penny. Her head is down, as if she's afraid to look the Pastor in the eye.

"Some of you out there are probably saying to yourselves right now, I know the Bible says you can't have sex before marriage. But why can't you, if you're in love with the person? Or you might be saying, recently I had sex with a guy, thinking that it would bring us closer. I know now that was a mistake, and I feel totally ashamed. I feel cut off from God, I want to do what's right, but I can't seem to."

Penny's head shoots up, her eyes wide open.

I'm pretty sure she's said both of those things to herself. The pain in her eyes is so evident that I feel horrible for her. I'm pretty sure Pastor Summers can see it too.

He starts talking about his time in high school.

"Of course, there was always a lot of pressure to have sex," he says. "I was a football player, you know. And the girls—they really came after you. But the Bible is clear. No sex 'til marriage."

"But how did you do it?" one of the boys in the back of the room asked. "How did you fight the temptation? *Tell me.*"

Everyone laughs.

"The main thing that helped me to maintain a biblical standard of purity is that I could see where indulging in alcohol, drugs and even sex had taken a lot of my peers. Don't get me wrong—it wasn't easy. I had to stay prayed up. I knew what I wanted out of life and I didn't want to limit myself. Having babies or getting AIDS was not on my route. If y'all just stay focused on your goals, peer pressure shouldn't faze you."

Penny surprises me by raising her hand. Is she going to confess or something? I wonder.

"What happens to people who have sex but maybe don't get pregnant or AIDS? I mean, what if they still go to church and everything. Do you understand what I'm saying?"

Pastor Summers nods. "Penny wants to know what can happen beyond the physical costs of having sex. I've seen boys and girls who have had sex and while they still attend church, their spiritual lives become empty. They become fake. Your sin takes you further and further away from God."

Another girl raises her hand to speak.

"I'm going to wait until I'm married before having sex because I don't want to hurt God."

I'd never looked at it this way. Having premarital sex *would* hurt God. I've heard my uncle say that sin hurts God. While I'm pretty clear on the abstinence issue—thanks to my mom and Aunt Phoebe—I'd never really considered how God would see my other sins like muttering curse words under my breath, or thinking evil thoughts about my aunt and uncle when I don't get my way.

I send up a silent prayer. *God, I'm so sorry for hurting You. I'm not perfect, as You know, but I will try to do so much better. I promise. Amen.*

THE WEEKENDS DON'T last long at all. Before I've had a chance to even enjoy my time off—it's Monday.

"I'll be right back," I tell Alyssa. "I need to use the bathroom." I hand her my backpack and rush into the one nearest the cafeteria.

My classmate Deonne Massey is in there. "Hey girl," she greets. "I like that shirt you have on."

"Thank you. I like yours too."

"Did you get all the notes for English Lit?" she asks. "I couldn't write fast enough. That woman talks way too fast for me."

"I have them," I respond. "You can get a copy."

"Thanks." Deonne heads to the door. "I better go get me something to eat. My stomach was growling so loud earlier my boo thinks he had a tiger for a girlfriend." Grinning, she adds, "But that may not be such a bad thing."

I laugh. "You're crazy."

Alone in the bathroom, I enter one of the stalls. I hear someone come in while I'm doing my business.

Suddenly, I hear vomiting, which truly grosses me out. I'm not real surprised because the food isn't all that great. Most days, Alyssa and I bring something from home for lunch or we get Chance to bring us something from off campus. I look forward to the time when me and Alyssa will have off-campus privileges.

All that vomiting and gagging is making me queasy. "You okay?" I call out.

"D-Divine?"

I finish my business and flush the toilet before walking out of the stall. Trina's standing at the sink washing her face. "Girl, what's wrong with you? What did you eat?"

"I had some of the s-spaghetti in the cafeteria." She presses a wet napkin to her face. "I think the sauce was too greasy or something."

Concerned, I scan her face. "You sure you okay? Maybe you should go home."

Trina shakes her head no. "I'll be fine. I don't think I have anything else left in my stomach."

I offer her the tiny bottle of mouthwash I keep in my backpack, which she readily accepts.

"Thanks," she manages.

Trina and I walk out of the bathroom together.

"I was wondering what was taking you so long," Alyssa says to me. She glances over at Trina. "I didn't know you were in there."

"She was sick," I supply. "Alyssa, you may not want to eat the spaghetti today." I can't handle another person throwing up.

Trina presses a hand to her stomach. "I'll see y'all later. I need to get to the library before the bell rings."

"I don't know what they put in that spaghetti but it tore up Trina's stomach."

Alyssa glances over her shoulder, then back at me. "Trina's been looking kind of sick for a few days. She's losing weight too."

"Just the same—stay away from the spaghetti," I warn.

After lunch, I catch a glimpse of Trina on her way to her next class. Alyssa's right: she's lost weight and she's been looking real tired. I just figure it's all those late-night phone calls with Chance.

Aunt Phoebe would have a fit if she knew he was on the phone with Trina after eleven. I know because I hear them talking when I'm on one of my midnight runs to the kitchen or to gossip with Alyssa.

Trina is the last person on my mind by the time the bell rings, signaling the end of the school day. All I can think about is going home and taking a nap before dinner. I was up late myself, talking to Rhyann and Mimi last night.

Normally, I try to abide by my aunt and uncle's rules but this was just too important. Mimi was having boyfriend issues and she really needed me and Rhyann to be there for her.

The fact that Aunt Phoebe's cooking dinner makes me even happier. I've learned a lot since moving here and I can do a decent job in the kitchen, but if I don't have to cook—I'm thrilled.

I lie down and close my eyes. All I want right now is at least a half hour's worth of good napping time. I need some sleep before I have to dive into my homework.

I hear Chance's voice. He's right outside my window. Most likely watering the grass—something he has to do four times a week. I don't know why Uncle Reed won't just spring for a sprinkler system. Guess he thinks we don't have enough to do—that's why he refuses to get a dishwasher, a sprinkler system or a gardener.

"Trina, what do you want me to say? I don't know what to do either."

The tone of Chance's voice forces my eyes open. I sit up in bed, listening.

"I didn't expect this to happen."

Didn't expect what to happen? I wonder.

He moves away from my window but not before I hear him say, "What do you mean you gon' have it?"

Have what? The shock of the truth hits me full force.

Trina's pregnant. I should've realized it before now. All the signs were there—Chance crying like a girl, his mood swings, Trina vomiting and looking all washed out—even the way Chance was acting during TeenTalk. Like he was guilty of something.

Chance and Trina . . . having a baby? Wave after wave of shock wash over me.

My body is propelled off the bed. I have to tell Alyssa. This is way too big a secret to keep from her. I can't believe Chance hasn't come to us with this, or Trina. We're all friends and we hang out a lot. Well, we used to until Trina and Chance started dating.

I walk inside Alyssa's room, not bothering to knock.

She's sleeping so I give her a light shake.

"It's me. Get up. I need to tell you something."

Alyssa sits up in bed, rubbing her eyes. "Girl, this better not be about something you just read in *Seventeen* magazine. Or about the time you dreamed you won *America's Next Top Model*."

"Alyssa, hush . . . will you? I think I know what's going on with Chance and Trina."

"Okay . . . what do you think is going on?"

"Alyssa, I think Trina's pregnant."

Her mouth drops open in shock and she just sits there. "Why do you think that?" She asks after a moment.

"Chance was just outside my window and he was on the phone. From what I heard, it sounds like Trina's pregnant."

"Divine, you're wrong on this. I think they're just having problems. Maybe they're about to break up." It's obvious that Alyssa isn't that convinced. "What exactly did he say?"

"He was asking if she was going to have *it*."

"That's it?"

I nod, still trying to wrap my mind around the whole idea.

There is a long, brittle silence.

"You really think Chance got Trina pregnant?"

I nod again.

Alyssa is as stunned as I am by this revelation. "I didn't know they were having sex."

"Alyssa, it's not like they're going to tell us something like that. It's too personal."

Placing a hand to her face, Alyssa falls back against her pillows. "Oh Lord . . . Mama and Daddy . . . when they find out . . . Oh Lord."

Just the mere thought of Aunt Phoebe and Uncle Reed finding out is enough to scare me. "I'm so glad I'm not Chance right now."

Alyssa sits up. "Divine, they are gonna kill him. I don't think there's enough forgiveness in the Bible to save my brother."

I totally agree. That boy is dead for sure.

"What are we gonna do?" Alyssa asks.

"I don't know about you, but I'm going to sit back and watch the fireworks."

"Divine, I'm serious. Chance is in big trouble."

"And I feel bad for him, but he should've kept his clothes on. He wouldn't be in this trouble if he had."

"I'm so scared for him."

"We should pray for Chance," I suggest. "He'll need prayer."

Alyssa eyes me. "Why? Because he sinned?"

I shake my head no. "Because he's going to meet Jesus as soon as your parents find out about the baby. And you don't want to even think about what Trina's dad is going to do to him. That man is as mean as a bulldog."

"Chance, what have you done?" Alyssa moans softly.

"He got busy," I respond softly. "But at least he won't die before ever finding out what it's like to be in a real relationship."

chapter 5

The next morning, Alyssa and I stand outside of the house waiting for Chance, half in anticipation and half in dread.

"I'ma ask him if Trina's having a baby," Alyssa announces. "This is a big deal."

Anxiety spurts through me, prompting me to say, "Maybe you shouldn't say anything yet. You know he'll get mad."

"I have to, Divine. This is my brother and I care about him."

"Please don't say anything," I plead. "He's going to know that somehow I found out and told you. He's going to be mad at me."

"How will he know?"

Shrugging, I respond, "I don't know. Or he might think Trina told us and then he'll get upset with her. The last thing they need is to be fighting at a time like this. Besides, I don't want to be in the middle."

"Then maybe you shouldn't've told me. Chance is my brother and I don't want him going through something like this alone."

Chance walks out of the house, putting an end to our conversation. He takes a bite out of a piece of toast. He never leaves the house without making toast and eating it on the way to school.

"Y'all ready?"

The morning weather is nice—not too hot—but to me, it suddenly feels like I'm on a volcano on the verge of erupting. I just know that Chance is going to freak the moment Alyssa opens her mouth.

Before I can stop her, Alyssa walks back into the yard, meeting him halfway. "Chance, I need to talk to you."

"About what?"

"I think you know already."

Biting my bottom lip, I walk over to where they're standing. Chance is really going to have it in for me if he finds out I told Alyssa. I just know it.

"Girl, what are you talking about? Look, I don't have time for this." He turns to leave, but stops when Alyssa says, "I know that Trina is pregnant."

"Did Trina tell you that?" His tone is chilly all of a sudden.

I've never seen Chance look so mad. I just pray my name doesn't come up.

Alyssa doesn't waver. Her eyes never leave his face when she answers, "No, she didn't tell me anything. I just know."

"Then how do you know?" he demands. "Trina says she ain't told nobody but me. Now she must've told you. I'ma call her right now. Involving you in our business."

My nerves tense immediately. I don't want him upsetting Trina for nothing, so I decide to confess. "Chance, she didn't say anything. I was the one who told Alyssa."

His eyes meet mine. "What did you do? Listen to my phone calls? You too doggone nosy, Divine."

The boy is practically growling at me. I take a step backward because in his current situation I'm not real sure what the baby daddy might do.

"I didn't listen to your conversation on purpose," I quickly interject. "Chance, you were standing outside my window."

"So why'd you go running to my sister? She didn't have to know."

"Because we care about you and—"

He shoves me hard. "Just get out my face, Divine. I hate your guts right now."

His harsh words don't hurt me as much as his shoving me does. No way I'm going to let him get away with this. "Don't you ever put your hands on me again," I warn. "*Ever.* You will get hurt. *Trust.*"

Chance gives me this look like he's not totally convinced I won't take him out.

"Look, I'm not the one who got you in this trouble. Don't go getting no attitude with me. Don't let these designer clothes fool you."

"You just need to mind your business. If I hear this at school it's gon' be me and you. I don't care nothing about you taking tae kwon do."

"Whatever," I mutter. "If you'd kept your—"

"What in the world is going on between you two?" Aunt Phoebe demands from behind us. "Why y'all out here carrying on like this? Anything I need to know?"

We were so busy fussing, none of us heard her when she came outside. I scan Aunt Phoebe's face, looking to see if I can gauge just how much she might have overheard.

"It's nothing, Aunt Phoebe," I say. "I guess I just get on Chance's nerves from time to time."

"Chance, did I hear you correctly? Did you just threaten your cousin?"

"Yes ma'am." He ground the words out between his teeth. Chance is not sure whether I'm going to spill my guts. I can see the desperation in his eyes.

"Come here, boy."

Shoulders slumped, Chance turns around slowly and walks back to where Aunt Phoebe is standing.

I'm too angry with him right now to really sympathize. I hope she cleans the yard with him, personally.

"We better leave," Alyssa says in a low whisper. "Mama don't look like she's in a good mood. When she's done with Chance—he gon' be in a worse one, so let's just get on outta here."

Alyssa's not going to get an argument from me.

I feel even guiltier for telling Alyssa when I see Trina. Maybe it wasn't a good idea to spill their secret to her. I should've kept my big mouth shut.

"I'm not gon' say anything to Trina," Alyssa tells me.

"You won't have to. I know Chance is going to tell her and then she'll hate me too. Why didn't you just listen to me?"

"I didn't know he was gonna trip like that, Divine. I'm sorry."

I direct my anger at Alyssa because she's an easy target. "What did you think was going to happen? Did you really think Chance would be *happy* about us knowing? I don't know why you had to say anything to him in the first place. You talk too much, Alyssa."

The tension between us begins to melt after a moment.

"He's my brother, Divine. I care what happens to him."

"I care about Chance too."

Alyssa holds up a hand. "You know what? Let's stop talking about this. I don't want to argue with you all the way to school. We didn't do anything—this is Chance's problem."

Although we're not discussing it, Chance's situation is still in the forefront of our minds. We're both afraid for him.

For most of the day, I go out of my way to avoid Trina. I'm

not in the mood for another tongue-lashing. I'm just not up to it today.

Alyssa and I decide to walk home alone since it's pretty clear that Chance is still mad at me. He arrives home about ten minutes behind us.

I hide out in my room.

Somewhere between finishing my history homework and starting my English literature assignment, there's a knock on my bedroom door.

"Yeah?" I call out without looking up.

"Hey, Divine. Can I come in?"

My gaze travels to Chance then down to his hands. I want to make sure he's unarmed. "For what?"

He enters the room, closing the door behind him.

I stand up, my arms folded across my chest. "I don't see what we need to talk about," I huff. "You already said more than enough."

"Divine, I came in here to apologize. I'm sorry for the way I jumped all over you this morning. I just got a lot on my mind."

"And that's my fault?" I snap. "You the one going around here . . ." My voice dies at the pitiful expression on his face. "Look, you really hurt my feelings, Chance. I wasn't trying to be nosy like you accused. You were the one running your mouth outside my window the other day. I only told Alyssa what I thought after hearing you ask Trina if she was going to keep it. I thought that maybe you might need somebody to talk to. You know, I actually thought the three of us were pretty close but I guess I was wrong."

"I know y'all care about me. I just wasn't ready for anybody else to know about the baby."

"I hope you know that you were a major jerk."

He nods. "I'm sorry."

My tone softens toward him. "I know that this has to be hard on

you. And I understand totally that you're stressed, but Chance . . .
don't you ever shove me like that again."

"I wouldn't ever hit you, Divine. You know that."

"Shoving a girl is just as bad. My mom says so all the time."

"I'm really sorry."

Satisfied, I give a slight nod.

"We cool?"

I embrace Chance. "Yeah. We're cool."

"Divine, I really don't want Mama and Dad to know. Not until
Trina and I figure something out."

I don't think I've ever seen Chance look so scared. I don't
blame him for being afraid—his mom is crazy when she wants to
be. "I'm not saying a word. Alyssa isn't going to tell them either."
I pause for a moment before asking, "So what are you and Trina
going to do?"

Alyssa knocks on the door. "Can I come in?" When I say she
can, she questions, "Have you seen my blue earrings and the matching bracelet? I can't find them anywhere."

"I haven't seen them," I respond. "Did you go through your
backpack and your purse?" Alyssa loses stuff often.

"Close the door behind you," Chance tells her.

Alyssa sits down on the edge of my bed. "Y'all get everything
straight?"

"Yeah," we respond in unison.

She looks at Chance. "Sit down and talk to us. Let's see if
there's something we can do."

I give Alyssa a brief recap. "I was just asking him what they're
going to do."

Shrugging, Chance says, "I don't know. Trina doesn't want to
have an abortion."

"And you want her to?" Alyssa demands. "Chance, that's a sin.
It's—"

"So is having sex when you're not married," he interjects. "Trina and I already sinned. That's why we're being punished like this."

"I know you've been a Christian a lot longer than I have, but what I understand is that no matter what we do God still loves us and He forgives," I say. "I don't think He punishes us, but I could be wrong. I'll have to ask Uncle Reed."

Chance suddenly looked panicked.

"I told you. I'm not going to say anything about this. I wouldn't betray you like that."

"We only did it a couple of times."

Holding up my hand, I say, "Whoa . . . *way* too much information. I definitely don't want *that* image in my mind. Talk about gross."

Chance sighs heavily. "I wish there was something y'all could do to help me, but there isn't. This is a problem only me and Trina can fix."

Alyssa hugs him. "Sorry."

He nods. "I don't know how to tell Mama and Dad about this. I just sent off my application and stuff to Georgetown University." Shaking his head, he says, "Man . . . this is so crazy. I just want to graduate and go off to college in the fall."

"You gotta tell them before they find out some other way, Chance," Alyssa advises. "You know how Mama gets over stuff like that."

"I can't tell her this," he practically whispers. "I can't tell her."

I feel so bad for my cousin. He's done nothing but dream about going to Georgetown University and now—now he's about to become somebody's daddy. I bet life must really suck for him right now.

AUNT PHOEBE AND Uncle Reed suspect something's going on with Chance because they've been asking a lot of questions and trying to get him to open up. Aunt Phoebe's even come to me and Alyssa but we keep quiet. I'm not about to let her know that I'm privy to anything between Chance and Trina.

Wednesday afternoon, as we're walking home from school, I say to Alyssa, "I didn't see Trina today. Did you?"

Shaking her head no, she replies, "I don't think she came to school today."

We turn around to ask Chance about Trina but he looks deep in thought. Instead of bothering him, Alyssa and I resume our pace.

Just as we round the corner, we see Trina's parents pull up in front of the house and park the car. Both the van and the Cadillac are there, which means Uncle Reed is home too. This can only mean bad news.

I glance over my shoulder at Chance; he looks like he's about to be executed. Things are definitely not looking good for him.

Alyssa stops walking, waiting for him to catch up. "Chance? Do you know what's going on?"

"They must know . . ."

He sounds tired. Like he's just given up on keeping this secret. "I'm so sorry, Chance," I murmur.

He shrugs and sighs in resignation. "It's not like they wasn't gon' find out. I just wanted time to tell Mama and Dad myself. Now, Dad's gonna kill me, if Mama don't beat him to it." He releases another long sigh.

When Trina climbs out of the car, she's looking about as sad as Chance. I'm almost positive that she's probably wishing she was dead right along with him.

Trina's parents are usually smiling and talkative but not today. Her father just stands there at the edge of the yard, glaring at Chance, who seems to be shrinking right before my eyes. Her mother looks like she's been crying.

"Hey, Trina . . . Mr. Winston . . . Mrs. Winston," Alyssa greets. I throw up my hand in a wave before rushing into the house. Behind us, I hear Mrs. Winston say, "Hey . . ." in response, but Trina and her father say nothing.

Aunt Phoebe meets us in the hallway. I note that she's not smiling either. Things are about to get real ugly around here.

"I want you two to stay in the back while we're talking in the family room. Don't come out until we call you. I mean it."

"Can I at least get a glass of water?" Alyssa asks.

Aunt Phoebe eyes her hard before saying, "Get your water and then get yourself somewhere."

"Does she know already?" I whisper. "Aunt Phoebe really looks angry."

"She probably guessed it. What other reason would Trina be coming over here with her parents for?"

We decide to hold a vigil in my room since it's the farthest down the hall. I wanted to stand out in the hallway and listen, but Alyssa doesn't think it's a good idea. I'm really disappointed that we have to miss out on the drama.

Two hours pass before we finally hear the front door open and close.

"I think Trina and her parents just left," I state. "C'mon, let's go out front."

Alyssa shakes her head, folding her arms across her chest. "Nope. I'm staying right here. Mama said she'll call us when it's time for us to come out. I don't want to get on her bad side right now."

Before I can respond, we hear a sharp, shrill scream echoing around the house.

"What is that?"

"Mama," Alyssa explains. "I think she's about to have one of her hissy fits."

I frown, completely baffled. "What's a hissy fit?"

"Just listen."

"Boy, what in the world were you thinking?" Aunt Phoebe screeches at the top of her lungs. "How could you do a fool thing like that? Getting that girl pregnant. You still wet behind the ears yourself. Oh Lord . . . I just can't believe this is happening. Do you realize that you've just ruined your life?"

Aunt Phoebe is so upset that she's talking nonstop. Well, actually, it's more like she's screaming the words. I ease out into the hallway to hear better. Uncle Reed is saying, "Honey, calm down . . ."

"Calm down? How in the world can I *calm down?* I didn't intend on meeting none of my grandchildren until much later. Chance—boy, what were you thinking?"

Before he can say a word, Aunt Phoebe comes back with, "You weren't thinking. You were doing all that kissing and messing around . . . getting all hot and bothered. See what happens when you get hot and bothered? You start acting on them feelings and now look—you gon' be a daddy."

I've never heard Aunt Phoebe ramble on and on like this before. I figure I'll time her and sure enough, fifteen minutes later, Aunt Phoebe is still talking—if you could call it that.

Alyssa joins me in the hallway. "I feel sorry for Chance. Mama is mad."

"Like *yeah.*" I've never heard Aunt Phoebe sound so mad. She's really upset.

Aunt Phoebe finally calms down to the point that we can't hear her talking. Uncle Reed must have stuffed a sock in her mouth or something. But knowing them, they were probably in there praying.

Ten minutes later, Alyssa and I are summoned to the family room. I go through a mental checklist to make sure I haven't done anything that could come back to haunt me.

Only Uncle Reed and Aunt Phoebe are sitting in the family

room on that ugly striped couch. Chance is probably hiding in his room in shame.

Uncle Reed gestures for us to take a seat on the sofa. "I'm sure you heard some of what's going on."

Alyssa and I don't respond. We dare not say a word with Aunt Phoebe in the fragile state of mind she's in.

"Chance is going to be a father," Uncle Reed announces.

Aunt Phoebe suddenly falls apart, crying loudly. Uncle Reed comforts her by wrapping a thick arm around her. She wipes her face with a tissue and runs her fingers through her hair, which is a wild mess of curls. Aunt Phoebe looks like she's been in a bar fight. I glance at the double crease in her pants and the shirt that should've been thrown away years ago; she's a fashion disaster, but under the circumstances it's allowed.

After what seems like eternity, she says, "I know you two have been waiting for us to decide if we're going to let you have boys visit. Well, we've talked and we prayed over it. We thought about changing our minds but after all that's happened, we've decided to keep the rules as is."

Alyssa and I look from Aunt Phoebe to Uncle Reed.

"But why?" I question. "What did we do?"

"You didn't do anything. We just feel that after all that's happened with Chance, it would be better that y'all wait until you're eighteen to date. You and Alyssa are only fifteen—you're not ready emotionally."

I can't believe what I'm hearing. This is so unfair and I have every intention of telling them so. "I don't get it. We're not asking to go out anywhere with a boy—just have one come over every now and then. It's not a big deal."

"Oh, it's a very big deal, Divine," Aunt Phoebe counters. "Right now the only thing you need to focus on is your education. There will be enough time for boys after you finish your schooling."

"Are you saying we won't be able to have boyfriends until we graduate from high school?" Alyssa inquires. "That's not fair. Chance was able to do it. He didn't have to wait until he turned eighteen."

"And Chance has made a big mistake," Uncle Reed blurts. "He and Trina are going to be parents. Well, we're not about to let that happen again."

Aunt Phoebe surveys us. "I get the feeling that you both already knew about the baby?"

"We found out a couple of days ago," Alyssa says.

I could have hit her. Especially after the look Aunt Phoebe gives us. Her gaze travels first to me, then Alyssa. "So you didn't think we should know? Keeping something like this secret just tells me that you two are just as irresponsible as Chance."

"Aunt Phoebe, you can't blame us for what Chance did," I argue. "It's so not fair."

"Is it fair to keep things like this away from us? Huh?"

I really don't care about Chance and his issues right now. I'm more concerned about my social life. "Nothing would happen if you let us have boys over. You and Uncle Reed could sit in the room with us."

"Have you ever heard the saying that if you give a dog an inch—he'll take the whole foot?"

"Yes ma'am."

"See, when you get too much freedom too soon—you don't know how to act," Aunt Phoebe explains. "You lose yourself in your emotions and things just get crazy."

"Mama, we not gonna lose ourselves with you and Dad sitting in our faces."

"The answer is *no*. Now, I don't want to have this discussion again. My pressure is up and I just need to calm down."

I can't stand my aunt and uncle right now. I'm so mad I could just start screaming, but I don't. Aunt Phoebe is barely holding it together.

"You two can go to your rooms. Reed and I need to talk about some things."

I can't believe it. We've just been dismissed. Banished to our rooms for all of eternity.

Alyssa fights back tears while I clench and unclench my fists. I was mad enough to punch a hole in the wall, but I certainly wasn't about to ruin my nails or push Aunt Phoebe to the brink of murder. "I'm calling my mom," I tell Alyssa. "Aunt Phoebe's really trying to punish us for what Chance and Trina did and that's not fair. Maybe Mom can talk some sense into her."

"I hope she can. My mama's really tripping right now. *Eighteen.* She wants us to wait until we're practically out of high school."

"She sure is. I can't believe even Uncle Reed is siding with her like this. I thought he'd be more objective. He's usually real fair when it comes to things like this."

"He probably just don't want to upset Mama. He knows how she gets."

"This is all Chance's fault. We wouldn't be going through this if it wasn't for his mess."

"Don't matter really," Alyssa states.

"Well, when I talk to my mom, she'll get this all worked out," I assure her. "Just wait and see. This will soon be a nonissue."

I SPEND THE rest of the evening waiting on my mom to call me back. I really need her to straighten out Aunt Phoebe and Uncle Reed. They are being totally wrong about this all thing.

Alyssa is sitting on the floor in my bedroom, wiping away her tears. She's such a crybaby. I've told her over and over again that Mom is going to straighten this out. She's cool like that.

My cell phone rings.

I answer the phone before it can ring a second time. "Thanks for calling me back, Mom. I really need to talk to you."

She's immediately concerned. "Honey, what's wrong? You sounded so upset on your message."

I get straight to the point. "Mom, Aunt Phoebe is seriously buggin'. She and Uncle Reed just found out Chance is going to have a baby and—"

"Whoa!" Mom yells into the phone. "Slow down. Now what did you just say?"

"Chance and Trina are going to have a baby."

"*Oh my goodness.* I know Reed and Phoebe have to be devastated. Lord, what was that boy thinking about?"

Sex . . . *duh.*

"He needs to be focusing on his education," Mom fussed.

"Chance isn't all that happy about it either," I tell her.

"That poor boy."

I don't want to discuss Chance anymore, so I change the subject by saying, "But anyway, me and Alyssa presented our case to them—just like they asked us to—and they said they would think about it."

"You're losing me, honey. About what?"

"We'd asked Uncle Reed and Aunt Phoebe if Stephen and Madison could come over sometime. Especially since Alyssa's turning sixteen in a couple of weeks. They first said that they'd pray about it and get back to us. Now they're saying we have to wait until we're eighteen. I don't believe God told them that."

"Okay. So what do you think God *did* tell them?"

"I'm sure it was okay with Him but then they changed their minds because of what Chance did. What was the point of bothering God with this in the first place if they're not going to listen to Him?" I pause for a moment before asking, "Why do I have to pay for what Chance did?"

"Hon, they're upset right now and probably in shock. Maybe in a few days they'll calm down and you can talk to them again."

"Aunt Phoebe was pretty firm. I don't think she'll be changing her mind. You know how she is."

"Then she and Reed are doing what they think is best for you and Alyssa."

"I still think it's wrong. Alyssa and I should be given a chance to show that we can be trusted. It's not like we're going to just strip down and start doing it. Uncle Reed and Aunt Phoebe will both be around."

"It's their house, Divine. Whatever they say goes. You have to remember that."

"But you could talk to them, Mom. Eighteen is more than two years away."

"I'm not getting in the middle of this situation. Besides, I actually agree with what they're doing. We've had this discussion before. Reed and Phoebe have always said that you and Alyssa had to wait until you're at least sixteen years old anyway."

I gasp loudly. "*Mom.* I can't believe you. How can you do this to me? You're ruining my life."

"How?"

I didn't really know the answer to that so I say, "Mom, I'm almost sixteen years old. I'm not some baby."

"Nobody is treating you like a baby. We're just trying to protect you."

"Everybody is acting like I can't be trusted. Like I'm a tramp or something."

Mom laughs. "Divine, that's not it at all."

"Why can't I have a boy come see me then? What is the big deal? Why do I have to wait until I'm eighteen? What's going to make the big difference?" A tear escapes my eye. This is so frustrating.

"Hopefully, you'll be more mature emotionally."

"I'm mature now," I argue. "What difference is two years going to make? *None.*"

"You might want to tone down your attitude, Divine."

"Mom, why won't you speak up for me? Do you think you did that bad of a job raising me? Do you have to let Uncle Reed ruin my life—is this how you're trying to stay on his good side?"

I realize way too late that I'd actually verbalized my thoughts. "Mom . . ."

"Girl, you better be glad you're about three thousand miles away from me. I—"

"All I'm trying to say is that since I've come to live with Uncle Reed and Aunt Phoebe, you just seem to take a backseat to raising me," I interject.

"Divine, I'll talk to you tomorrow," Mom practically growls. "I need to get off this phone before I come through it."

My little dig had gotten to her. "Mom, why won't you help us?"

"Divine, I stand by Phoebe and Reed. You have the rest of your life to meet boys—it's not like they're going anywhere. Baby boys are being born every day."

I'm furious by the time Mom and I end our conversation, to the point that I'm crying. I can't believe she turned on me like that. This is worse than being in Mom mode. Those are the times when she suddenly remembers that she's supposed to give me guidance. She picks the worst times to slip into Mom mode.

"She's not going to do it, is she?" Alyssa questions.

Wiping my eyes, I shake my head no. "Mom thinks they're right."

Alyssa drops down on the edge of my bed. "What did she say about Chance?"

"Nothing much about that. She was too focused on ruining my life. I can't stand her sometimes." I angrily brush away a tear.

"I know what you mean. I feel the same way about my parents. I'll be glad when we're grown and on our own."

I agree totally. I can't wait to graduate and move out on my own. There's nothing I want more than my freedom. I hate being a teenager. I'm too old to be treated like a child but not old enough to be considered an adult. Life sucks.

chapter 6

We let a couple of hours pass before gathering in Chance's room to talk. I make myself comfortable on the black, overstuffed beanbag chair while Alyssa sits cross-legged on her brother's full-size bed.

I glance around the room, trying to picture a baby crib near the window, pale pink or blue walls instead of the current gray color, with little teddy bears or lambs on top of the posters featuring some of Chance's favorite athletes. One thing's for sure, I'm not giving up my room and I'm not letting Alyssa move in with me.

"You know we got lectured big-time because of you," Alyssa says in a low whisper. "Why couldn't you just keep your pants on?"

Chance rolls his eyes at her. "Leave me alone."

Alyssa glares at him, frowning. "No, I'm not gonna leave you alone. You were sinning. Don't you know you can go to you know where? Don't you care? What's going on with everybody—seems like everybody I know is having sex."

"I'm not," I state.

"I didn't set out to do this. I . . ." He sighs in resignation and shakes his head. "Y'all don't understand."

"What about birth control, Chance?" Alyssa asks. "Ever heard of a condom?"

"It wouldn't matter if he used a condom or not," I contribute. "It's still a sin. Like Jesus is going to give him points for using protection. Not."

Alyssa swings her head around to look at me. "Nobody asked you anything."

"Hey . . . I'm on your side. I called him a sinner too."

"Get out of my room," Chance demands. "Y'all getting on my nerves."

"He's stressed," Alyssa explains.

I totally agree. "That's because he's about to be a daddy."

"Why me . . ." he moans, falling back on his bed.

Since he obviously doesn't have a clue, I decide it's my duty to tell him. "Because you decided to have sex. Duh."

Chance's brows are drawn together in an angry frown. "Divine, shut up."

"Truth hurts, huh?"

"Why are you buggin', Chance?" Alyssa demands. "You *did* know this was a possibility, didn't you? I mean, every time Mama talked about sex she mentioned getting pregnant."

He shoots her a twisted look. "I'm not discussing my sex life with a bunch of kids."

"Actually, you don't have to because the whole world knows your business now," I counter. "Everybody knows you did the nasty."

Alyssa bursts into laughter.

"Get out of my room," yells Chance. "Just leave me alone."

I'm not about to give him any peace—especially since his actions are ruining my love life. "Chance, this is serious stuff. You're going to have a little kid. What about college? Are you still going or do you plan on marrying Trina?"

He suddenly looks like he's about to be sick. "I'm not ready for marriage. I wanna go to school but Dad says I have to get a job so that I can take care of the baby. I really want to go to Georgetown."

I've never seen my cousin look so sad. "Chance, I'm really sorry. I wish there was something I could do."

He says, his expression tight with strain, "I made this mistake all on my own."

Playing with her hair, Alyssa says, "Can I ask you something, Chance?"

He glances over at his sister with a look I interpret to be half anticipation and half dread. *"What?"*

"Was it worth it? Is having sex so great that—"

He shakes his head. "No. Listen to me . . . You and Divine, don't do it. Wait until you get married like Mama says. Y'all don't wanna deal with this. Having a baby is no joke."

Alyssa embraces him. "I'll help you and Trina. I can maybe babysit while you work or something. Mama might be mad right now, but she'll be there for y'all. This is her first grandbaby. You'll see. She really likes Trina and you know how much she loves you."

"I don't know. Right now, Mama can't even look at me. She's really mad."

"Chance, you know she won't be that way for long. Mama just wants the best for us. That's why she's so upset."

I expect him to burst into tears at any moment.

"Can y'all just leave? I got a lot to think about."

I rise to my feet and say, "C'mon, Alyssa. Your brother is kicking us out."

We leave and walk across to Alyssa's room.

"Chance looks so down. I feel bad for him."

"I do too."

"You know, I'm always hearing about how great sex is. Chance didn't seem like he enjoyed it much. Maybe it's because he's upset about the baby?"

"I have no idea, Alyssa. I was actually wondering about that myself. Even on television, people make it out to be something fierce. But after hearing how Aunt Phoebe carried on and knowing how crazy my mom can get—I think I'll just wait and find out. I don't like the idea of diseases and having babies."

"Remember how crazy Mama got when she caught me kissing Stephen that time at the movie theater? I'm not going through that again. I barely escaped with my life."

Shaking my head in confusion, I say, "First Penny and now Chance . . . Two people I never thought would be having sex anytime soon. I still can't believe it."

I RUN INTO Madison bright and early the next morning. In fact, he's the first person Alyssa and I see when we step on campus.

My cousin spots Stephen and runs off, leaving me alone with Madison. Normally I'd be in heaven, but not today.

"So did y'all talk?" are the first words out his mouth.

Reluctantly, I give him the bad news.

He wraps an arm around me. "What did they say?"

"They're not going to let you come over." I didn't want to spread Chance's business, so I left it at that. "They said no."

Madison drops his arm. "Why? What can we do if they sitting around watching us?"

I can tell he's upset. "I know, Madison. I asked the same question. My aunt is seriously tripping right now, though."

"She don't like me or somethin'? Is that it?"

"That's not it, boo. Aunt Phoebe is just . . . she's just trip-ping. She thinks me and Alyssa are too young to have boyfriends. Madison, you know she's real strict."

"Divine, I'm crazy about you, but I can't do this no more. Girl, I need to see you . . . I wanna spend some time with you. You know?"

"I want the same thing, Madison."

"You sure?"

"Yeah, I'm sure. Why did you ask me that?"

"Because you don't seem to be putting forth any effort."

"Boy, what are you talking about? I went to my aunt and uncle and asked—that's all I could do."

We sit on a nearby bench in silence.

After a moment, Madison says, "If this is how its gon' be . . . I think we need to just chill for a while. I can't handle just seeing you in school. I need some quality time with my girl. You know? We need to just call this thing off."

My head jerks up. I *know* I can't have heard him correctly. "Excuse me?"

"Baby, all I'm saying is that if you can't come see me and I can't come see you—we need to chill. Maybe when you get a little older we can—"

"I don't believe you, Madison," I snap in anger. Standing up, I say, *"You're breaking up with me?"*

"I'm a man, Divine, and—"

"You're a jerk," I rudely interject, fighting back tears. I work hard to maintain my fragile control but it's not easy with my heart being ripped to shreds like this. I can't believe this is the same guy I've been talking to all this time. We've been together almost two years now. "I'm not stupid, Madison. This isn't about your coming over to the house—this is about sex. You just mad because I won't let you—"

"I'm tired of just talking to you on the phone," he responded. "I'm just being truthful, Divine. I'm human."

"I'm not going to have sex with you, Madison."

He stands up and shoves both hands in his way-too-big jeans. I wish they'd just fall down around his ankles, humiliating him.

I take my attention off his clothes and back to his words. "Divine, I need more than holding hands and kissing."

I can't hold back my tears any longer. Wiping my eyes quickly, I say, "I can't believe you're doing this to me."

"Divine, you're cool. I really care for you, so it's not like we can't still be friends."

No he didn't just say those dreaded words to me. He might as well have called me the "b" word.

People are walking all around us; my face is wet from my crying and the sobs are building up in my throat—I'm about to lose it big-time. But before I humiliate myself, I walk away from Madison.

He calls out for me, but I keep walking and rush to the nearest bathroom.

I can't talk to him right now. I just want to die, my heart is so broken.

I meet up with Alyssa at lunchtime. "Divine, Madison wants to talk—" she begins. Taking a long look at my face, she changes what she was about to say. "What's wrong?"

"Madison broke up with me. I'm surprised he didn't tell you."

"He didn't say anything about that." Alyssa is surprised. "What? Why?"

I meet her gaze. "He didn't tell you what just happened?"

"No," she responds. "What happened?"

I angrily wipe away my rush of tears with the back of my hand. "Madison just broke up with me because of Aunt Phoebe and her stupid rules. I really hate your mother right now."

Alyssa tries to embrace me but I'm not interested in being comforted right now. I'm mad at the world.

"Divine, he'll probably change his mind and be running you down after school."

I wave my hand in dismissal. "I don't care. I hate Madison Hartford and even if he begs me to take him back—I'm not. Nobody dumps *me.*"

"Didn't you tell me that your last boyfriend dumped you?"

"Nobody in this little town dumps me," I amend. "I don't feel like wasting any more words on Madison, who is the scum of the earth. I hate him."

"Divine, we're not supposed to hate anyone."

I glare at Alyssa. "I don't need you preaching to me. Just don't do it."

"Maybe Stephen can talk to Madison for you."

"I don't want you talking to anyone about me and that jerk."

"Madison's gon' come back, Divine," Alyssa tries to assure me. "He's crazy about you."

"Really?" I ask. "Doesn't seem that way to me. I never thought he'd dump me." Right now I didn't know much about anything anymore. I felt like my whole world had just been turned upside down.

AUNT PHOEBE STICKS her head inside my room. "Divine, I know you're still upset with me, but sugar, you should come to the table. You really need to put something in your stomach."

"I'm not hungry," I respond without looking at her.

She steps all the way into my room. Uninvited.

"Alyssa told me what happened with Madison. I know you're hurting right now but let me assure you that you'll get past this little crush on Madison. There will be plenty of time for boys and dating."

I roll my eyes heavenward, wishing Aunt Phoebe would just leave. I don't want to hear her voice or see her face right now.

Just get out of my face, I want to yell, but I'm not crazy. Aunt Phoebe would sling me all over this room and then Uncle Reed would pick up where she left off.

"You and Alyssa just need to focus on your studies and your relationship with the Lord. Y'all think parents are mean and that we don't want our children to have fun, but that's not true at all. God created parents to shape the values of children—He holds us responsible. We as parents need a heart to follow God and not the ways of the world. I'm not gonna try to be your friend. I'm not gonna try to be popular—I'm going to teach you what's right, whether you like it or not. Humph. One day you'll thank me for it."

I seriously doubt that.

Aunt Phoebe continues talking and I continue to ignore her. It doesn't matter to me what she's saying because I've heard it so many times before. It's times like this that I miss living at home with Mom and Jerome. Although Mom is about as bad as Aunt Phoebe when it comes to boys. I already know that she'll side with Aunt Phoebe on this.

Parents truly suck!

"Divine, I told you already that I haven't seen any dead models walking around."

"I'm not hungry right now, Aunt Phoebe. I don't have an appetite."

"Don't let that boy stop you from living. He's not going to be the only boy you'll ever develop feelings for."

"How do you know that? Aunt Phoebe, you don't know what I feel."

"Sugar, I've been down that road before. I know what it's like to have a crush on a boy."

"My feelings run deeper than a crush."

"Oh, so you think you two are in love?"

"I thought so."

"Don't you think that if this boy really loved you . . ." Her voice softens. "Sugar, don't you think he'd still be around?"

I don't want to answer her question. It's something I've asked myself a million times since Madison broke up with me earlier today and it just hurts so much.

"If that boy couldn't wait for you, Divine, then maybe this is for the best. You can bet Madison's moving on with his life. Sugar, you need to move on with yours."

"Aunt Phoebe, I'm fine. Really I am. I'm just not hungry right now."

She sighs. "Okay . . . I guess I'll cover your plate with some foil and stick in the refrigerator."

"Thanks, Aunt Phoebe."

"One day you will understand."

Like never.

I don't care how nice she tries to be, I'm never going to forgive Aunt Phoebe for ruining my life like this. If I didn't like school so much, I'd just pack up and move back to California.

IT'S FRIDAY NIGHT and I'm so bored. I'm too depressed to go to the football game. Alyssa wanted to go until she found out Stephen was staying home. Besides, I know Madison will be there and I don't want to see him.

I peek into Alyssa's room and frown. She's still on the telephone talking to that stupid boy. All she ever does is talk to Stephen. It didn't bother me before because I had Madison.

Arms folded across my chest, I stand in her doorway, vying to get her attention. Tonight was supposed to be about us. Facials, manicures, pedicures, comfort foods and a movie.

Kicking back in the middle of her brightly colored bed, Alyssa spies me and holds up one finger.

My lips pressed in anger, I roll my eyes heavenward. I've been waiting on her for the last hour or so to get off the phone so we could get started.

"C'mon, Alyssa," I plead. "Get off the phone. We're supposed to have a girls' night. You promised."

"In a minute," she says.

Whatever Stephen says on the phone makes her giggle. She's so stupid. When she glances over at me, I can't help but assume Stephen is saying something about me.

"I know that old ugly thing is not saying anything about me," I say loud enough for him to hear.

Alyssa rolls her eyes at me, her mouth twisted into a threat.

Fuming, I stalk out of her room.

Half an hour later, I'm back at her door. Alyssa's still on the phone gabbing away.

"Get off the phone," I whisper as I climb into bed beside her. "Tell that boy you have better things to do."

I don't care that he can hear every word I'm saying. Alyssa promised me this evening would be our time and I need her to keep her word. I'm depressed and could really use a friend.

"Alyssa," I say an octave higher than usual. "Get off the telephone."

She tries to shush me with her hand.

I lay back against the stack of pillows in hues of hot pink, purple, green and yellow, hoping that my presence would be enough to annoy her to the point of hanging up, but no . . . She acts like I'm not even in the room. She's still yapping nonstop to that ugly Stephen. I don't know what she sees in the guy.

The conversation is boring at best.

When fifteen minutes pass, I decide to give up on our pampering session and just call it a night.

"We'll do it tomorrow night," Alyssa whispers.

"Whatever."

It's pretty clear to me that Stephen is more important to Alyssa than I am. Rejection leaves a bitter taste in my mouth and I vow never to speak to my cousin again.

Alyssa appears at my door, thirty-five minutes later. "Divine, why was you trippin' like that?"

I ignore her.

"Divine, I'm talking to you."

"It should be obvious that I'm *not* talking to you." Pointing my finger at her, I add, "What you did to me tonight was wrong and you know it. You made a promise to me and you didn't keep it."

"I didn't promise you. I just said we could kick it together, but Stephen and I had a lot to talk about. Divine, we live in the same house. We see each other all the time."

"And?"

"And we can get together any time we want."

"You talk to Stephen every day, Alyssa. I could see if the boy lived in another state. You're wrong for what you did."

Alyssa sighs. "You didn't have to come in my room with that stank attitude."

"If anything stinks it's that telephone with all the talking you been doing on it. You might want to spray it down with some Lysol."

Folding her hands across her chest, Alyssa responds, "That wasn't even called for, Divine."

"After the way you treated me tonight . . . Humph. All bets are off in my books."

"Divine, I'm sorry I didn't sit around with you, holding your hand because you got dumped. I'm sorry I still have a boyfriend and I'm sorry I want to talk to him."

Her words wound me. "Get out of my room, Alyssa. I don't even want to see your face again."

"Divine—"

I shake my head. "No—just get out of my room. You don't have to worry about me ever asking you to do anything with me. From this point on, our lives are separate."

"Divine, you're really buggin'."

"Whatever . . ."

Alyssa stands there a moment while I slip on the headphones attached to my iPod. I lay back on my bed, listening to Heather Headley. At least she feels my pain; the lyrics she's singing soothes my wounded heart. I love Mom's music but I'm still mad at her. The last thing I want is to hear her voice.

AFTER A RESTLESS night, I wake up in a cranky mood. It doesn't help that Alyssa dissed me for Stephen. When she walks into the kitchen, I make a point of not speaking to her.

"Morning, Divine."

I continue pouring cereal into my bowl, pretending that she simply doesn't exist in my world.

"What's up with you?" she asks. As if she doesn't already have a clue. Alyssa knows that I'm mad at her.

"Okay," she mutters. "Don't talk to me."

I'm not. I pour milk into my bowl, pick up a spoon and begin eating my breakfast. I don't even bother to sit down at the table.

Chance walks into the kitchen and fixes himself some toast. I've never seen anybody love toast so much. He eats it practically every day. "Why y'all so quiet?" he questions after a moment. "We usually can't shut you up."

The room is dead silent.

He looks from me to his sister. "Oh . . . y'all must be mad about somethin'."

"I'm not mad," Alyssa says pointedly. "She's the one not talking."

I finish my cereal and leave the kitchen after rinsing out the bowl. I can hear them discussing me, but I don't care. All I know is, they'd just better leave me alone. I can't stand them sometimes.

Trina's family invited us over for a Labor Day barbecue—I guess it's because Chance is almost part of their family now.

I'm not really in the mood to go, but haven't been able to figure a way to get out of it. At least Madison won't be there. I can get through this better if he's not around.

After our Saturday morning chores are done, we prepare to leave for the barbecue. Aunt Phoebe is doing her best to be cheerful, but we can tell that it's all an act. She's still very upset.

She's not the only one. Mrs. Winston looks just as sad. I'm surprised she's able to be so nice to Chance. Just to be on the safe side, I warn him to be careful. "You don't know if she put something in your food."

He gives me this crazy look. "Girl, she's not gon' do somethin' like that."

"How do you know? You did get her little girl pregnant," I remind him.

I pick up a can of soda and walk over to an empty bench, sitting down. Alyssa joins me there a few minutes later.

"They got a lot of people here," she says.

"That's what you do when you're having a barbecue. You invite people over."

"Why you always got to be such a smart mouth?"

Giving her a sidelong glance, I respond, "Because that's what I do."

Alyssa's response is halted when Trina joins us. We make room for her on the concrete bench in their backyard. She's been acting kind of embarrassed since we found out that she was pregnant.

"Hey girl," Alyssa greets her. "How're you doing?"

"Okay," she responds. "Chance told me that your mama is still mad about everything. She probably hates me now."

"No, she doesn't," we say in unison.

"I can't believe this is really happening to me. I'm going to have a baby. I'm going to be somebody's mama."

Like, *yeah.*

Alyssa plays with one of her braids. "Are you ready for this?"

Trina sighs in resignation. "I don't have any other choice. The baby's coming whether I'm ready or not."

Stacy arrives right before the food is ready. She comes over to where we're sitting and says, "I see your mama got herself another man. She's seeing that fine Kevin Nash."

I stare at her, confused. "My mom's not seeing anyone. You need to stop reading that trash," I say, pointing to the tabloid she's carrying.

"Maybe you should check out these photographs. They sure look lovey-dovey to me. I don't know why you trippin' anyway. I wouldn't mind having Kevin Nash for my stepdaddy."

"He's not going to be anything to me," I respond dryly.

"Well, if your mama don't want that fine man—send him to me, girlfriend."

As if. My eyes travel to the latest edition of the *National Enquirer*. Stacy catches me looking at it and offers it to me.

I shake my head, refusing it.

We get up to fix our plates after the children are seated. Trina abandons us for Chance, which is not unexpected. I notice Aunt Phoebe watching them like a hawk—Mrs. Winston too. Don't they have a clue that it's already too late?

Despite my sour mood, I manage to have a pretty decent time at Trina's house. The unspoken truce between me and Alyssa ends as soon as we are back at home. I'm still stewing over the way she treated me the night before.

I go straight to my room and get on the computer. I check Instant Messenger and see that Rhyann and Mimi are both online. I immediately IM them, telling them about my breakup with Madison.

> **HollywoodQT:** Can u believe my bf dumped me like that?
> **SexyRhyann:** r u ok? Girl, he's a jerk. Don't u go back 2 him for nothing.
> **SweetMims:** Rhyann's right. Leave that farm boy alone. Leave him 2 the animals.
> **HollywoodQT:** He's my boo. He was supposed to b mine 4ever.
> **SweetMims:** ur better off without him. ur too good 4 him.
> **HollywoodQT:** thx
> **SexyRhyann:** wan2 talk about something else?
> **HollywoodQT:** yes
> **SexyRhyann:** brb panb

I know BRB means be right back but PANB. It takes me a moment to figure the meaning. Parents are nearby. Rhyann's mom doesn't like her using Instant Messenger at all.

I see at the bottom of my IM window that Mimi's typing a message on her end.

> **SweetMims:** I told u that u should leave those boys down there alone. U need someone on ur level.
> **SexyRhyann:** ok. Coast is clear.

I'm definitely ready to talk about anything else but Madison and the way he broke up with me. I still get upset thinking about it.

It really feels like a bad dream I just can't wake up from. How can we be truly over?

I don't know how I'll ever get through this. He's the love of my life and even though I hate his guts right now, I really miss Madison so much.

I've picked up the phone a couple of times to call him, but my pride just won't let me reduce myself to begging. I'm a Hollywood princess and we don't look back—we look for the next prince. I hate to admit it, but Mimi's probably right. I'm not going to find one down here in Temple. I've learned the hard way that farm boys do not make great princes.

Madison had potential, but then he had to go and destroy my life.

> **HollywoodQT:** What have u guys been up 2? U don't respond when I IM u but I c u online sometimes. Must b flirting with boys r something.
> **SexyRhyann:** We've been checking out a new site called TeenSpot.net. U should ck it out. I even have some of my poetry and short stories posted on a blog there. I heard that publishers read some of the blogs, so I thought I'd give it a try. I'll send u a link right now, so u can go there l8tr.
> **SweetMIms:** Rhyann's been getting a lot of hits with her blog. Everybody's loving her stories.
> **HollywoodQT:** I'll check it out.

We IM a few more times before calling it a night. I get up from my desk to retrieve my textbooks and handouts from my backpack. Since I don't have a life I might as well practice being a nerd by studying.

My cell phone rings and I check the caller ID.

It's Madison. My heart leaps in my chest.

"What does he want?" I ask myself. My curiosity is trying to get the best of me, but stubborn pride won't let me answer his call. I just couldn't handle it if he's calling for any other reason than to beg for my forgiveness.

Madison so needs to pay for hurting me. After he begs for my forgiveness maybe I'll take him back—although I try not to make the same mistake twice.

I sit, waiting for Alyssa to come running to my room. I heard the house phone ring a couple of times. I'm pretty sure Madison called her and asked her to plead his case with me.

No Alyssa.

Nearly twenty minutes pass. Sighing my disappointment, I return to my laptop. Since I have nothing better to do, I decide to check out Rhyann's blog.

I click on the link for TeenSpot. I follow the instructions to become a member so that I can gain access to my friend's blog.

PARENTS R ALIENS 2

Sometimes I think life would be better if the Aliens traveled to earth and kidnapped our parents. They belong on another planet because they are so strange and very controlling. My mom needs a life of her own so she can stop trying to live my life for me. And they punish you because you won't buckle down underneath their control.

If ET came and whisked her away, I can promise you even though I'll miss her, my life would finally have some meaning.

Think about it. Don't your parents seem a little strange in their behavior? They don't remember what it's like to be a teen-ager. All of sudden they think they know everything and that they have all the answers.

Strange, if you ask me.

I burst into laughter. Rhyann must have really been upset with her mother to write this. "Maybe I should start a blog about over-protective relatives."

Alyssa laughs in response, entering the room. "I heard you. You better be careful what you say. You know Mama's always roaming the halls."

I knew it. Madison called her. My heart leaps with joy. He still wants to be with me.

"Okay, what did he say?" I can't help grinning from ear to ear.

Alyssa looks at me in confusion. "Who?"

"Madison. Didn't he just call you?"

"No. Was he supposed to?"

"Then who called? I heard the phone ring twice."

"First Miss Hattie called to talk to Daddy and then Stephen called me."

"He probably called and since you were on the phone with that boy you didn't click over."

"Divine, Madison hardly ever calls on the house phone. I'm sure he would've called you on your cell." Folding her arms across her chest, she asks, "Are you two getting back together?"

"No. He called me earlier but I didn't answer. I thought maybe he'd call you next." Hurt, I glance over at her. "I'm surprised you're not still on the phone with your boyfriend."

"C'mon, Divine, just stop it. I'm sorry about last night. I promise I'll make it up to you."

"Well, you can make it up to me by buying my ticket to the Nicole Mullen concert."

Alyssa's smile disappears. "You're the one always claiming to be rich. I only get twenty dollars a week for allowance."

"But this way I'll know you're truly sorry."

"Fine, I'll buy your ticket so I can get off this guilt trip you got me on." She plops down on one of the beanbag chairs. "What are you in here doing?"

"I was just reading Rhyann's blog. This is a really cool site. You should check it out. You can even sign up for a free email address," I tell her.

"Oooh . . . I might get me another one." Alyssa gets to her feet. "Rhyann has a blog?"

I nod. "You should read it."

She walks over to my desk and leans over my shoulder to read Rhyann's next entry.

BALL OF CONFUSION

I have millions of questions about life. The answers so confusing,
I can't help but wonder if I'm losing my mind?

The world is filled with millions of decisions I know I can't make. I hear nothing but criticism from my parents and it makes me wonder if I'm losing my mind?

I know I can't please everybody no matter how hard I try. I don't know why all the pressure's being brought down on me but I can't help but wonder if I'm losing my mind?

This world is a ball of confusion

"So what do you think?" I ask.

"Wow, Ryhann's pretty good. How long has she been writing poetry?"

"For a while. I think she started like when she was in the fourth or fifth grade. She wants to be a writer when she graduates. She's thinking about getting a college degree in journalism or English."

"I can see Rhyann as a reporter. She'd be good at it. She's tough." Alyssa heads to the door. "I'm going to my room and register. Let's try one of the chat rooms."

"Okay. Just IM me with your screen name."

Before our registration is complete, we have to fill out a profile questionnaire. After I complete mine, I check my inbox for the verification email.

Once I'm approved, I log into TeenSpot and visit some of the other pages while waiting to hear from Alyssa.

"Girl, what is taking you so long?" I whisper. "I don't have all night."

A small window pops up. Alyssa's online *finally*. "It's about time," I mutter.

I pull up the link Rhyann sent me and forward it to Alyssa. I check out the different forums and chat rooms while I wait for Alyssa to complete the member registration.

We spend the rest of our evening IMing each other as we discover what TeenSpot has to offer. Alyssa wants to enter one of the chat rooms, but I'm not much into them. Me and my friends usually IM each other back and forth. Only losers do chat rooms, in my opinion. Losers and perverts.

TODAY IS THE absolute worst day of my life. It's only been five days since Madison and I broke up and he sure didn't waste any time moving on. The dog just walked past me all hugged up with this girl named Brittany Wilkes. She has a reputation for sleeping around so he won't have any problems getting sex from her.

"I can't believe Madison is messing around with her. Brittany's not even as cute as me," I whisper to Alyssa. "He was probably messing around with her all this time."

"I don't think so. He really liked you, Divine."

"Well, he doesn't anymore," I snipe back. "He just acted like he didn't even see me."

"Well, didn't you tell him not to talk to you ever again?"

"So?"

"Divine, he's doing what you asked him to do."

"I can't believe you're even still friends with him. You're my cousin, Alyssa. You're supposed to be on my side."

"He and Stephen are best friends. What do you expect me to do?"

"I want you to hate him like I do. What he did to me was foul. *You know it.*"

"It wasn't right," Alyssa agreed. "But he and Stephen *are* friends, Divine."

"Fine. *Be his friend.* I don't care."

"Madison and I don't really talk that much anymore. Besides, I already told him what I thought about the way things went down between you."

"You did?"

Alyssa nods. "He knows I don't like what happened."

"He probably don't take you seriously because you're always laughing and talking to him when you're with Stephen."

"I'm not trying to have problems with my boyfriend, Divine. I told Madison what I thought and I'm done with it."

Alyssa doesn't get what I'm saying. She doesn't understand that I feel betrayed. "Forget it," I tell her.

After school, Alyssa has a student council meeting, so I walk home alone. Chance is with Trina at a doctor's appointment.

I hate going home without them because Aunt Phoebe's there and I know she's going to try and talk to me. I don't want to hear anything from her because I'm still really mad at her.

"Divine, I was just talking about you. The Youth Ministry group at church would like to have a fashion show for the annual Mothers' Luncheon," Aunt Phoebe announces as soon as I enter the house. "Do you think you can help me coordinate one?"

It's a bribe and I know it. But since it's so obvious that they desperately need help in the fashion department—how can I say no?

We KICK OFF Alyssa's birthday weekend at a gospel concert on Friday night. Nicole C. Mullen is all that. I am now such a big fan of hers.

Looping her arm through mine, Alyssa says, "I really enjoyed Micah Stampley. That man knows he can sing. I love his song "War Cry."

"Mary Mary was good but Nicole . . . now she showed out. I didn't care too much for her at first, but now since seeing her live, I'm going online and ordering her CD," I tell her. "I had a good time tonight. I'm glad Aunt Phoebe and Uncle Reed let us come."

" 'Let us come,' " Chance repeats. "Girl, what are you talking about? They didn't let us come—they brought us here. They didn't sit with us, but they're here just the same."

"At least they let us sit away from them." Alyssa stops walking and turns, pulling me with her. "I didn't want Mama embarrassing me with her shouting all over the place."

We laugh. Aunt Phoebe loves to get her shout on. I can hear her now talking about how the spirit was moving. We stand in the designated waiting area for my aunt and uncle to show up. While we're waiting, I smile at a couple of cute boys passing by. I get a few winks and one boy blows me a kiss, but no one comes over to say anything.

What's wrong with me? I'm still cute.

I have on a tight Elie Tahari cream-colored beaded blouse with a pair of brown linen pants. My hair is falling in waves around my face and my makeup is perfect. I look good.

I love my cousin but she pales in comparison to me. She's taken to wearing microbraids and I can't get the girl to buy something other than jeans. I mean, the pair she's wearing is tight. The embellished pants and matching denim jacket were a gift from my mom.

Aunt Phoebe didn't even want to know how much they cost. She said her heart couldn't take it.

A few minutes later, I glimpse Aunt Phoebe's tall frame. She must have really loved Uncle Reed because I would never date a man shorter than me. But in spite of that, they do look happy and in love.

I don't remember my parents ever looking like that, except when posing for the media.

We meet up with Uncle Reed and Aunt Phoebe before walking to the car. We're in for another surprise when they take us to a nearby restaurant for dessert.

After we place our orders, Aunt Phoebe glances over at Chance and asks, "Have you made any decisions?"

"Yes ma'am. I'm going to try and get into Morehouse or Clark."

Alyssa and I remain silent.

"That way I can be nearby for the b-baby."

Those words almost seemed to choke Chance. Uncle Reed nods in approval. "I think you're making the right decision, son."

From the look on Chance's face—he didn't seem so sure.

I release a short sigh of relief when the conversation turns to Alyssa's birthday party tomorrow.

"We thought we'd just have a barbecue," Aunt Phoebe was saying. "The last one of the year."

Alyssa perks up. "I love cookouts."

"Barbecues are nice and all, but I have this thing about bugs—I don't like them," I contribute. "A huge fly landed on my hamburger when we were at Trina's house. I had to throw my plate away. Then they ran out of hamburgers. I really wanted that burger."

"I don't bother them and they don't bother me," Aunt Phoebe declares.

"I guess I need to set up the same arrangement with the bugs,"

I say before sticking a forkful of strawberry cheesecake into my mouth. "I'm not ready to eat with them."

Chance and Alyssa crack up with laughter.

We are still talking about the concert when we arrive home. Uncle Reed and Aunt Phoebe head to their bedroom, while me and Chance gather in Alyssa's room. He ends up falling asleep on her floor. Alyssa keeps me up late talking because she's excited about turning sixteen.

Since we're not able to date, what's the big deal?

"Party hats?" I glance over at Alyssa. "What is Aunt Phoebe thinking?"

Alyssa laughs. "Mama must have found them somewhere in the house. She knows I'm not going out like that. I'm way too old for party hats."

Aunt Phoebe had the backyard decorated in a sea of pink, yellow and purple. Tables from the church banquet hall had been brought over and covered in striped tablecloths. There were chairs everywhere. "I hope you didn't invite Madison to the cookout," I tell Alyssa.

"Divine, I wouldn't do that to you. He asked if he could come and I told him no."

"Good. The last thing I need is to see him and Brittany over here."

"You know, since you and Madison broke up you've been acting kinda funny with me, Divine."

I meet Alyssa's gaze. "No, I haven't."

"Yeah you have," she insists. "And you're always making little smart comments. I know you hatin' on me and Stephen."

I wave my hand in dismissal. "Girl, pleeze. Hatin' on you and that boy for what? I'm not hatin' on nobody."

Even as I deny it, I can't help but wonder if what Alyssa is saying is true. I am upset that she seems to ignore me. I'm hurting over being dumped by Madison and Alyssa just doesn't seem to care.

My mood continues on a downward spiral as guests start to arrive. I go back inside the house to see if I can help Aunt Phoebe with anything.

"Need help?" I ask.

"Can you get the lemonade for me, dear?" she responds.

I take it out of the refrigerator and set it down on the counter. "How many people are coming over?"

"I think about twenty-five or thirty."

The doorbell rings.

"I'll get it," I say.

I open the door to find a grinning Stephen standing on the porch. A wave of irritation washes over me and my mood sours. We've been cool all this time but now—now I can't stand the boy. Mainly because he's still friends with Madison.

"What's up, Divine?"

I can't stand the cocky grin on his face. I give in to a mean streak. "Everybody's out back," I tell him before slamming the door right in his face.

That felt so good.

Before I can walk away, Stephen knocks on the door. I don't bother to answer—I already know who it is and I already told him to go around back. How difficult can it be? Duh.

"Who's at the door?" Chance asks me as I pass him in the hall on the way back to my bedroom.

"Why don't you answer and find out," I snap, brushing past him. He's getting on my nerves too. I'm not sure why I'm suddenly so angry, but I know it has to do with the fact that I'm feeling lonely and rejected. I'd never say as much to anybody, though. I'm not a loser.

I barely turned on my computer when Alyssa blows into my

room demanding, "Did you just slam the front door in Stephen's face?"

I don't even glance her way. "I told him the party was in the backyard."

"Why you trippin' like this, Divine?"

Meeting her angry gaze, I say, "Alyssa, go enjoy your boyfriend and your little birthday party. Okay? Just leave me alone."

"I'm not gon' let you ruin my birthday, Divine."

"Good-bye, Alyssa," I say, waving my hand in dismissal.

"I can't stand you sometimes," she yells on her way out of the room.

"The feeling's mutual," I shout back. Deep down, I'm shaking because Alyssa and I are fighting. I don't like being mad at her, but I just can't help myself. Everybody is running around so happy—it's like nobody knows I'm even alive or even cares how I feel. It's all about Alyssa and her stupid birthday. It's not like it's a major deal or something. *It's just a birthday.*

An hour passes, then another.

I'm bored out of my mind, but I refuse to go outside and join Alyssa's stupid party. I can't stand her right now. I can hear them in the backyard, laughing and talking. I don't care because I don't want to be a part of their little celebration.

"Divine, what are you doing in here?" Uncle Reed inquires when he bursts into my room, practically giving me a heart attack. "How come you're not outside with the rest of us?"

I decide to be honest. "I'm not in a party mood."

He enters my bedroom. "Do you want to talk about it?"

I shake my head no. "Not really. I don't want to be a damper so I think I'll just stay in here, if you and Aunt Phoebe don't mind."

He heads back to the door, saying, "I'll have Phoebe bring you a plate."

"Thanks, Uncle Reed."

Before he leaves, he says, "You know, birthdays are special. It's a day we celebrate life. Whatever is going on between you and Alyssa—work it out. You're family."

"Yes sir." Uncle Reed doesn't miss a thing. He walks around the house like he's oblivious to all the stuff going on, but he isn't— Uncle Reed knows everything. I think God whispers in his ear. Either that or he's bugging the whole house.

Hmmmm. I get up and thoroughly check out my room. I peek under and around my bed, the furnishings and even the lamp. Satisfied, I decide that it could only be God telling Uncle Reed what's going on under his nose.

I walk into the closet and retrieve the present I bought Alyssa from Martinique. Instead of taking it outside, I slip inside her room and leave the wrapped gift on her bed.

Because of the way Alyssa treated me earlier, a small part of me feels like I shouldn't give her the present but that would be mean. I'm not totally heartless.

By the time seven o'clock rolls around, everyone has gone home. I can hear my family in the backyard—cleaning up, I suppose. I'm definitely not about to go out there offering my help.

I lie back on my bed and dial Mimi's number. I get her voice mail. That girl is never around when I need her. She's dating now and so she's hardly ever home anymore.

Alyssa comes knocking on my door, fifteen minutes later. "You missed a great party," she tells me.

"I'm glad you had a nice birthday."

"Thanks for the present. I love the necklace."

I feign a yawn. "Mom picked it out."

Alyssa comes over to my bed and sits down on the edge. "Divine, what's up? I can't believe you wouldn't even come out to the party. You really hurt my feelings."

I'm feeling a little catty so I say, "I'm sure Stephen kept your mind off my absence."

"Why do you have such a problem with Stephen? You two used to be friends."

"I just want to be left alone, Alyssa. Can you do that for me?"

"Fine." Alyssa storms out of my bedroom. I resist the urge to follow her or call her back. I'm mad at her—and the truth is I'm not exactly sure why.

chapter 8

Mom is in town for a few days; Uncle Reed offers to drive me to Atlanta so I can spend the weekend with her. She usually comes to Temple to spend time with all of us, but I wanted to go to Atlanta. I'm actually glad to be getting away. Things are a little shaky between me and Alyssa right now—have been since the barbecue a week ago. I guess everyone's tired of my constant mood swings and my some-timey attitude.

Uncle Reed turns into the historic neighborhood of Tuxedo Park. Mom made the right decision when she bought this house—it's tight. I practically jump out of the car while it's still moving when we pull up in front of the Tuxedo Drive home.

Mom comes outside wearing a pair of jeans and a red sweatshirt. I'm a little stunned at first by the fact that she's wearing glasses. Makes her look like a nerd.

She smiles. "You like?"

"You don't have to wear them all the time, do you?" I ask. "You can always get contacts, you know."

Mom laughs. "I only use them for reading. Y'all come on inside."

We follow her into her Atlanta home filled with nine-foot ceilings, hardwood floors, six bedrooms, seven baths and an awesome swimming pool.

Uncle Reed and Mom have a talk while I get settled in my room on the second level. I unpack before heading back downstairs.

After Uncle Reed leaves, I tell Mom, "I'm so glad you're here. Things have been so crazy for me lately." I drop down on the sofa beside her. "Can you believe Madison dumped me? Me."

"Sweetie, in time you won't even remember that boy's name."

"I'll always remember Madison. Mom, I really liked him."

"If he really cared for you, Divine, he wouldn't have ended the relationship. Sounds like he was just looking for sex. He knew he wasn't going to get it from you, so he dumped you." Mom eyes me. "Tell me the truth . . . did Madison try to have sex with you?"

"No ma'am. Not really. He wanted me to sneak out of the house so that we could spend time together. He tried to get me to skip school with him one day."

"You know he wanted sex. That's why he was trying to get you to leave school. You didn't—did you?"

"Mom . . . no, I didn't skip school. I wasn't going to have you or Aunt Phoebe trying to knock me into the next year."

After listening to me whine nonstop about Madison and his new girlfriend, Mom decides that the only way to shut me up and get me out of my depression is to take me shopping. We change clothes and head to the mall.

In the Mercedes, Mom asks, "How is Chance doing?"

"Working hard," I respond. "The boy barely takes time to eat, he's working so hard."

"I guess I can understand that. Having a baby so young—it's hard. He's trying to do the right thing and I'm sure he's scared."

"I bet he regrets having sex now." I lean forward, switching the radio station. "Alyssa and I asked Chance if he thought it was worth it to have sex. He said no."

Mom glances over at me. "Really?"

I nod. "Do you think he's lying?"

Shrugging, Mom responds, "Hon, I don't really know. What do you think?"

"I think he'll do it again. Everybody at school is always talking about sex. It's everywhere. On the television and the radio. People say sex is so good. But to me, it just sounds icky."

Mom laughs. "Sex is special. It's a gift from God to a husband and wife. People have abused it—taken it and turned it into something vulgar, nasty and just downright perverted. It can be wonderful between a husband and wife. But for kids—teenagers—it just becomes something to do; something to talk about. Nobody is thinking about the consequences."

"Like babies."

"Not just that. There are diseases too. But even more important, is that God says it's wrong. To teenagers, it's cool for them to tell their friends they're involved in a physical relationship and maybe they actually believe they're in love, but the chances are that most relationships don't last long after the sexual act."

"Sounds like you really can't win. Boys dump you if you don't have sex with them and then they dump you if you do."

"If a boy really cares about you he won't dump you—he'll wait for you. Think of it this way. Getting dumped is God's way of moving those guys out of your life. He's weeding out the good from the bad."

"Humph. I never thought of it that way. I thought Madison was crazy about me. Now he's going with this girl with a bad reputation. I guess you're right."

"If he doesn't appreciate you, then you were much too good for him anyway. You are a jewel, Divine. You should be treated as such. You want a guy to value not devalue you."

My eyes water so I blink rapidly to keep the tears at bay. My heart still hurts. "But I really liked him, Mom."

She reaches over, taking my hand in hers. "I know. I'm sorry that he hurt you, hon."

"Do you think you could have your bodyguard take him out?"

"Divine . . ."

"They don't have to kill him—just pound him a few times."

"I know you're kidding. Right?"

"Mom . . . Madison broke my heart and he needs to pay."

"What does my brother say about forgiveness?"

"The same thing the Bible says, but I'm too mad at him right now to forgive." Shrugging in nonchalance, I add, "Maybe later."

"You can't really move on with your life until you do. You give that boy power over you by holding on to that anger. Believe me . . . I know from experience."

"I don't think I'll ever trust another boy again. I don't know if I'll even meet anybody else. There's not a whole lot to pick from down here."

"I'm sure you will. You're a beauty with a personality to match. Some young man is going to be very lucky to have you, sweetie."

"Mom, I'm going to wait until I get married. I think having sex is way too much trouble."

"I'm really glad you said that, Divine. That's what every mother wants to hear. However, I know the flesh and it's much easier said than done."

"Well, I plan to wait, but then again, if I get all hot and both-

ered like Aunt Phoebe says . . . that might fly out the window." I
can't resist trying to wreck her nerves a little.

Mom laughs. "You might not want to say that around your
Aunt Phoebe. She's not exactly in a joking mood when it comes to
stuff like this. If she heard you say this, she'd probably keep you in
the house until you're twenty."

"But I'm only kidding."

"Oh I know that. At least you better be."

"But definitely before I do anything, I'm getting birth control."

"There are a lot of other things out there that you need to
worry about—not just babies. But I want to make one thing clear.
Sex before marriage is a sin, Divine. The Bible tells us that."

After a moment, I inquire, "Mom, can I tell you something
without you buggin'?"

"Sure. You know you can tell me anything."

"Madison and I kissed." My hands on the door handle, I close
my eyes, waiting for to her to hit the brakes, then come after me.

"I kind of figured as much."

I'm totally surprised that my Mom didn't start freaking out and
yelling. She's totally being cool about the confession. Maybe her
Mom mode is out of order.

"How did you know?" I question.

"A mother knows."

"I felt all tingly inside. Is that what you and Aunt Phoebe are
talking about when it comes to those feelings that lead to sex? I'm
trying to figure out if I was on my way to doing it and didn't realize
it. You and Aunt Phoebe are making me paranoid—always talking
about these feelings we might get."

Mom throws back her head, laughing.

"It's not funny."

Reaching over, she grabs my hand, squeezing it. "My sweet

baby. I'm not laughing at you. I just think you have such an interesting way of looking at life. And you're smart. Don't try to grow up so fast. Enjoy being a teenager, sweetie."

"How am I supposed to have fun as a teen when there are all these rules?"

"You can still enjoy your life within the guidelines. That's what rules are—guidelines."

I follow Mom into Caché. She heads straight to the back of the store where the gowns are hanging.

"I can't do anything that I want to do," I complain.

Mom picks up a dress and presses it against her body. "I don't think you're being honest about that. You get to do a lot of things you enjoy."

"You know what I mean, Mom."

"Divine, this is the best time of your life. You're young. You don't have any worries."

I know what my mom is trying to do. She's trying to make it seem like a grown-up's life is just so boring. Sorry, but I don't see it.

"I love you so much and I'm so proud of you. I just want you to have the best life has to offer. I want you to enjoy your time as a child—a teen."

"Mom, I get all that. I just want to be able to do what other girls my age do. I want to be able to hang out with boys. I want to be able to go to a dance without Aunt Phoebe being there watching every move I make."

We leave Caché and head to another store in the mall.

Mom inquires, "Do you think your aunt is cramping your style? Is that the problem?"

I think about her question for a moment, then respond, "Yes ma'am. I'm not a baby."

Embracing me, Mom says, "You'll always be my baby. I don't care how old you get."

"You're embarrassing me," I mutter.

Our conversation ends when we leave Lenox Square Mall and drive over to Phipps Plaza. I can't wait to get to the Gucci store.

Two hours later, we return from our shopping spree at Phipps Plaza weighted down with shopping bags from Gucci, Sisley, Theory and Juicy Couture.

Setting my Gucci bag near the staircase, I say, "Now today was a good day."

The telephone rings, cutting off our conversation.

"It's Alyssa," Mom announces when she answers the phone.

"I'll call her back," I respond, wondering why she didn't just call me on my cell phone. That's what she usually does. I'm actually surprised she called me at all with things being so tense and all. I'm not ready to talk, though.

"Okay, what's going on between you two?" Mom questions when she hangs up.

"Nothing."

"I don't believe you, so you might as well tell me the truth. What happened between you and Alyssa?"

"Mom . . . it's nothing."

"It's *something*."

After a moment, I tell her, "She's still friends with Madison. Even after the way he treated me. That's so not cool. She's my cousin."

Mom nods in understanding. "Oh, I see. You want her to be mad at Madison because you're upset with him."

"Why not?" I ask. "I want you to be mad at him too. I want everybody to hate Madison's guts because he's a big jerk."

"Honey, life isn't like that. Don't do that to your cousin."

"I'm not doing anything to her," I counter.

"Just because things didn't work out for you and Madison, don't expect Alyssa to get upset with him too."

"But she's supposed to be loyal to me."

"Okay, what if things were the other way around? What if you and Madison were still talking and she and . . ."

"Stephen," I supply.

"What if she and Stephen stopped talking. Would you be mad at him?"

"Yes ma'am. I would. Nobody dumps my cousin."

"That's easy to say, Divine. I don't think you'd want to make any waves between you and Madison, if you were still together."

"My loyalty is to Alyssa."

"Honey, listen to me. Don't let a boy come between you and your cousin. You hear me?"

"Yes ma'am," I reply sullenly.

"Blood is thicker than water."

"I just wish she'd be mad at him for a little while. I get so upset when I see Madison at school with that Brittany Wilkes. Then Alyssa's over there talking to them like she's their friend."

"It sounds to me like you're a little jealous."

"Jealous? Over what?"

"Alyssa still has her friend and, well, you don't."

"I'm not jealous," I say. "Me, jealous? Humph."

"Just think about what I've said. I think you're being a little unfair to your cousin. Alyssa loves you like a sister. She would never do anything to hurt you."

"She hardly spends time with me anymore."

"You two live in the same house, Divine honey. You see each other all the time."

"All she wants to do is talk to that boy on the telephone."

"Well, that's all she can do. Isn't that what you did with Madison? I know when I was there, you would be on your cell and Alyssa would be on the other phone."

"But I didn't ignore you."

"Actually, you did a little, but I understood."

"Mom, did I really?"

Smiling, she nods. "You meet a boy and lose your mind. I did it and even your Aunt Phoebe did it. Man, she and I used to argue like nobody's business because she and Reed used to tie up the telephone line. We didn't have cell phones back then."

"I forget you were walking around with the dinosaurs."

Mom laughs and throws a pillow at me.

THE NEXT MORNING, Mom drives me to the College Park area to see my half-brother, Jason. Normally, she just drops me off so that I can spend a few hours with him, but not this time. Mom actually parks and climbs out of the car.

"What are you doing?"

Slipping her purse on her shoulder, Mom says, "I think its time I met Mrs. Campbell face-to-face."

I hope and pray that Mom isn't going to ruin this for me. I love my little brother and I want a relationship with him. But I worry that his grandmother may not warm up to Mom because of what happened with her daughter, Jason's mother.

"Why?"

"Well, I didn't do anything so I have nothing to be ashamed of. You're my daughter and Jason is your brother. He's part of my family, the way I see it."

Mrs. Campbell greets Mom warmly, a gesture that surprises me. I wasn't so sure if my mom would be able to handle an ugly reminder of what happened with Shelly and Jerome.

Jason takes to her as well. He's growing up to be such a cute little boy. I can see some resemblance to Jerome but mostly he looks like Shelly. I feel sad that she couldn't be alive to see him grow up.

I wonder if he remembers her at all. Probably not. He was only a couple of months old when she died.

I had no intentions of liking her but from the way Mrs. Campbell talks about her Shelly wasn't that bad of a person. She just fell in love with the wrong man.

Shortly after one, Mrs. Campbell serves us lunch. Mom offered to take us to a restaurant, but that suggestion was quickly vetoed. Mrs. Campbell loves to cook and she's good at it.

While Jason and I eat, she and Mom venture into another room to talk.

"Dee, you pray wit' me?"

"Huh?" Jason's almost two so it's still a little hard to understand him at times.

"You pray wit' me?"

"You want me to play with you?" I ask.

Smiling, he nods.

"Finish your chicken and we'll play when you get done. Okay?"

My friends would crack up if they could see me now—crawling on the floor with my brother, pushing toy trucks around. I love being around Jason.

He loves being with me too. When it's time for us to leave, Jason cries, begging me not to leave.

"Please don't cry," I beg. "I'll be back, Jason. I will. I promise." I pick him up, hugging him tight. "I love you, cutie."

"Me wuv you too."

I'm so done.

Tears in my eyes, I gently place him in Mrs. Campbell's arms. "I'll be back to see you real soon."

When we walk out the house, my mom surveys my face and shakes her head. "You big softie."

On the way back to Mom's house, we stop at the grocery store.

I pause at the magazine rack containing the tabloid newspapers. On the front of a couple of them is a picture of my mom and her supposed boy toy, Kevin Nash.

"I've told you—pay that trash no mind," Mom tells me. "Nothing but a bunch of lies."

"Why are you suddenly gracing the covers of all the tabloids?" I ask. "Are you having an affair?"

I'm not sure I really want to know the answer to my question. Not quite sure how I feel about my mom seeing someone.

Mom looks like she's about to slap my face into the next year. Instead, she takes a deep breath before saying, "Kevin and I are friends, Divine. You know how these people operate. They're always looking for a scandal."

"Isn't he married?"

"Kevin just separated from his wife a few months ago. But it's not what the tabloid reporters are making it out to be. They just want to sell papers. Remember what they did to your father and Ava?"

"Yes ma'am. I remember."

Jerome and Ava's prison romance was the main scandal last year. Ava, a high-profile news reporter, lost her job after her romance with my dad became public.

"Well, now they need something else to print, so now the cameras are focused on me." Mom gives a short laugh. "You know your dad and I have given them so much to write about in the past."

"Kids at school read these things. They believe every word of it."

"I'm sorry, hon. Unfortunately, it comes with the territory. I don't like my personal life splashed across the news for the whole world to see, but because of what I do my life is no longer my own. That's one of the reasons I wanted you with Reed and Phoebe. I want your life as normal as possible."

I shrug. "It's fine. I can handle it. I don't believe this mess," I tell her. "I know you'd tell me the truth."

ALYSSA'S IN HER bedroom reading when I return Sunday evening. I knock on her door before entering.

"Can we talk?" I ask.

She lays down her book. "Sure. What about?"

"The way I've been acting. Alyssa, I'm sorry. I've been such a jerk."

"Tell me something, Divine. What did I do? Why have you been so mad with me?"

"I guess I was jealous of you. You still have Stephen and I'm alone. I just couldn't stand it. Deep down, I wanted you to break up with Stephen because me and Madison aren't together anymore. That wasn't cool."

"I love you, Divine, and I'm so sorry about the way Madison treated you. Believe it or not, Stephen doesn't think it's right either—he even told him so."

I shrug nonchalantly. "It's not your problem or Stephen's. It's just that I really liked Madison and he hurt me."

"Daddy always says that you may not see the reason why things happen when they do, but God will eventually reveal it to you."

"Well I already know that Madison is a dog so God doesn't have to waste His time with that. I'm just real sorry for being so mean to you. I love you too, Alyssa."

"So we're cool again?"

I nod. "We're cool. I'll send Stephen an email in a little while and apologize to him too."

Patting the empty space beside her on the bed, Alyssa says, "Sit down and tell me about your weekend with Aunt Kara. I know y'all had a good time and I hope you brought me back some of that perfume you had the last time. You promised to get me some."

Laughing, I respond, "Let me tell you everything first. You know the rules: I brag, you get jealous and then I give you your gifts. And since I was such a jerk—I got you something extra special this time."

chapter 9

"*Did* you hear about the girl that's missing in Atlanta?" Alyssa asks me in the middle of setting up for our family game night the following Thursday. We have a weekly tradition of playing Scrabble. Actually it's not my tradition, but I've adopted it because we have a lot of fun.

Confused, I question, "What girl?"

"Divine, don't you ever watch the news? It's been on practically every day this week. The police are searching for a fifteen-year-old girl who left home last Friday and hasn't been seen or heard from since. Her parents think that maybe she met somebody on the internet. They said she spent a lot of time on her computer in the past couple of months."

"She could've just run away," I say. I feel like Alyssa's trying to throw hints at me because I've been spending a lot more time on my computer.

It's because I don't have a boyfriend to talk to like she does. She'd probably laugh if she knew I've been going to an online psychic to find out if Madison and I are going to get back together. I've been to a couple of them and right now they're split on the answer. One says yes and two others say no. I've even been reading up on relationships to find out where mine went wrong.

"Or she might have been kidnapped," Chance counters.

I don't like the way Alyssa is watching me, so I ask, "Why do you keep looking at me like that?"

"I hope you're not giving out your personal information over the internet, Divine," Alyssa states. "You're always signing up for stuff and joining groups."

My hands on my hips, I demand, "Who died and made you my boss? Tell me."

"My sister's right. Divine, you really have to be careful. It's some crazy people out there."

"You two need to stop watching the news," I advise. "It's making you creepy."

"All right, Miss Know-It-All."

"I'm not a know-it-all," I argue. "I'm not negative all the time either. I think positive. Something you should try every now and then, Alyssa."

"Humph. Instead of all that *positive thinking,* you need to use your brain."

"I do use my brain," I retort. "Stop picking on me."

"Nobody's picking on you, Divine," Chance offers. "We're just trying to get you to understand that the world is crazy."

I'm truly offended now. They think I'm stupid. "I know that terrible things happen. I know that, but I try not to dwell on stuff like that."

"We're not telling you to dwell on bad stuff," Alyssa counters. "Just to be careful."

Our conversation ends abruptly when Uncle Reed enters the family room.

"Everything set up?" he asks, referring to the game.

"We're all ready," Alyssa responds. She picks up the dictionary. "I'm definitely ready."

"You can't be cheating," I tell her. "I'll be watching you, Alyssa."

"It's you and Chance that need to be watched. Y'all the ones who'll try to slip in something that's not even a real word."

I laugh.

Aunt Phoebe joins us at the table. I notice that Chance always seems to tense up some whenever she comes around. I can only assume it's because he's embarrassed or he still feels really guilty about him and Trina. He knows that this pregnancy really broke her heart.

Watching everyone laughing and teasing makes me long for times like this with my mom. Why couldn't we have been a normal family? Why couldn't we have family game night? Why did Jerome have to be in jail?

I blink rapidly to keep my tears from falling. I'm not about to break down crying in front of Alyssa and Chance. It's so totally not cool.

"Divine, you okay?" Uncle Reed inquires.

I can feel everyone watching me, so I put up a front. "Yes sir. Just ready to get my Scrabble on. C'mon, let's get it started."

After the game ends, Alyssa and I get on our computers. We end up checking out one of the chat rooms on TeenSpot.net.

She IMs me a few minutes later.

> **HollywoodQT:** They r having a stupid conversa-
> tion n here. And whoever Meow7777 is—she is
> so stupid. Letting a boy hit on her like that. I can't
> believe she won't tell her father.

> **SimplyMe:** She won't listen 2 everyone n the chat room telling her 2 break up with that boy. Girl, we need 2 leave b4 I tell her off. Then there's that girl, girl2girl, who is afraid 2 tell her parents she's a lesbian . . . Let's find another room. I can't handle all these issues right now.
>
> **HollywoodQT:** They have one 4 teens livng n GA. Let's ck it out.
>
> **SimplyMe:** I'll meet u n there.
>
> **HollywoodQT:** ok

Alyssa joins the chat at just about the same time I enter. We lurk, reading the different streams of conversation.

Scanning down the list of visitors in the chat room, one screen name catches my eye: NiceGuy16. He doesn't seem to say much, just kind of lurking like me and Alyssa are doing.

After a few minutes, I can't take this anymore.

Boring. This is exactly why I don't do chat rooms. The conversations are hard to keep up with because there are usually several going on at the same time. It's too confusing. I send an instant message to Alyssa.

> **HollywoodQT:** Everybody Is n2 blogging. A few people n this chat room have blogs.
>
> **SImplyMe:** Yeah I kept noticing that. But what exactly is a blog? Do u know?
>
> **HollywoodQT:** I think it's a online journal or something. Maybe we should check out some of the others. I like reading Rhyann's blog.
>
> **SimplyMe:** Rhyann is crazy
>
> **HollywoodQT:** True

Aylssa IMs me that Stephen's on the telephone, which means she's about to abandon me. So much for our exploring TeenSpot.net together. I decide to read some of the blogs on my own.

In the space of three days, I've managed to get myself grounded, lose my allowance and my boyfriend.

    I have a hard time at school because most of the females there are so jealous of me. I'm the cutest girl in school so all the boys like me. I was in two fights already this week and even though I didn't start them—I got suspended right along with the other girls.

    One of the girls went and told my boyfriend that I slept with her brother, which is so not true, but the jerk actually believed this girl. She's his ex-girlfriend.

    All I feel is major depression.

I shake my head after reading that entry. I feel sorry for the girl. Talk about having a run of bad luck. Sometimes girls can be jerks too. She's a pretty girl and they were probably just hatin' on her because of it. How stupid is that?

It's not like she made herself like that. Why don't people who think that way take it up with God? He's the man in charge.

I'm compelled to post a short note of encouragement before selecting another blog to read.

I watched the Oscars today just to see what everyone was wearing. I am a fashion diva and I love to shop . . .

"Now, she's my kind of girl," I whisper to myself. We have a lot in common in that she's as much of a diva as I am.

    . . . of course I want to study fashion design when I graduate high school. I dream of actresses wearing my gowns at the Grammys and the Oscars . . .

I post a short note on her blog as well. I read one more random blog before getting off my computer. Glancing around the room, I suddenly realize just how lonely I feel when I'm not playing around on the laptop.

I almost miss sharing space with Alyssa. Now that we have our own rooms, she stays closed up in hers a lot talking to Stephen. For a moment, I contemplate calling Madison but I'm not that desperate. I'm way too cute to be chasing after that dog, I tell myself. I can do so much better.

But until then, I have to suffer. I have to be the dreaded A word.

Alone.

The truth is that this is so hard for me. I'm cute, very fashionable and I'm rich. Why can't I get a decent boyfriend? What's wrong with me?

Just as I'm about to sign off, I get an instant message request, prompting me to accept IMs from NiceGuy16.

Flattered, but mostly out of curiosity, I give permission for him to IM me.

> **NiceGuy16:** I tried 2 catch u b4 u left the chat room. I like ur screen name. Cool.
>
> **HollywoodQT:** thx. I don't really do chat rooms. 2 busy 4 me.
>
> **NiceGuy16:** same here.
>
> **HollywoodQT:** well it was nice talking 2 u but have 2 go. I have church tomorrow and need 2 get my clothes ready.
>
> **NiceGuy16:** nice talking 2 u and hope 2 c u online.

Smiling, I sign off.

ON FRIDAY, ALYSSA and I walk home from school; Chance had to leave early to accompany Trina to her doctor's appointment. I have to say that I'm pretty proud of the boy for being responsible.

"Why are you so quiet?" Alyssa questions.

I glance over at her. "I was just thinking."

"Oh boy . . ." she moans. "Watch out, world."

I give her a playful shove. "You're stupid."

Chance is in his parents' room talking to Aunt Phoebe when we arrive.

"I'm glad they're talking," Alyssa whispers. "Mama must be getting used to the idea of being a grandmother."

I'm glad as well. There's been too much tension in the house already. We've been walking around on eggshells for the past three weeks.

We go to our rooms.

I find a letter from Jerome lying on the dresser. I open it immediately. When I see Ava's name, I frown. I don't know why he always wants to bring her into our relationship. Nobody cares about her.

He and Ava are planning on getting married as soon as the divorce is final. *So what?*

Before starting my homework, I sit down and write Jerome a letter. If I don't do it right now, it might not get done for a while.

My letter done and stuffed in an envelope, I pull out my history textbook. I have a paper to write on slavery.

Uncle Reed stops by my room shortly after he gets home. "What are you working on?"

"A paper on slavery."

"How's it going?" He asks.

"Good," I respond. "I'm doing my report on William Still."

"He was an abolitionist, right?"

Smiling, I nod.

We talk until Aunt Phoebe calls us to the dinner table.

My eyes travel to Chance as soon as we sit down. He seems more relaxed—his conversation with Aunt Phoebe must have gone well.

The pork chops make my mouth water. My aunt can really throw down in the kitchen. I have to give her that. Conversation is kept to a minimum because we're enjoying our meal.

Alyssa and I help clean up the kitchen because we need to set up for family game night. I've learned some great new words and I can't wait for the opportunity to use them when we play Scrabble.

Chance is going to get whipped tonight.

I SPEND MOST of Saturday morning on the phone with my mom. She's in Los Angeles for a couple of days, then she's off again. This time she's taking Miss Eula to Mexico for a mini vacation.

Picturing our cook in Cancún with Mom almost makes me laugh out loud. The two of them are going to look like the odd couple for sure. Mom is sophisticated and very fashionable while Miss Eula is round, the color of dark chocolate and loves wearing straw hats and bright-colored caftans. She always wears her snow-white hair pulled back into a bun. Miss Eula is full of wisdom, I always heard Mom say. She's full of something. That woman don't know how to keep an opinion to herself.

Alyssa opens my door. "Mama wants to know if you're going to the wedding."

I shake my head no. "Are you?"

"Naw. I don't really know Miss Mary's daughter like that. She's been living in Chicago a long time. I think I was in elementary school when she went away to college. What are you about to do?"

I sit up in bed. "Probably just get on the computer. Not much else to do."

Alyssa nods in agreement. "Well, let me know if you want to watch a movie or something."

I bite my lips to keep from saying, "Like I can pull you away from the phone and Stephen. He's her favorite pastime these days.

Her gaze reaches mine. "I know what you're thinking. Stephen is going to Atlanta today. I won't be talking to him until later on tonight."

"He's got a cell phone now. I'm sure he'll be calling you before then."

"Stacy was telling me about this guy who lives three doors down from her—he wants to meet you."

"How does he look?"

"I think he's cute," she replies. "He's tall, wears his hair cut short and he plays in the band at school. Saxophone, I think."

"I'll think about it," I say.

Alyssa grins. "You know you want to meet him."

"Let's go to Stacy's house so that I can see what he looks like first." The idea motivates me out of my bed and into my closet searching for just the right outfit. Who knows, I might be meeting my next boyfriend.

Two hours later, we are walking up the steps leading to Stacy's house. She greets us warmly, then ushers us into the house.

"So who is this guy that wants to meet me?" I ask as soon as we sit down in the family room.

Alyssa and Stacy burst into laughter.

I roll my eyes. They are like so immature.

"Okay . . . okay," Stacy begins, still cracking up. "His name is Nicholas Crawford. He's a nice guy."

"As in he looks like a dog 'nice guy'?" I want to know. "C'mon, tell me the truth."

"Nicholas is cute, girl. If he wasn't like a brother to me—I'd be his boo."

I didn't hide my suspicions. "If you two are so tight, why haven't I heard you mention him before?"

"I don't tell y'all about all my friends. Besides, Alyssa knows Nicholas."

Glancing over at my cousin, I ask, "You know him?"

"We're not friends but I do know who he is. He's on the quiet side and pretty much keeps to himself."

"Which house is his?" I get up and peek out of the window, scanning the houses in the area. I don't recall any cute boys living on her street. "Is it the one down there? The green and white house with the brick? I've seen a boy down there a few times sitting on the porch."

"Yeah, that's it."

A tall, slender boy walks out of the yard.

"Is this him?" I ask.

Stacy and Alyssa rush over to the window. "That's Nicholas. See, he's nice-looking."

I walk to the front door and open it, stepping outside just as Nicholas nears the house. Alyssa and Stacy join me outside.

"Hey, Nicholas," Stacy greets. "Come here for a moment."

I jab her in the back. "Why'd you do that?"

Alyssa whispers, "You want to meet him, don't you?"

Nicholas walks up the steps and is soon standing right in front of me. I glance over at Stacy, chewing on my bottom lip. He's so cute. I'm surprised I never really noticed him before.

"Nicholas, this is Divine," Stacy says, making the introductions.

"It's nice to meet you," he remarks.

I'm just as dopey. "You too." I don't know why I'm acting so dorky with this boy. It's not like he's a celebrity or anything—he's just a plain boy. I run my fingers through my hair, trying to think of something else to say. Thankfully I'm looking fierce.

We just stand there looking at one another. Stupid . . .

"So what have you been up to?" Alyssa asks after a tense moment. I guess she's trying to strike up a conversation.

He's extremely quiet, I note silently. "Stacy says you play the saxophone."

He nods. "I'm in the band."

Duh. Does this guy think I'm an idiot? "I kind of assumed as much," I respond. I can tell already that this isn't going to go anywhere—the boy won't even talk to me.

Bored from lack of conversation, I make up an excuse to go inside the house. Five minutes later, Alyssa and Stacy follow me.

"Girl, what happened? Why did you leave like that?" Alyssa questions. "You don't like him?"

I shrug. "How do I know if I like him or not? The boy hardly said anything. I have to wonder if he can string a sentence together."

Stacy giggles. "Girl, he talks. Nicholas is quiet, but he'll start talking more after he gets to know you."

"I don't know if he'll get the chance. I don't have time for this."

Alyssa eyes me. "What else do you have to do?"

I sit down on the loveseat in Stacy's family room. "I'm just not interested in Nicholas. All right?"

"Sure. Whatever." Alyssa drops down beside me. "He's probably not your type anyway. Every time I see him he's got his head stuck in a book or he's playing his sax."

"You're right—he's definitely not my type, then. I need a boyfriend who is mesmerized by me—he only thinks of me—he'll die for me . . ."

Alyssa and Stacy break into loud peals of laughter.

Grinning, I ask, "What? What's so funny?"

"You might be waiting on a boy like that for a long time, girl." Alyssa chuckles. "Unfortunately, I think they're only in romance novels."

Leaning against her, I remark, "Well, that sucks big-time."

chapter 10

It's Youth Sunday; normally, Pastor Michael Summers is the one who gives the sermon, but he's on a monthlong sabbatical, which according to my dictionary means a leave. I didn't know what it was, so I looked it up.

After we sing, Uncle Reed stands up and makes his way over to the pulpit in that long black robe he loves wearing. I think he'd look so much better if he just wore the dark suit he has on beneath. But maybe the robe makes him feel more preacher-like.

I glance down at Aunt Phoebe, who's planted herself on the front pew in her olive green suit with the wide-brim hat and matching olive green shoes.

Who wears green shoes?

I wish she'd just let me help her with her clothes. I could have Aunt Phoebe dressing so sharp. She'd look like a true first lady.

I bite my bottom lip to keep from laughing when I notice the poor woman sitting behind Aunt Phoebe keeps moving her head, trying to see what's going on in the pulpit.

"Good morning, church."

We return Uncle Reed's greeting.

As usual, he bends his head in prayer before starting his sermon.

"Most of what parents teach their children about God will never come from a Bible, but rather by their actions and the way they respond to life situations." He gives a little chuckle. "It's a scary thought, isn't it? Our children are watching us for cues on how to live their faith. It's a huge responsibility. It's a privilege. It's one of the responsibilities that many parents overlook . . ."

My eyes travel over the congregation, surveying the expressions on the church members' faces. A few drop their eyes, causing me to wonder why. Are they feeling guilty about something?

"As parents we are entrusted to nurture, love, guide and mold our children's lives. It's a very humbling responsibility but it's good news nonetheless. You see, God has a plan for your child's life. So, what is your part in that plan? What do you teach your teens about God?"

Uncle Reed's stepping on some toes today. He draws my attention back to him when he asks, "Church, can I get real with you this morning?"

The response is a positive one. If Uncle Reed is about to tell his business, then the church members are definitely going to listen. A few of the members have gotten wind that Chance is a baby daddy, although no official announcement has been made. And no one's really summoned up enough courage to ask Aunt Phoebe about it.

"My hopes are that my children might see God in me and continue to be drawn to Him, even though I am far from perfect. I want my children to see a flawed human being whose heart's desire is to love and serve God." Uncle Reed's eyes travel over to Chance, who's sitting at the piano.

"I want my children to hear my apologies when I mess up. I want them to know without a doubt that they are the recipients of the truth when I confess. I want them to know that while I may not know how to handle certain situations, I have faith that I will figure it out with God's guidance. I want my children to see in me everything they need to make it in this world today."

I get the feeling that Uncle Reed's talking directly to Chance right now. I steal a peek at Aunt Phoebe and catch her dabbing at her eyes.

Uncle Reed turns back around to face the congregation and finish his sermon.

After what seems like an eternity, I finally hear him say, "Before I close, I'll like to leave you with this: Rather than looking at your child's life today, take a minute and examine your own. If you never spoke another word about God, what would your actions and life say about Him to your children?"

I think about my mom and Jerome. Mom is trying to get her life straight, but Jerome—I think God Himself would have to come down and have a little talk with my dad.

After service ends, I walk back to Uncle Reed's office. I stand in the doorway, my eyes traveling around the medium-sized room lined with floor-to-ceiling bookcases. I thought he had a lot of books at home, but Uncle Reed has a lot of books here, all of them dealing with biblical studies.

"Hey you," he says when he glimpses me standing in the doorway.

I walk into the room and sit down in one of the burgundy-colored visitor chairs, facing him. "That was a good sermon this morning."

My teddy bear of an uncle smiles at me. "You mean you were actually listening?"

I pretend to be offended. "I can't believe you just said that to me, Uncle Reed. I always listen to you preach."

"So what did you like about this one?"

"The fact that you were talking to the parents. I wish my mom and Jerome could've been here this morning. I need to buy a tape and send it to them." I pick up a crystal paperweight off his desk to read the inscription. It was a gift from the senior choir. "This is pretty," I say.

"What is it that you think they should hear?"

"Basically how their actions can affect their children's lives." Putting the paperweight back on the desk, I tell him, "I didn't know anything about God until I moved in with you. Just think . . . I could've gone straight to you-know-where all because of my parents. That's scary, Uncle Reed."

"You're not going to be judged on your parents' actions."

I release an audible sigh of relief. "That's good to know. Whew."

"You *will* have to answer for your own sins, however."

"You just had to go there. Didn't you?"

Rising to his feet, Uncle Reed laughs. "Ready to go home?" He picks up his notes and places them in a nearby file cabinet.

"Yes sir. Aunt Phoebe's sweet potato pie is calling my name."

He holds the door open for me. "Divine, your mom is going to be all right. She's on the right track. I think Jerome is gonna be fine too. I keep praying for Him and I know that through God, all things are possible."

"You're not about to start preaching again, are you?"

"You might need an extra sermon or two. What do you think?"

"Uncle Reed, I think you really need to throw away that black robe you wear. You look nice in this suit. Just get rid of the robe. Save it for something like a funeral or a wedding."

"Miss Diva, I don't know what I'm gonna do with you."

I laugh. "I make your and Aunt Phoebe's life worth living. You know I do."

He hugs me. "You keep us on our toes, that's for sure. But I have to tell you: I never thought I'd love you as much as I do. You are a very special young lady and God has a special plan for your life. I don't know what it is, but He'll reveal it to you when it's time."

"I hope it doesn't mean that I have to give up something like shopping. I live for the mall."

MY WEEK STARTS off badly when the first thing I see as I round the corner of the cafeteria is Madison in a lip-lock with Brittany. I try to rush off before they see me but no such luck. The rest of my day goes downhill from there.

I can't find my homework for math and have to take a zero as my grade. Then I lose my wallet out of my backpack. I run into Nicholas, who treats me like I have the plague—my life sucks right now.

I'm so ready for the bell to ring so that I can go home and relax. The sooner I get this day over with the better I'll feel.

My prayers are answered forty-five minutes later, when school lets out.

But my streak of bad luck continues.

From the moment I arrive home from school, it becomes clear that she's got it in for me.

"Divine, you had a package arrive from some store in Los Angeles," Aunt Phoebe announces as soon as I step into the kitchen.

I jump up and down in my excitement. My day isn't so bad after all. "I've been waiting on that."

"You're gonna have to send some of that stuff back. It's too old for you. What in the world were you thinking ordering that mess?"

"You opened my package?" I can't believe she invaded my privacy like that. She had no right to open up my stuff.

Aunt Phoebe pulls up to her full height. "I sure did. Why?"

"I don't think that's right. It was addressed to me. I know you wouldn't like me opening up your stuff."

Aunt Phoebe dismisses my comments with the wave of her hand. "I'm not the child around here. This is my house and I have every right to see what you were ordering. Now you know good and well I'm not gon' let you walk around in those see-thru shirts." Her expression changes to one of disgust. "I don't even think Kara would let you wear that mess. What you planning on doing? Going to work on the street somewhere?"

I'm still tripping off the fact that she opened my package in the first place. Then she has the nerve to say that I'm trying to dress like some streetwalker—*no she didn't*.

She still walking around fussing. "And those skirts—you gon' wear something under them? 'Cause they barely reach your panties. Girl, what you thinkin'?"

I'm thinking you need to mind your own business.

"That stuff cost way too much money and you don't even get enough material to cover up anything." Inclining her head, Aunt Phoebe asks, "How'd you pay for this stuff anyway?"

"I had it put on my mom's account."

"Well, you can just have it taken right back off. This stuff is going back to that store."

It's no use arguing with Aunt Phoebe so I just storm off to my room. There's no point in calling Mom either because she'd side with Aunt Phoebe and probably fuss me out for using her account without permission.

I stay in my room until dinnertime to avoid any more scenes with Aunt Phoebe.

"I've noticed that we all take turns saying grace," Aunt Phoebe begins. "All of us except you, Divine."

Here she goes again.

"I don't feel like praying today."

"If you want to eat dinner today—you'll have to. It's not that difficult to offer thanks for the food we have."

"Then why don't you do it?" I snap.

Aunt Phoebe shoots up from the table. "What did you say to me?"

Before I can respond, she yanks me up by my collar, her dark eyes boring into mine.

"I didn't mean anything by it, Aunt Phoebe." The words rush out of my mouth.

She gives me a withering stare before releasing me. "Divine, I think you need to go to your room. I can't deal with you right now."

You can hear a pin drop, it's so quiet. I don't even think anyone is breathing. Aunt Phoebe's clearly lost her mind.

"I'm sorry. I didn't mean to be rude," I say a second time.

Aunt Phoebe takes my hands in her own. "Divine, praying is like talking to one of us—only you're talking to God. If you don't know how to pray, I'll help you."

"I know how to pray. I just don't like doing it in front of everybody." Tears slip from my eyes. "I'd like to be excused now."

Aunt Phoebe wraps her arms around me, holding me tight. "I love you, sugar. I want you to know that."

I leave the dining room as fast as I can. I'm just not comfortable praying aloud. It's a private thing for me. What's the big deal? I want to ask but right now it's not the right time.

I turn on my computer and click on the icon linking me to the internet. I need to calm my nerves.

After reading entries from various blogs on TeenSpot, I decide I have something I'd like to get off my chest as well. I sign up for my own personal blog space.

I already know what my first entry is going to be about, so I type away, putting my innermost feelings on the internet.

PARENTS: KNOW-IT-ALLS OR POWER-TRIPPING?

I don't know about you but I am so sick and tired of grown-ups thinking they know everything. God didn't have to bother with giving us brains if we have to follow our parents' rules.

I think it's all about power. Control. It's not so much that they want to protect us—they want to control our every move. Think about it. They were young once although they try to act like they were oh-so-perfect—at least in my household. My mom is cool until she gets in Mom mode and then she tries to tell me what to do with my own life.

There are times I just want to tell her about all the mistakes she's made in her life but my mom's not ready to hear the truth.

What really gets on my nerves is when she tells me how smart I am and then turns around and tells me I'm not mature enough to do something or just wait until I'm a little older. I HATE IT!!!

Writing those words felt so good. Smiling, I sit back in my chair, proofing my first entry. I love it. I feel empowered. That's my word for today.

Alyssa walks into my room without knocking. "Hey, Divine, what are you doing?"

"Come here . . . I want to show you something." I point to my computer screen. "I started a blog."

"About what?" Alyssa wants to know.

"Read," I tell her.

When Alyssa's done, all she can say is, "Wow. I guess you had something on your mind."

"It's what I feel right now."

She chuckles. "You better hope Mama don't ever come across this. She'd chase you all over Temple."

"Like your mom is going to surf the internet. Aunt Phoebe thinks it's full of nothing but sex and drugs."

"No, she doesn't," Alyssa counters. "She knows there are a lot of good educational sites too."

"I don't ever hear her talking about any."

"You know you tune out when my parents are talking to you. You zone out quick."

"I listen to them . . ." Grinning, I add, "Sometimes anyway." Pointing back to the computer screen, I say, "You should try it. Blogging is fun."

Alyssa shakes her head. "I don't know. I'll think about it."

"Do you think your mom's still mad with me?" I've stayed hidden in my room for the past two hours.

"She's not. But Divine, you know you lucky. If I'd said something like that to her—she would've killed me without blinking an eye."

"I just didn't want to say the blessing."

"Why not?"

"Because I really don't know one. I hear you all saying them all the time, but I don't really have anything special that I say."

"Well, what do you say?"

"Thank you, God, for the food. Amen." I wait for the laughter and teasing to come but it doesn't. Instead, Alyssa says to me, "Then just say that. That's still giving God the thanks. It's okay."

"You sure?"

Alyssa nods.

"You think I should go talk to Aunt Phoebe?"

"I would." Alyssa checks her watch. "While y'all talking, I'ma go call Stephen."

"Like you'd do anything else. That's all you do—talk to Stephen," I complain.

"Divine, don't start that again. You know I can't see Stephen unless we're at school. All we can do is talk on the phone. Just wait until you get another boyfriend. I bet you won't be giving me the time of day."

I laugh.

"You should go talk to Mama," Alyssa advises.

Nodding, I get up from my desk and head to the door. "Wish me luck," I say over my shoulder as I walk out of the room.

Aunt Phoebe is in the kitchen. She turns around when I enter. She still looks a little upset with me.

"I was just putting away the food. Are you hungry?"

"A little," I confess. Actually, I'm starving.

I walk over and take Aunt Phoebe by the hand. "I'm sorry for being such a pain. The truth is that I don't really know why I bought those clothes. I knew you wouldn't ever let me wear them—it was just something to do. And with the blessing . . . Aunt Phoebe, I thought it had to be, like, a certain amount of words or something. I was embarrassed because I can't pray like you and Uncle Reed. Even Alyssa and Chance can throw out some tight prayers."

She hugs me. "Sugar, you just speak from your heart. That's all. Now you're a part of this family and in this family—we pray. A family that prays together, stays together. Remember that."

"I'll say the blessing tomorrow when we eat."

Aunt Phoebe strokes my cheek. "Good girl."

"I love you, Aunt Phoebe. I'm sorry for being such a pain."

We hug again.

I take my plate to the microwave to warm up my food. If I don't eat something soon I'm liable to just pass out on the kitchen floor.

BOYS CAN BE SO STUPID!!

Sometimes I really hate boys. I had a boyfriend that I thought really liked me—at least that's what he told me all the time. Actually he used to tell me that he loved me. That I was his boo. LIAR.

We were very happy together and then one day he decides that he wants to dump me and the reason is so stupid. I mean really, really stupid. It's too stupid to even write it here.

But it's okay. My broken heart is mending and one day I'll find somebody new. One day he'll look back at me and really really want me back. It'll be way too late though.

He had his chance and he missed it.

Big mistake!!

My mom comes to mind. Some kids at school were talking about her and Kevin Nash today. They are still leading the rumor mill. Why? I don't know. It's not like what the tabloids are saying is true. He and mom are just friends—at least that's what she keeps telling me.

There are times I wish she was just a normal person—then her business wouldn't be plastered all over the *National Enquirer*.

Before I realize it, my fingers are flying over the keyboard.

TRUTH OR GOSSIP

I just read something in a tabloid about someone I know really well. This person is always telling me that I shouldn't believe what I read in papers like this, but I'm not so sure she's telling me the truth. I mean the pictures look real.

I know her very well and I trust her. But when I see and read this stuff, I have to wonder if she's being honest with me. Grown-ups are always so big on honesty but are we supposed to believe that they always tell the truth?

I'm careful not to mention that the person I'm referring to is my mother because I don't want my identity revealed. Besides, my mom would kill me if she knew I was telling her business on a blog.

Although it's really not that much difference than having her personal life splashed all over newspapers and tabloids the way I see it.

THE NEXT DAY, I ride with Aunt Phoebe to the church for rehearsal after school because we have to get there early. Alyssa will be coming with Penny and Stacy later because she needs to finish a school project.

Since it's just the two of us, I tell Aunt Phoebe about something that's been on my mind.

"I know this is a luncheon for the mothers, Aunt Phoebe, but the clothes you want to use from Susie's Fashions are boring—not to mention cheap-looking. Let's jazz it up some."

"These dresses are nice, Divine."

I decide to use the direct approach. "Nice and ugly maybe. Aunt Phoebe, just because you're not young anymore and you've put on a few pounds . . . you can still be cute. You don't have to dress like somebody's great-grandmother."

"I have not put on a few pounds," my aunt argues. "Maybe a couple of pounds but that's it. And I think I dress just fine. Reed never complains."

Apparently Aunt Phoebe has forgotten I go shopping with her and jumping from a size twelve to a sixteen in like, two days, is more than a couple of pounds. As far as Uncle Reed's taste in clothes . . . well, he's in desperate need of a fashion makeover himself. I make a mental note to give them both consultations with image consultants for their wedding anniversary next year.

"Aunt Phoebe, you know I'm right. You don't even shop at Susie's."

She breaks into a big grin. "Okay, so if we take these back to the store, where should we get the clothes from?"

"Mom has this designer friend who has a wonderful collection. She—"

Aunt Phoebe cuts me off by saying, "Sugar, we want clothes that the women will be able to purchase. Remember, this is supposed to be a fund-raiser. We're raising money for college scholarships."

"Aunt Phoebe, I'm telling you—they can afford these. Kiani's clothing is very reasonable. She wants her line to be affordable."

"So why do you think she'll let us use her stuff?"

"Because we have the hook-up, Aunt Phoebe. She'll do anything for Mom. That's how she got her start. She dressed Mom until she got saved—her style changed after that. Trust me, she'll do it."

"Uh-huh," Aunt Phoebe mutters.

I make a call to my mom's cellular but am immediately transferred to her voice mail. I call Stella, her assistant, next.

"Hello, Stella, do you know where my mom is? She's not answering her cell."

"She's been on the set all morning taping. I'm sure she'll give you a call back as soon as she can. Is there something I can do for you, dear?"

"I need Mom to call Kiani Sams and see if she'd be willing to let us use her clothing line for a fashion show here in Temple."

"Why don't I call Kiani myself?" Stella suggests. "I'm sure she'd do the show if it fits in her schedule."

"That'll be great. Thanks so much, Stella." Since I don't have to spend so much time with Stella anymore, I kind of like her better. She's really not that bad.

"How are you doing?"

"I'm fine. How's the baby doing?"

Stella laughs. "She's getting so big or maybe I should say I'm getting bigger and bigger. I'll be glad when she comes out."

Who in their right mind looks forward to childbirth? I wonder silently. I make a mental note to ask Trina if she's looking forward to labor and delivery. I guess after having to carry a baby in your belly for nine months—labor doesn't sound that bad.

ON WEDNESDAY I walk into the house, heading straight to my room. I'm so angry I could scream. Instead I decide to post an entry on my blog. I find it a great place to vent these days. For me, it's like a journal. I don't care if other people are reading it because they don't know me.

It's not like I really have anyone around here to talk to. Alyssa is into Stephen and Penny is having her own drama. Not to mention Chance and Trina dealing with the baby thing. Trina's not much fun these days because she seems to stay sick.

I think she's getting a little excited about the baby. Chance even talks about it sometimes. Before, he would hardly mention it. So far, we've been able to keep it off the school's grapevine but I know it won't be for much longer. People have been asking questions about Trina throwing up all the time.

I turn on my computer and log into my webspace. I know just what I want to say.

BOYS: WHAT ARE THEY THINKING?

I met a boy today at school and he was so cute. He walked me to my first class and then we met again at lunchtime. He even spent his money to buy my soup and salad.

It was actually funny watching my ex-boyfriend's expression.

He couldn't seem to concentrate on his ugly and trampy-looking girlfriend for totally being in my business. Just kept watching us while that thing holding onto him was trying to keep his eyes on her.

Anyway, things are going great until this boy just out of the blue asks me to skip the rest of my classes with him.

He thought we should get busy, as he put it.

Now I'm thinking that I just met him TODAY and I barely know his last name. He doesn't know much about me except what he's heard. He doesn't know if I like hot dogs or if I'm a vegan. The boy doesn't even know who my homeroom teacher is.

Why would I want to skip school with this fool? I mean he is fine and I mean FINE, but I don't really know him and he doesn't know me. I'm insulted that he would even think I'd actually consider doing something so totally stupid.

I know what'll happen if I did. I'd lose my membership in the big V (Virgin) club and then I'd go back to school and all my business would be everywhere.

And if I somehow survived not getting pregnant or getting a disease I'll still be labeled as being easy.

Just ask my ex-boyfriend's new girlfriend.

chapter 11

There won't be a family game night because Uncle Reed is preaching at a revival in Villa Rica. I'm grateful we didn't have to go with him. Mainly because we have mountains of homework. Aunt Phoebe says we have to go with them tomorrow night since it's Friday and we have all weekend to do homework.

We ordered pizza and after eating went our separate ways. Chance is in his room with the door closed—probably talking to Trina. Alyssa is in her room studying for a test when I last checked on her.

I finished my work and with nothing else to do at the moment, I turn on my computer.

"Somebody responded to my entry." I rush to the doorway of my bedroom, yelling, "Alyssa, come here."

"What's up?"

136

"I got a response on one of my entries. Somebody read my blog."

Alyssa sits down in my chair. "Looks like a lot of people read your blog, Divine. This person that calls himself NiceGuy16 actually commented a couple of times."

"It sounds like he's really liking my entries," I mumble as I read the comments he left. "He's really feeling what I wrote."

I go back over NiceGuy16's comments when Alyssa leaves the room to check her laundry.

Feeling bold, I send an email to NiceGuy16, thanking him for leaving a response on my blog.

Thanks for commenting on my blog. It's good to know that I'm not the only one dealing with issues like these.
    Me.

Alyssa strolls back into my room carrying a basket of freshly dried clothing, which she drops on the edge of my bed before plopping down beside it.

"You still reading your own blog?" She picks up a T-shirt and starts folding it.

"Nope. I wrote that guy back."

She picks up another T-shirt. "You did?"

I push away from my desk. "Come read it and tell me what you think."

Alyssa stands up and walks the short distance to the computer.

"Nice and short. *Good*," she compliments. "That's all you need to say to him."

"Alyssa, why must you be so negative? With you it's always doom and gloom."

"That's not true."

I disagree. "I know bad things happen in the world, but not everybody you meet is a bad person."

"It doesn't hurt to be a little cautious, Divine. You don't know that guy."

I raise my eyebrows a fraction. "I hope you know that you sound just like your mom."

Alyssa's gaze meets mine. "And you think that's a bad thing?" She rumbles through her laundry basket, looking for what I don't know. She's always losing stuff.

"Divine, you need to keep up with what's going on outside of Hollywood and the fashion world. You know they're still looking for that girl and now there's another one missing from somewhere in Savannah. The world is not as safe as it used to be."

"I'm not going to live my life in fear," I tell her. "I believe God will look out for me."

"I'm not saying you should be scared, but Divine, God wants us to use wisdom . . ." She pauses. "Now I really sound like Mama."

I laugh. "You do."

"All I'm trying to say is that you have to be careful. You can't take anything for granted—not anymore. Besides, I don't want anything to happen to you, Divine. I'd die."

I smile. "I don't want anything to happen to you either. Look, I'm not a stupid person. I know to be careful." Pointing to the basket of laundry and the tiny stacks of folded clothing, I say, "Get your stuff out of my room. Fold your clothes in your own room."

"You getting ready to go to bed?"

"In a few. I'm tired."

Alyssa yawns. "I'm kinda tired too, but I still have one more load of clothes to do."

I would offer to help but I'm just not feeling it. Besides, I have to do my own laundry tomorrow night.

She stays for a few minutes more, then leaves.

Yawning, I stand up and stretch.

It doesn't take me long to shower and change into my pajamas. The last thought before I close my eyes is a hope that NiceGuy16 responds to my email. I need my deflating ego stroked.

THE NEXT DAY, I come home from school and the first thing I do is check my email to see if NiceGuy16 has responded.

I decide that I must be pretty lonely and desperate. This is the only explanation for rushing home to see if I've heard from a complete stranger. I'm pathetic—I admit it.

I break into a grin when I see the email from NiceGuy16.

Hey Me
Thanks for emailing me. I was surprised to hear from you but I'm glad because I really like your blog. You speak the truth and that's cool. Don't stop now because you've got some fans out here.
Sean

I immediately set out to reply to his email. Eventually our going back and forth will fizzle out and I'll probably never hear from him again. Guys have been such jerks lately. But I'm okay with it. I just need somebody to talk to until I meet someone new.

Sean
Do you have your own blog? If not, you should consider creating one. It sounds like you have something on your mind—free yourself.
Dee

Sean sends me yet another email. It comes so quickly that he must be sitting in front of a computer too.

Dee

No, I don't have a blog. Thought about it but then I just don't know what I'd talk about. Outside of living in the Buckhead area of Atlanta all my life with my parents and four brothers.

My name is Sean Tyler and I'm sixteen. Tell me more about yourself. You sound like a pretty cool person and I'd like to get to know you better. Don't worry. I'm safe.

Sean

My fingers dance across the keyboard, typing out my response. I envision him sitting there in front of his monitor just waiting to hear from me.

"I really am pathetic," I murmur with a short laugh. My email finished, I reread it, checking for errors before I hit the send button.

Sean

I didn't expect to hear from you so quickly. You must be sitting at your computer. You don't live that far from me. I'm living outside of Atlanta with my aunt and uncle. I'm fifteen—well, almost sixteen. My birthday is in December.

I don't have any brothers or sisters, but I do have two cousins that sometimes drive me crazy. I'm sure you can relate to that.

You sound like you're a nice person so I don't mind getting to know you. Write back when you can.

Dee

To my disappointment, I don't receive another email from Sean. Maybe he had to get off the computer, I tell myself.

After dinner, I alternate between doing my homework and checking my email, looking for one from Sean.

I don't hear back from him until the next day. Right before we sit down to play Scrabble, I sneak into my room to check email because Mimi was supposed to be sending me a picture of her and Bow Wow.

Instead, I find the email from Sean, explaining that there had been a family emergency, which is why I'm just hearing from him.

I'm relieved. I thought maybe I'd done something to scare him off.

"Divine, we're ready?" Alyssa calls from the hallway. "You playing tonight?"

"Yeah," I shout back.

Shutting down my email, I decide not to tell Alyssa anything about my budding friendship with Sean. The last thing I want to hear is that he's some pervert trying to lure me into his madness. I need some positive energy right now.

UNCLE REED AND I sit in his office after dinner on Sunday. Aunt Phoebe and Alyssa are in the family room watching some stupid romantic movie. Chance had to go to work, so he won't be home until late. That poor boy is going to work himself to death.

"Your aunt tells me that you've arranged for us to have a real fashion designer for the Mothers' Luncheon."

"Yes sir. Kiani Sams. She's an up-and-coming designer, so this is a great opportunity for her to get her name out. Aunt Phoebe is really going to love her clothes."

"Thank you for helping out like this, Divine. I really appreciate it."

"I don't mind, Uncle Reed. You and Aunt Phoebe do a lot for me. I'm just glad I could help. Besides, you can't have a fashion show without . . . well, *fashion*. You know?"

He laughs. "What am I gonna do with you?"

"Raise my allowance, maybe? There are these killer shoes by Baby Phat that I want. I—"

Uncle Reed interrupts me by responding, "No, I think the amount you get now is more than fair."

"You're not listening to me. Uncle Reed, I'm a fashion icon. I need to stay on top of my game."

"That's fine. Just do it on a shoestring budget."

"You're so not funny, Uncle Reed."

He leans back in his chair. "So Miss Diva, what did you want to talk about? I know you're not just in here to keep me company."

"Have you seen the *National Enquirer?* They keep talking about Mom and Kevin Nash. What do you think?"

"What do *you* think?"

"Mom says they are only friends. But they are saying that Mom broke up Kevin's marriage. And supposedly his wife caught them together in bed."

"Have you asked your mother about this?"

"I told you. She just says that they're friends. Nothing more."

"I gather you don't believe her?"

"I want to," I confessed. "But Uncle Reed, I don't really know what to believe. Some of the pictures are looking suspicious. And the kids at school—I'm so tired of them talking about this. It's like they don't have anything else to talk about."

"I don't read those kinds of papers, Divine, for a reason. I think they play up shreds of the truth and fill the gaps with speculation."

"Sometimes I wish I just had a normal mom. One that wasn't famous."

"Divine, people will always attack your character no matter what you do."

I look up at my uncle's face. "You don't have to worry about that."

He laughs.

"What's so funny?"

"I have come under attack a few times in my life. I've had people tell my wife things that were not true."

I sit straight up. "Really?"

"If I were you, I wouldn't listen to all this stuff going around about your mother. My granny used to tell me all the time that your true self will come through—no matter how hard you try to hide it."

"It's not that I believe it. I'm just tired of hearing about it. I wish the media would just leave my mother alone."

THE WEEK PASSED by in a blur. I can't believe that in two days, it will be October. The days seem to go by fast—sometimes I feel like life is just passing me by. I take care of my laundry as soon as I come home from school. I don't want to deal with it after rehearsal.

One more day until the fashion show. We had our last rehearsal earlier. I really enjoyed working with the models and Kiani. This just confirms that the fashion world is where I belong. I can't wait for everyone to see the new outfit I'll be wearing tomorrow. Because it's Kiani's fashion line, I have to wear something from her label. She designed something just for me, and I love it.

Aunt Phoebe is so giddy with excitement she didn't hesitate in letting me and Alyssa hook up with Stacy and Penny at the movie theater.

We invited Trina along, but her parents hardly let her leave the house now that she's pregnant. Seems to be a moot point now, but that's just me.

Chance is working today so it's just us girls hanging out at the movies.

"Hey, you want some popcorn?" Stacy asks, cutting into my thoughts.

"Yeah," I respond. "A small one, and a root beer."

"Oh no he didn't . . ." I hear Penny mutter.

I turn around, following her line of vision. Her boyfriend James is here with some other girl. I groan because all I want to do is enjoy my night out with my girls. But I can feel it—it's about to get ugly up in here.

"Penny, c'mon. Don't make a scene," I whisper between clenched teeth.

Alyssa scopes out the situation and walks over with drinks in both hands. "Let's go. The movie will be starting soon."

I grab Penny by the arm. "He's so not worth it."

"What you looking at my man like that for?" I hear a female voice yell out. "Yeah, you better go on. And keep yo' eyes to yo'self."

Penny snatches her arm from me. "I know you ain't talking to me. As for your man—you need to ask him about me."

I can't believe this. I look over at Alyssa, silently urging her to do something. I have on a brand-new outfit and I don't want to get it ruined in a catfight. From the looks of things, the cow with James has some backup. It's a group of them all coupled off.

"Penny, c'mon. Don't even waste your time with them. Let her have the dog."

"Hey, who you calling a dog? I ain't no dog. I don't know what your girl been telling you but she and I—we weren't nothing but friends. That's all. Right, Penny?"

Penny launches into a string of vile curses, calling James some of everything. I've heard her cuss from time to time but never like this. Even Jerome would be put to shame and I didn't think there was a person alive who could outcuss my dad.

I'm so relieved when Security appears. We are ushered toward one entrance while James and his crew are led into another direction. Thankfully, we're not going to be in the same movie location.

Penny cries through most of the movie, which nearly drives me up a wall. That guy is so not worth her tears. He looks like a jerk.

Afterward, we try to console her.

"I can't believe he treated me like this," she cries. "I thought he really cared about me. I really did."

"Boys can be such jerks," Stacy utters.

I totally agree.

"I can't believe I actually had sex with him."

"I can't believe you did either," I blurt. "That's all guys like him really want."

"Divine, shut up," Alyssa huffs. "She feels bad enough."

"I'm not trying to make her feel bad, but Penny . . . you only knew him for what? A few weeks?"

"I met him in June."

"And you slept together when?"

"The end of July."

"I'm not trying to be mean or nothing, but girl, that was way too soon."

Her eyes flash in anger. "I know that now, Divine. But back then, he was so nice to me and he just kept telling me how much he loved me and wanted to be close to me. I was really feeling him. I believed him . . . it's stupid, I know."

I reach over and take her hand. "It's not stupid—just human. Now you've got to pick yourself up and move forward. Leave that no-good you know what alone. You see he's got a girlfriend. A *big* girlfriend."

Stacy utters, "Yeah, girl. That thing was huge. She could've whipped all of us with one hand. What were you thinking? You wear a size one."

"I was mad. Hurt, angry and I just wanted to wring his ugly neck. Did you see the way he was just standing there laughing at us?"

Alyssa pulls up her braids in a ponytail and wraps a black hairband around them. "It probably made his day to have two girls fighting over him."

Seeing the pain on Penny's face reminds me of how I felt when I first saw Madison with Brittany. I know how betrayal feels, only I imagine her pain to be much worse because she'd given so much of herself to James. I vow to never make that same mistake.

chapter 12

$\mathcal{I}$ *go* back through my notes one more time before the fashion show begins. The last thing I want to do is make a fool of myself. I've been bragging for days now how this event was going to be the talk of Temple.

Aunt Phoebe must be able to see how nervous I am, because she comes over and tells me, "Sugar, you're going to do just fine. Just do it the way we practiced."

Mom flew in for the luncheon and fashion show and she looks beautiful in her deep lilac suit with fringed hemline, a Kiani Sams design. She's cut her hair off and it really looks cute on her, although I initially had my doubts how she would look with short hair.

She really came through for me with getting Kiani to showcase her new fashion line here in Temple. Ticket sales went through the roof, so Aunt Phoebe's really loving me right now. The proceeds go toward scholarships for students wanting to attend college.

I can barely eat the stuffed chicken and wild rice entrée, but I did finish my dessert before having to freshen up before the fashion show. I make a quick run to the bathroom to brush my teeth. With people taking pictures, I can't take the chance of standing up there onstage grinning and then find out there's something between my teeth. I get grossed out just thinking about it.

As soon as I walk back into the banquet hall, Mom ushers me up to the podium. It's time.

I take a deep breath, releasing it slowly before welcoming everyone and thanking them for their support. Aunt Phoebe's idea—not mine.

"All right ladies, there is definitely a charm in this three-piece suit," I commentate as the first model makes her entrance on the runway.

"The jacket has a one-button closure with a matching tank underneath. The skirt has a handkerchief hemline with tiny silver charms sewn all around." I pause while the model strikes a pose for photographers.

The flashing lights reminds me of Hollywood and I find myself slipping back into the old routine of making sure my best side is photographed and not looking like I'm posing for the camera. Some habits just never die.

"Our next model is wearing a radiant suit with a lovely gold metallic hat." I can't resist adding, "Aunt Phoebe, I know you love this outfit."

"I sure do, sugar," she responds.

Amid the chuckles, I continue describing the outfit.

While the model is at the end of the runway posing, I steal a peek over at the table where Mom and Aunt Phoebe are sitting. Mom winks at me and waves. I smile and relax. The show is going well.

Midway, I'm comfortable enough to ad lib my way through the rest of the show. People are smiling and enjoying my comments, including my top ten fashion tips—little things I've picked up over the years from various makeup artists and fashion consultants, not to mention *Glamour* and *Vogue*.

"Here's fashion tip # 4: Don't be a fashion disaster by wearing the wrong colors. Ladies, I'm telling you—not everybody can wear yellow and orange. And blue eye shadow . . . Trust me."

I can hear Mom laughing. I'm so glad that she's here with me.

"Fashion tip # 5: Don't get a Japanese character tattoo unless you can read Japanese—or at least have a good translator. It's important to know what you're having permanently stamped on your body."

One of the male models, the drummer from church, walks on the runway. The way the women are carrying on right now, you'd think he was really something special. He is kind of cute, though.

He's followed by another boy and then Chance. I was worried that my cousin was going to mess up—he did at each rehearsal, but today he's making me proud. *Chance looks good.*

Right before the finale, I give my last fashion tip. "Here's fashion tip # 10: Your clothes say a lot about you, so keep that in mind while building your wardrobe."

The model wearing the dress for the finale is about to make her entrance. It's gorgeous, one of my favorites. Kiani's dresses are more for women Mom's age so I'm not crazy about much of her clothing.

"Now, this piece is called Rouge Fire and ladies, you know why. This gown is *hot*. Two riveting pieces give this ensemble its edge. This open-shoulder style has bronze sequin trim on the neck, front and along the sleeves. You'll note that the lined, ankle-length skirt has the matching sequin trim . . ."

I finish my commentary and welcome all the models back onstage. I wink at Alyssa when she sashays back down the runway.

Kiani walks out to join the models and bows gracefully amidst the thunderous applause and standing ovation.

I'm grinning from ear to ear because the fashion show is a major success.

Mom comes over to me. "You did a beautiful job," she compliments. "I'm so proud of you."

"So when do you have to leave for Miami?"

"On Tuesday. We start taping my new movie on Friday. We're filming a sequel to *X-Factor*."

"Are you excited?"

Mom nods. "Actually, I am. I get to do some singing in this one. Gospel music. It's about a woman who returns to her gospel roots after the death of her twin sister."

"Uncle Reed's going to love this movie. Aunt Phoebe too."

Mom pushes a curl away from my face. "I'm going to miss you, baby girl."

"Me too. I like having you close by like this."

"At least we'll see each other next weekend when you come out to Los Angeles for the premiere of *Moonshadow Lake*."

I nod. "Alyssa and Chance are really excited. I think Uncle Reed and Aunt Phoebe are too. We could use some excitement around here." Glancing up at her hair, I say, "Mom, you never told me . . . why did you cut your hair?"

"I figured it was time for a new attitude. I wanted a makeover." Mom places a hand to her head. "You don't think it looks good like this?"

"I like it. I was just wondering why you did it." In the back of my mind, I recall seeing Kevin Nash with various women before he got married and they all wore their hair short—like my mom's.

"What are you thinking so hard on?"

I blink rapidly. "Nothing. Mom, I'll be right back. I need to check with Aunt Phoebe on something."

I rush back to Uncle Reed's office and pull out my cell phone.

"Mimi, this is Dee. I need you to do some detective work for me. Yeah. I need you to find out everything you can about Kevin Nash, his wife and my mom. I know your mother hangs out at the same spa as Kevin's wife. Thanks."

I hear voices in the hallway, so I say, "I'll call you back. Bye."

Aunt Phoebe walks into the office with Mom.

Pasting a smile on my face, I say, "I was just looking for you, Aunt Phoebe."

IF SHE DOESN'T shut up soon I'm going to throw her off this plane. Alyssa's been talking nonstop since we boarded. We are on our way to Los Angeles for the premiere of my mom's new movie. The whole family's going and it's a first for them. I just hope they don't get all starstruck and embarrass me.

"Aren't you tired?" I inquire. "We had to get up at the crack of dawn."

"I'm too excited to sleep. I can't wait to get to Los Angeles. Will we see Rhyann and Mimi? I really want to see Rhyann."

Holding up my hand, I say, "Alyssa . . . like, chill for a minute."

Our flight lands five hours later. I practically drag myself off because I'm so tired and Alyssa wouldn't let me get any sleep. I'm so ready to murder her.

After we retrieve our luggage, I lead them outside where a driver and stretch limo are waiting for us.

"This is the way to travel," Alyssa gushes. "I love Los Angeles. I hope Aunt Kara stays out here so that I can come to visit often."

"You mean you don't want to move out here?" I ask.

Alyssa shakes her head no. "I know me. Girl, I'd lose my mind."

The limo enters the 405 freeway, heading toward I-10 West. It feels good being back home until I see the backed-up traffic. This is what I *don't* miss about California.

Aunt Phoebe zooms in on our conversation. "In what way, Alyssa?"

"I don't know, Mama."

"I don't know why you even running your mouth. You know you don't want to leave Mama and Dad," Chance states.

Alyssa corners him by asking, "And you do? You want to get away from our parents?"

I burst into laughter over the funny look on Chance's face. "I wouldn't answer that if I were you. Your parents are eyeing you down."

Laughing, he shakes his head.

"Oh, you won't be hurting our feelings if you want to get as far away from us as possible," Aunt Phoebe says. "I'm planning on turning your room into a sewing room. The same day you move out."

Alyssa and I bow over in laughter.

"And your room will be an exercise room, and Divine, I'm turning your room into a guest room."

"You're only going to have one guest room?" I ask. "What about when we come to visit? And what if we have families by then . . . well, Chance will already have a child, so where do we all sleep?"

"Sugar, they got plenty of hotels all over."

"Aunt Phoebe—we're family."

She smiles. "We'll still be family. Just won't be staying all up under each other."

"I just had an epiphany."

"A what?" Alyssa asks.

"An epiphany. It means a sudden manifestation of the essence or meaning of something. That was my word of the day yesterday. Only I'm just getting it today—the meaning. Anyway, I just realized that all the remodeling you and Uncle Reed did has nothing to do with me. This was all about getting ready for when you kick us out of the house." I place a hand to my chest. "I feel so betrayed."

Everyone in the limo cracks up in laughter, including me.

The driver makes a right turn on Temescal Canyon Road and then another right on West Sunset Boulevard. We turn left on Swarthmore Avenue.

"We're almost there," I tell them.

We pull into the circular driveway of my home, a huge twelve-thousand-square-foot house surrounded by expansive lawns, brightly colored flower gardens and trees. We're just a few blocks from the bluffs and the ocean.

Mom greets us at the front door. "C'mere, baby girl, and give me a hug."

"You just saw me last weekend," I tell her, reminding her of the fashion show.

"I know that. I still missed you." She holds out her arms to me. "Just hush and give your mama a kiss."

I do as she requests.

Mom hugs her brother first, then Aunt Phoebe. "I'm so glad y'all are here. I really think this movie is going to be a blockbuster."

After Mom gives love to Chance and Alyssa, we take our luggage upstairs. Alyssa takes the bedroom across from my mine while Chance is staying right next door. We can hear Aunt Phoebe losing her mind over the master bedroom. Mom's room is tight.

She has it decorated in black and gold with leopard accents.

We can hear Aunt Phoebe's scream when she is taken to the media room. Alyssa and I bust into a round of laughter. My aunt is too funny. Like her daughter, she trips out over my leather floors. They're just floors. Duh.

I'm so ready for a nap, but Alyssa wants to call Rhyann and Mimi. "We'll see them tonight. Now leave me alone. I just want to sleep."

Alyssa isn't trying to hear me. "You can sleep when we get back home," she tells me. "C'mon, Divine . . . you're supposed to be the party animal."

I give Alyssa Rhyann's phone number and practically push her out of my room, locking the door behind her. I just want to sleep.

But just before my nap, I open my laptop and check my email. I almost fall out from the shock to see an email from Nicholas. He hasn't said two words to me since that day we were at Stacy's house. Now I get an email from him?

He apologizes for not really talking to me. It's actually a sweet email. I shoot him one back thanking him. I'm not interested in him being a boyfriend, but maybe we have a shot at being friends.

I break into a smile when I discover that I have one from Sean. We've been talking almost every day. And he always comments on my blog entries. More and more teens are reading them, which thrills me. I love being popular.

Dee

I hope you're having a wonderful day at school. As for me, I'm so bored with my classes. I'm in college prep classes because my parents feel I need to be challenged more. They want me to go to Morehouse just like my father did, but I don't know if I really want to go to college at all.

What I'd like to do most is be able to think for myself. I want to experience life for myself and not through my parents' eyes. I know you feel what I'm saying. Why can't they see that they don't know everything?

Enough of my madness. I want to concentrate on you. Do you feel comfortable enough with me to send a picture? I don't want to freak you out but we're sharing so much—I'd like to know what you look like.

Think about it.

Sean

I'm psyched about sending him a photo but then I worry that he'll recognize me. I'm not ready for him to know anything about my life as Kara Matthews' daughter. I want to know that he likes me for me. So for now, I decide against sending pictures. Maybe when I get to know him better.

Me, Alyssa and Chance stay up late talking in my room while Mom, Aunt Phoebe and Uncle Reed are downstairs in the media room with Stella and her husband. We're all excited about the premiere tomorrow night. Mom's scheduled appointments for us with her hairdresser and for manicures and pedicures. We're going to be stunning.

We are forced to go to bed shortly after midnight when Mom and everyone come upstairs.

Morning comes much too soon.

Mom wakes me up, rushing me to get dressed so that I don't make us late for our hair appointment. Uncle Reed and Chance are going to hang out with Miss Eula while we get all beautiful.

Five hours later, we return home to rest for about an hour before having to get dressed. The limo is scheduled to arrive promptly at five, so Mom wants all of us ready to leave. She gets real bossy when she's nervous.

"Do you like my hair like this?" Alyssa asks when she comes into my room.

I nod. "Your braids are all real shiny. You look nice."

She walks over to the mirror. "But do you like my hair up like this?"

"Yeah." I eye my reflection in the mirror, fingering my hair. "I should've had her cut a little more off the top, don't you think?"

Alyssa shakes her head. "No. You need to leave it just like that. You look good with your hair styled like that. It's not really curled—the layers fall in just the right place."

I check the clock. "We'd better get dressed. Mom will be knocking on my door soon."

Alyssa goes to her room.

Smiling, I take off my robe and slip on my black-and-white dress by Noelle Black. Mom and I found some black-and-white shoes to match perfectly. I can't wait to see Alyssa in the black dress my mom bought her. It's a Ya-Ya Love and I'm hoping she won't mind my borrowing it. The dress is tight.

After we're dressed, Alyssa and I meet up with everyone downstairs. Aunt Phoebe looks like a walking flowerpot in her hand-painted, iridescent-colored, velvet evening coat with matching gown. Her outfit is definitely making a statement—what it is, I have no clue. . . .

Mom is so beautiful in her Luly Yang couture dress. I'm beaming with pride as I watch her move about the room. I feel so lucky.

"The limo's here," Chance announces.

"I'm so excited," Aunt Phoebe gushes. "Will there be lots of celebrities there?"

Mom laughs. "Some. Okay, let's head to the car. We don't want to be late."

HIGH-INTENSITY SEARCHLIGHTS CRISSCROSS the night sky. Stretch limousines line up in in front of the Village Theatre in Westwood Village to the applause of a growing and adoring crowd.

As soon as Mom steps out of the limo, reporters are trying to interview her before she heads inside to watch the film.

"There are a lot of stars here," Alyssa whispers. "Even some that aren't in the movie with Aunt Kara."

"Some celebrities come to stuff like this because their agent thinks they should be seen in the spotlight," I explain.

"This is too cool," Alyssa says. "I feel like a celebrity myself—the way the media's been snapping pictures of us."

I glance over at Chance. "So what do you think about all this?"

"It's okay."

I give him a slight nudge in his elbow. "Are you okay?"

Nodding, Chance whispers, "I was just thinking about Trina. She wasn't feeling well when I called her earlier."

I wrap an arm around him. "The baby's healthy and growing. They just want Trina to be careful and take it easy since she's sick."

"The doctor said she has the flu. She can't really take anything for it though because she's pregnant."

"She and the baby will be okay so stop worrying. Don't worry, Chance. Tonight we're supposed to party."

A tall slender girl with long hair waves at Chance.

He smiles and waves back.

We pose as a family with Mom, Uncle Reed and Aunt Phoebe standing behind us.

"We're gonna be on television," Alyssa whispers. "On the E!, I bet."

"We should definitely make *People* magazine or *Jet*." I toss my hair back and strike a pose.

Stella waddles out of the theater, coming to lead us to our seats, which are located down near the front of the theater.

Mom is still granting interviews but she'll be joining us soon.

I'm a little surprised when Kevin Nash escorts Mom down the aisle, holding her a little too close for my liking.

"Your mom and Kevin do look close. Do you think—"

I cut her off. "Don't even go there, Alyssa. They're just friends."

But deep down, I have to wonder what's really going on between them.

After the screening, we attend the gala with Mom, who keeps a respectable distance away from Kevin. But I notice that he's constantly watching her.

Inside, I see Mimi sitting with her parents. She jumps up and comes over to where we are.

"Did you find out anything?" I ask in a low whisper.

She nods. "Kevin and his wife broke up two months after they got married. They just kept it out of the press."

"If that's true, then he didn't really know my mom back then."

"I don't think you should worry. Besides, Kevin is a hunk. He'd make a sexy stepfather."

"Don't say that," I tell her. "I don't want to hear that." I don't want to share my mom with anyone right now—I don't want her losing herself in another man like she did with Jerome.

I can't fully concentrate on the gala because I'm watching Mom and Kevin. I'm not sure what's going on between them, but I intend to find out.

MOM AND I get up early the next morning to make the ninety-minute drive to the California State Prison in Lancaster to visit Jerome. While we're doing that, Uncle Reed has a rental car and is taking Aunt Phoebe and my cousins to do some sightseeing in Los Angeles.

As usual, we have to endure the humiliation of being searched by the prison guards.

Jerome has been promoted to contact visits, which means we can sit without a huge glass partition separating us from his side of the table.

"Hey baby girl," Jerome greets me. He reaches over and covers my hand with his own.

"Hello, Jerome."

"You looking good. I see Reed and them taking real good care of you."

"They are," I respond, eyeing his long dreadlocks. He doesn't look half bad with them. They must be growing on me because I didn't like them before.

"You doing okay?" I inquire politely.

"Yeah. I guess you can call it that. Just doing what I can so that I can try and leave this place." Jerome leans forward. "Ava and I been talking. We want to go on and get married. I don't know when I'ma get out of this place . . . I need to know I got somewhere to come home to." His eyes travel to Mom's. "I feel like I ain't got no home no more."

She doesn't respond and neither do I.

"Me and Ava. We getting married this coming Tuesday, October seventeenth. Y'all gon' be around?"

Both Mom and I shake our heads. I don't want to witness the misguided actions of my dad and I know Mom definitely isn't interested in playing bridesmaid to Ava. I say, "I'm leaving tonight on a red-eye. Tomorrow's a teacher workday but I have to be in school on Tuesday."

"That's too bad," Jerome says. "I'll send you a wedding picture."

"You get wedding pictures?" I ask.

He nods. "Just a couple. We gon' have a big fancy wedding when I get out. Ava's really been sticking by me—she deserves better."

Mom gets up and excuses herself. "I need to go to the ladies' room. I'll be right back."

I wonder if somehow Jerome is trying to take jabs at Mom for divorcing him. I glance over at her, but her facial expression is blank. Oh yeah . . . Mom's an actress now.

When she walks away, he announces, "Ava and I want to have a baby together."

My mouth drops wide open in my shock. Jerome's just full of surprises.

After I compose myself, I meet his gaze and say, "If that's what you want to do, then cool. But you might want to hurry since you're not getting any younger."

"What are you two talking about?" Mom questions when she returns ten minutes later.

"Jerome just told me that he and Ava want to have a baby."

She glances over at him. "Really?"

He nods.

"Congratulations, Jerome. I hope everything works out for you and Ava."

"Me too," he admits. "I want this one to work out for me."

After visiting hours end, Mom drives us back to Pacific Palisades.

"Mom, are you upset?"

"Upset about what?"

"About Jerome marrying Ava. Does it bother you?"

Mom shakes her head no. "Hon, your daddy and I are divorced. I want him to be happy."

"It doesn't bother you just a little?" I still hurt whenever I see Madison with Brittany, so it makes me wonder just how much Mom really loved Jerome—seems like his being with another woman would still bother her.

"I have my moments," Mom confesses. "I really loved your daddy and there's a part of me that will always care about him, but he's a part of my past now. No point in dwelling on what can never be."

I silently consider her words. Mom actually has a point. It doesn't do any good to dwell on the past. Just makes the hurt last that much longer.

Miss Eula has dinner ready and on the table when we walk into the house. Uncle Reed and everybody's in the media room watching a movie. I go in to announce, "The food's on the table. I don't know about you all but I'm starving."

During dinner I watch my mom. In a few hours I'll be getting on a plane heading back to Georgia. I've enjoyed my time here with her and especially at the movie premiere.

Lately, I've been feeling lonely and the thought of leaving my mom once again just makes it more intense. I'm strong enough to get through this. With God's help, I'll survive my high school years and eventually my feelings for Madison will be erased from my heart.

After all, I'm cute, intelligent and rich. *He's* the loser.

chapter 13

 $\mathcal{T}he$ first thing I think of when I wake up Tuesday morning is that it's Jerome's wedding day. I wonder how Mom's feeling about it but it's way too early to call her.

I'm feeling kind of down so I throw on a pair of jeans and a sweatshirt for school—which is so not me. I decide to pull my hair back in a ponytail and debate for a moment whether I'm going to do without any makeup. Okay, I'm not that depressed.

Alyssa is still hyped about our weekend in Los Angeles; it's all she can talk about. *She's driving me nuts.*

"Can we please talk about something else?" I plead as we make our way to school. "The movie premiere is over—let's move on."

"You do this all the time, Divine. This is my first one and I'm sorry, but I'm still excited over it. I'll never forget it."

Whatever.

Trina is standing at the edge of campus when we come around the corner.

"Hey y'all," she greets us.

I give her a hug. "How are you feeling, Mama?"

"Tired."

"That's because you stayed up late talking to your baby daddy," Alyssa supplies with a chuckle.

Trina grins. "That's my boo."

We sit on a bench in front of the school talking until the first bell rings.

Madison and his crew come strutting by us, trying to look cool. I pretend I don't see him, although he's hard to miss with his fine self. I hate that he's so fine.

The bell rings and we head off to our separate classes.

"You looking good, Divine," says a voice from behind me. I glance over my shoulder.

Grinning, Madison winks at me.

I walk faster, wanting to get as far away from him as possible.

"You still mad at me?" he calls out.

I don't respond.

I release a long sigh of relief when I step into my first-period class. I take my seat, still bristling at the thought of Madison trying to talk to me. He knows I don't want anything to do with him. He's just trying to make me trip on him. He's so not worth it.

When class is over, I spot Nicholas in the hallway. Out the corner of my eye, I see Madison coming down the hall in my direction.

I make a beeline to Nicholas. "Hey." I try to sound cheerful and like I'm very happy to see him.

He looks surprised for a moment but recovers quickly. "I sent you an email last night."

"I got it. I responded to yours, but it was late."

Nicholas walks me to my next class while Madison stands nearby, glaring at us. I steal a look over my shoulder at him, a grin plastered on my face.

My time in second period goes by pretty fast because I have to take a test in English literature. By the time I complete it, the bell rings. On my way to my next class, I run into Penny and Stacy standing in the hallway talking. From the looks of it, they're in deep conversation and Penny looks like she's ready to fight somebody.

"Why do you look so intense?" I ask Penny. "Who made you mad?"

"James . . . he gave that . . . that . . . his girlfriend my phone number and she's been—oooh, she been c-calling my h-house acting a f-fool." She can hardly speak coherently, she's so mad.

I look at her in confusion. "When did this start?"

"She started calling last night acting all stupid. She even tried to get all funky with my mama. Her name is Kat or something like that." Her fists balled up, she adds, "You wait 'til I see that jerk. I'ma make him wish he was dead."

I try to envision that image of her punching out James in my mind, but Stacy's words draw me back to the present.

"She's threatening to bring her girls over here to the school so they can beat up Penny."

I glance over at Stacy. "Where are they from?"

"Carrollton."

"Do you think they'd really come here?" I ask. I'm checking because I need to know if I'm going to have to fight. I glance down at my clothing. Expensive, but comfortable enough to kick some behind in. I'd have to pin up my hair, though. I don't want somebody pulling it out by the roots.

"We haven't seen Alyssa yet."

"I won't see her until after school," I respond. "Aunt Phoebe is picking her up during lunch for an appointment. She'll be back, though, so just meet us by the gym."

When three o'clock rolls around, Alyssa and I meet Penny and Stacy outside of the gym as planned.

"I just told Alyssa about what's going on," I say when we join them.

"That's messed up," Alyssa remarks in anger. "How he just gon' give your number out like that?"

"He did," Penny responds. "He told her that I been calling, trying to get with him. I just called him last week to ask why he never told me he had a girlfriend."

Frowning, Alyssa questions, "Why'd you even do that? You should've just let it go."

"I wanted to know. It's not like I'm trying to be with him."

"Well, he thinks you are and that's probably what he's been telling his girlfriend." Shaking her head, Alyssa says, "I love you, cuz, but I don't like getting into it like this. People crazy now. I ain't dying over no mess you started."

Okay, that gets my attention. "Excuse me? Who's dying?"

"Nobody," Penny mutters. After a brief pause, she adds, "Alyssa, chill. I didn't do nothing except ask a question."

I look around. "Well, I don't see anybody, so let's just go home. The cow was just doing a lot of talking. That's all it was—a bunch of talk."

"Yeah," Stacy agrees. "You see she didn't even show up. She was scared."

We step off campus and are soon surrounded by a group of girls. *Big* girls. Girls who looked like they'd take you down without a sweat.

I count about six of them, wearing lots of bling and jeans with matching jackets; a couple of them have scarves tied on their heads. By this time, I'm pretty much speechless.

The leader of the pack steps up to Penny, saying, "Where you think you going? I told you I'd be here."

I take a step forward, standing beside Penny. "I don't know what you've been told, but you need to deal with your man."

The cow looks from Penny to me. "What you got to do with this?"

Gesturing toward the group of girls with her, I respond, "The same thing they got to do with it."

She looks me up and down. "You might want to step back 'cause I'll take you out."

"Because of James?" I ask with a laugh. "You mean you'd actually *kill* somebody over that no-good cheating dog? Look, Kit . . . Kat . . . whoever you are—the man cheated on *you*. He *knew* he had a girlfriend when he met my girl. He knew. *She didn't.* Why are you mad at her? You should be angry with him."

Penny takes over. "I didn't know anything about James having a girlfriend. If I did—I wouldn't have let him near me. Believe that."

Kat folds thick arms across her huge chest. "That's not what he told me. He say you're stalking him."

"Really? Well, I can show you my cell phone bill so you can see how many times he called me over the summer. I'm not interested in James so please, just leave me alone. The only reason I called him last week was to find out why he never mentioned having a girlfriend. Now I don't even care about that. I just want to be left alone."

"Did you have sex with him?"

I look at Penny, wondering how she's going to respond to this question. I have a feeling her answer will decide whether we leave unscathed or have to fight our way out.

My eyes slowly travel around the group, searching for the weakest link. *We break through there—we're on our way to safety, I think. Miss Dorie from the church lives right across the street.*

Doesn't this girl have any skinny friends?

"What did James tell you?"

"He said you tried to seduce him but he wasn't having it."

Penny sighs in resignation. "He lied to you. James and I had sex. It was one time."

"When?"

"Back in July."

"Was it that third weekend in July?"

"Yeah. Why?"

"I knew it. That old cheating dog . . ."

Alyssa and I look at each other, puzzled.

"I had a feeling something was going on. We was supposed to do something that weekend and he picked this old stupid fight with me. When I went by his house later, I saw the car there, but when I called—he wouldn't answer the phone. I *knew* he was there."

Penny nods. "The phone kept ringing a lot."

"You wait until I see him. I'm tired of this . . ."

"You go through this often?" I ask.

Alyssa elbows me in the arm.

Her hands on her hips, Kat questions, "What did you ask me?"

My cousin sends me a warning look, but I'm not worried about this girl. If she really wanted to fight we would've been rolling all around in the grass already. "I asked if you go through drama like this a lot with James."

"Why?"

"Because I think you can do so much better." I'm hoping and praying that we'll be able to walk away without fighting—I'd much rather do that. I like what I'm wearing and besides, these are some big girls.

"What she saying do make some sense, even though she kinda got a smart mouth," one of the girls behind me says. "Kat, you don't need this kind of drama."

"I didn't know he had a girlfriend," Penny says a second time. "I really hate his guts for putting not only me through this, but you too."

"Y'all killing me over here with yo' ladylike ways."

"What good would it do for us to act like idiots?" Alyssa inquires. "I don't know if you noticed it the other night at the movies, but when you were yelling across the theater, James was standing there laughing."

"He sure was, Kat. I saw him."

"Can't you see that he gets off on this stuff?" Alyssa questions. "He wants you getting upset and fighting over him. My question to you is do you think he's really worth all your efforts?"

Lifting her chin in defiance, Kat responds, "James and I been through a lot. I know he loves me."

"Then why is he cheating on you?" I ask.

Mr. Mincey, one of the assistant principals at Temple High approaches us, asking, "Is everything all right here?"

Penny looks over at Kat. "Are we cool?"

She nods. "We cool."

"Why don't y'all go on home now?" Mr. Mincey suggests. "Just go home and stay out of trouble."

Chance arrives shortly after Mr. Mincey. "What's going on?"

"We were just talking with some girls from Carrollton," I respond. "We're getting ready to head home." I turn to Kat and say, "Go handle your business. Just be clear on who you need to be dealing with."

We walk away with Chance demanding, "Okay. I ain't stupid. What was about to go down back there?"

"Probably us, but we would've put up a good fight," Alyssa states dryly.

* * *

"How is that fine cousin of yours?" Rhyann inquires during our three-way conversation with Mimi later that evening.

"He's about to become a daddy," I announce.

"*What?*" they shout in unison.

Rhyann cracks up. "That PK is going to be a daddy? I can't believe it."

"Rhyann, he's just like any other boy in this country," I retort. "Being a preacher's kid has nothing to do with it."

"I'm still in shock. I never thought he would be doing the nasty. Hey, he could've hung out with me." Rhyann chuckles. "That boy is so fine."

"Stop talking about my cousin like he's a piece of meat. And what do you mean by he could've hung out with you? Rhyann, you having sex?"

"Not yet, but you never know. I might."

It's now my turn to be shocked.

"C'mon, Dee, don't act like you've never thought about it."

"I think about it all the time," Mimi confesses. "Everybody's doing it these days."

"I've never been one to follow the crowd," I respond.

"Like, you're such a liar, Dee. If it's not seen in *Glamour, Vogue* or *Seventeen* magazine, then it can't be true fashion."

"That's different and you know it. One of my friends here recently lost her virginity and afterward the guy treated her like trash. We were almost beat up after school today by that boy's girl-friend and her crew."

"Do I need to come down there?" Rhyann asks. "Don't nobody mess with my girl. You better tell 'em."

"No, we got it all settled. It's just that the guy did all this lying. He was cheating on his girlfriend and my friend didn't know—it was crazy."

"That's like so wrong," Mimi contributes. "I've been in a similar situation and it doesn't feel good. Especially when the girl's a much better fighter than you are."

Rhyann and I crack up.

"But Mimi, you knew he had a girlfriend. You just didn't care."

"If I'd known she was a wrestler I wouldn't have bothered him in the first place. I had a black eye for weeks and a horrible bruise around my neck. She was trying to kill me."

"I keep telling you," Rhyann interjects. "Leave other people's property alone. It's safer."

"Amen," I mutter. "It's definitely not worth the drama."

"I heard your daddy got married today," Rhyann tosses out. "Did you know about it?"

"Of course I did. Jerome told me when I went to visit him last weekend. I don't think it's going to last, though."

"Why not?" Mimi wants to know. She's just looking for something to gossip about.

I say, "I just don't think it's going to work out. I'm leaving it at that." I don't really care what Jerome and Ava do—she'll never be a part of my family.

I STILL HAVEN'T told Alyssa much about Sean. We email regularly and he continues to ask for photographs. I have plenty of pictures, but I keep hearing Alyssa's words over and over in my head, warning me to be careful when it comes to posting pictures on the internet.

Sean and I have been emailing for a couple of months now. He's never been rude or asked me anything that would make me uncomfortable. He's been the perfect gentleman, as my Aunt Phoebe would say. I get some of the sweetest emails from him and Nicholas. The only thing is that Nicholas doesn't really talk or type. He just checks in on me and that's about it.

I'm going to be leaving in a few days to spend Thanksgiving with my mom and Sean says that their family will be taking a trip to see his grandparents in Michigan, so we won't be able to IM or email back and forth.

I hate chat rooms but Sean prefers to meet in one of the private chat rooms on TeenSpot.net. It's okay because it's only me and him, but I still prefer IMing over chat rooms.

After a ten-minute silent debate, I push my misgivings to the back burner and upload some of my more recent photos to my computer. After typing up a short email to Sean, I attach the pictures.

I hesitate a moment before hitting the send button. What if he's ugly? What if he thinks I'm ugly? Naw . . . he's not going to think that way about me—I'm too cute.

I click the send button.

It's done. Now all I can do is wait for his response.

Right before I climb in bed for the night, I check my email. I'm elated that I have one from Sean.

Dee

I love the pics you sent over. You are so cute. I've attached one of me and I hope you won't run away scared. I'm really feeling you and I hope you feel the same way about me. After seeing your pictures, I really believe that we're soul mates. I hope one day we'll be able to meet each other in person and just kick it for a while. This emailing back and forth is cool but I want to see your face and that beautiful smile.

I find myself constantly looking for an email from you or an instant message. I'm not trying to pressure you but I want so much to see you face to face.

Can't wait to hear from you.

Sean

I don't waste any time in replying to him. Before long a window pops up with a message from NiceGuy16.

> **NiceGuy16:** I luv ur screenname. How did u come up with it?
> **HollywoodQT:** I luv HW. I luv movies—everything about HW.
> **NiceGuy16:** I luv computers. I will probably be a computer hacker when I'm older.

What a nerd, I think. He and Nicholas should probably meet because he seems to love computers just as much as Sean does.

> **NiceGuy16:** u there?
> **HollywoodQT:** I'm here.
> **NiceGuy16:** It would be so much better if I could c u in person. ur so cute.
> **HollywoodQT:** thx. I feel the same way but it'll most likely never happen. My aunt and uncle r very strict. They need to gal.
> **NiceGuy16:** what is gal?
> **HollywoodQT:** get a life.
> **NiceGuy16:** brb P911

I guess he doesn't want his parents to know that he's online chatting with a complete stranger, which I totally understand. I know Aunt Phoebe and Uncle Reed would have a cow, if they knew about Sean.

On the bottom of my window, I see Sean typing out a message.

> **NiceGuy16:** why don't u live with your parents? r they dead?

> **HollywoodQT:** no they're alive. My parents travel
> a lot.
> **NiceGuy16:** what kind of work?
> **HollywoodQT:** sales

Although I can't really explain why, I'm just not ready to divulge the fact that my mom is Kara Matthews. Maybe it's because boys usually start acting silly when they find out. To them she's a sex symbol or something. Mom looks good—I can't deny that—but I'm not really that okay with boys I like thinking she's hot.

"I thought you'd be in bed by now," Aunt Phoebe says from behind me.

I never heard her come into my room. I quickly close the small screen showing my conversation with Sean. I don't want my aunt in my business.

"I just wanted to finish something. I'll be going in a little while."

"Well, it's late and you have school tomorrow."

I can't quite meet her gaze. "I'll be done in a minute, Aunt Phoebe."

"Okay." She stifles her yawn. "Sugar, I'm tired so I'll say good night and I'll see you in the morning."

"Good night."

"What's that little thing blinking down at the bottom of your screen?"

"It's nothing. Just a window that's been open too long."

I let out an audible sigh of relief when Aunt Phoebe leaves my bedroom. I get up and lock my door.

Sean and I chat for the next two hours. I probably would've stayed online much longer but I thought I heard someone moving around and figured it was Aunt Phoebe or Uncle Reed. It was almost two and I didn't want them buggin.'

* * *

CHANCE AND TRINA are sitting in the family room watching a baby video, of all things. It's part of some parenting class they're taking. They even have homework. While they are learning how to be parents, I stroll down to Alyssa's room to see if she wants to hang out.

She's on her computer IMing Stephen while she's on the telephone talking to Penny. Alyssa gestures for me to come in, but I refuse. I'm going back down to my room. I don't want to listen to her yacking all night to somebody other than me.

Aunt Phoebe comes to my room, asking, "Sugar, you wanna work one of the booths for the Fall Festival?"

"Sure," I respond. It's not like I have a life. I might as well spend October thirty-first surrounded by a bunch of kids and adults from the church. This is our answer to Halloween and trick-or-treating. There's going to be a costume party at school, but Aunt Phoebe already put her foot down about us going. We'd be embarrassed to have her there chaperoning—we know she's not going to wear a costume so she'll just stick out like sky blue eye shadow.

Bored out of my mind, I log on to my computer. I send emails to Stella, Mom, Nicholas and Sean. I spoke to Mimi earlier today and also with Rhyann. I find an ecard greeting that I think will make Trina laugh and send it to her.

Thankfully, our TeenTalk group is going skating on Saturday. I'm already looking forward to it. Stacy told them there were a lot of cute boys hanging out at the skate center. Well, that's exactly where I need to be.

WHILE I FOLD my laundry Friday evening in my room, Alyssa keeps me company. Aunt Phoebe and Uncle Reed are on a date. For what? They're old and married.

"Are you still emailing Nicholas and that Sean person?"

"Yeah. Nicholas is pretty cool—just too quiet for me. Sean is much more outgoing. We're friends."

Alyssa's eyes travel to my face. "Friends, huh? That's it? Divine, what do you know about this guy?"

"He's sixteen and he lives in Atlanta with his parents and his brothers. They are originally from Michigan. He loves football but can't play anymore due to a knee injury. His favorite color is black."

"Okay," she responds after a moment. "What does he know about you? Have you told him that your mom is Kara Matthews."

"No, I haven't told him that. All Sean knows is that my name is Dee and I live outside of Atlanta. He thinks that my parents travel a lot and that's why I live with you all. He knows my favorite color is purple and that I'm not crazy about sports, but that I love the mall."

"What about Nicholas? You still email him?"

I nod. "I've never met a boy that was so quiet. He doesn't even say that much on email." I chuckle. "He just pretty much says the same thing—How are you? Just wanted you to know I'm thinking about you."

Alyssa's eyes rose in surprise. "That's it?"

"Just about," I respond with a shrug. "I don't think he really knows what to say to girls. He's nice, though. Nicholas usually waits for me after second period and we walk to our next class together. His classroom is next to mine."

"I think he likes you."

I shrug nonchalantly. "He needs to tell me himself. I'm tired of hearing it from you and Stacy. I think Nicholas is just looking to be my friend. That's it." I pick up a shirt and lay it across my lap. "I'm okay with that."

"You don't really like him?"

Laying the folded shirt on my bed, I glance over at Alyssa, saying, "I like him. I just think we make better friends instead of trying to be a couple. I'm too Hollywood for him."

"How do you feel about Sean?"

I smile. "He's nice and he gives some great advice. Besides, he makes me feel good about myself. I really need that right now."

chapter 14

I feel someone tugging at me, pulling me away from the edges of sleep. I try to escape.

"Divine, get up."

I open my eyes upon hearing Aunt Phoebe's voice. From the looks of it, she's decided to go back to her roots in her tribal-inspired print dress with matching hat.

"You look nice," I mumble sleepily. "Like an African queen. I feel like I should bow down or something."

"Divine, what you need to do is get yourself up. What time did you go to bed last night?"

"I don't remember," I lie. Sean and I stayed up until almost four talking online.

"You should've been up an hour ago," Aunt Phoebe fusses. "I told y'all I had to be at church early today."

"I'm not feeling too well," I tell her. "Can I just stay home this Sunday?"

"If you stay off that computer all time of night you might be able to get your proper rest. You can't fool me, sugar. I know what you been up to—your sins will find you out."

I don't comment. I'm not about to incriminate myself. I'm pretty sure Aunt Phoebe's just fishing.

"I'm gon' have Chance drive me to the church, then come back for you and Alyssa. If you know like I know—y'all better be ready."

"Alyssa's not ready?" I ask.

"Just worry about yourself. Now get up, Divine. I want you up and showered before I leave this house. And don't forget y'all singing this morning."

I'd forgotten. I sit up, swinging my legs out of bed. "I forgot about that."

"See . . . messing around on that internet . . . can't think straight. Don't let that computer get you in trouble."

I bite my bottom lip before I retort, how can a computer get you in trouble? I'm too tired to run if Aunt Phoebe decides to come after me with that bat of hers.

Aunt Phoebe leaves with Chance shortly after I finish my shower. After I get dressed, I walk up to Alyssa's room.

"Hey."

"Did you say something to Aunt Phoebe about Sean?" I ask.

"No. Why?"

"Because she keeps making comments about me being on the internet. I've been the internet queen from the first time I stepped into this house. Why is she tripping now?" I notice that Alyssa's not looking me in the eye.

"You said something. I know you did. Why don't you mind your own business, Alyssa?"

"She asked me why you were spending so much time on the computer lately and I told her I thought that you were talking to a boy. That's all I said."

Rolling my eyes at her, I say, "You talk too much."

AFTER CHURCH, AUNT Phoebe and Uncle Reed ask me to join them in the family room.

"Okay, what did I do now? I'm sorry for oversleeping but I forgot to set my alarm. You both know that I'm not a morning person."

"We're concerned that you may be spending too much time on the computer," Aunt Phoebe tells me. "I know that Madison hurt you—"

"He didn't hurt me," I say a little too quickly. "I'm so over him."

"Have you met someone else?" Uncle Reed wants to know.

"I meet a lot of people."

He doesn't crack a smile. "Divine, I'm pretty sure you know what I mean."

"Yes sir. I met a boy and we talk online sometimes. It's not a big deal. I talk to Mimi and Rhyann a lot on the internet too." Pasting a smile on my face, I add, "It cuts down on my cell phone bill, which I'm sure Mom appreciates."

Aunt Phoebe reaches over to take my hand. "I'm not comfortable with the idea of you meeting someone over the internet, but I trust that you are playing it safe."

My eyes rest on her questioning gaze. "I am, Aunt Phoebe."

"We would like for you to spend a little less time on the internet. It's affecting your sleep and we hardly ever see you anymore—you're always in your room on the computer."

Frowning, I ask, "What's the big deal? I'm in the house."

"There are reasons y'all don't have televisions in your rooms. Do you remember why?"

"Yes ma'am. You don't want us excluding ourselves from the rest of the family."

"Exactly."

I look over at Uncle Reed, who interjects, "Use your internet time wisely, Divine. Because if you don't, then we'll be forced to take your computer out of the room. You will only be allowed to use it in our presence."

My lips pucker with annoyance. I really can't believe what I'm hearing. *Why are they tripping like this?*

I'm so angry that I tune out the rest of their words. I'm so not in the mood for this. As soon as I'm excused, I check my watch before placing a call to my mom. I really need her help.

"Mom, can you do me a favor?" I ask as soon as I hear her voice.

"What is it, hon?"

"I really need you to talk to Aunt Phoebe and Uncle Reed. They have been seriously tripping since Chance got Trina pregnant."

"What's going on?"

"They are just being way too strict. Mom, they don't even want me talking to anyone on the internet. Like I can do something over the information super highway. This baby thing has them acting all crazy."

"What do you mean when you say you can't talk to anyone on the internet?"

"Aunt Phoebe says I'm spending too much time in my room on the internet. They're buggin' out over chat rooms and I don't even really go into them in the first place. You know I'm always instant messaging Mimi and Rhyann. I even instant message Alyssa and Chance when I don't feel like walking down to their rooms."

"Well . . . I don't see anything wrong with that. I don't see why they should have a problem with that. I'll speak to them."

I release a short sigh of relief. "Thanks, Mom."

"Divine, you know your aunt and uncle love you. They really do, and they treat you like one of their own. I think maybe they're just trying to protect you and Alyssa so that you won't make the same mistakes Chance made."

"I'm not even trying to do anything like that. I'm just talking to people online. What's the big deal? Mom, I'm almost sixteen. Why can't I have a life?"

"I know how old you are, Divine. I was there the day you were born."

"Now you sound like Jerome."

Mom laughs. "I guess I do . . . by the way, have you talked to your father lately?"

"He sent me a letter last week and I wrote him back. He sent me a wedding picture."

"That's nice. I'm glad you're keeping the lines of communication open."

"What about you? Have you talked to him since he and Ava got married?"

"No, but I've been on the road so much. He did call Stella and asked her to contact me. He wants me to come visit him when I'm back in California."

"Are you going to do it?"

"I don't know. I don't think I should—he's Ava's husband now, so we'll just have to see. She may not want me visiting her man."

I hear a male voice in the background.

I listen, baffled. "Mom, do you have someone there with you?"

A slight pause, then she responds, "Actually, yes. Kevin came by to see me. He's in town for a few days."

I don't respond.

"Hon . . ."

"I'm still here."

"Divine, I've already told you that I don't have time for a relationship. Kevin and me—we're just friends. *That's the truth*. I'm taking time to know me and I'm working on a closer relationship with God."

"How does he feel about this?" Right now I'm just not sure what to believe. It seems to me that Kevin is around Mom a lot. My mind is reeling in confusion.

"Kevin understands, Divine. Hon, I don't have to lie to you. He has become a very dear friend to me."

"I have no choice but to believe you," I say but my head is swirling with doubts.

Our conversation comes to a close when Mom says, "It's late there. You go get some sleep and I'll give Reed and Phoebe a call tomorrow. I love you, hon."

"I love you too."

I hang up and get ready for bed. I'm not able to fall asleep quickly because of the disturbing thoughts running through my mind. Mom wouldn't lie to me about Kevin, would she? Jerome just got married and it's not a big deal. I'm not like happy about it, but it's his life. There's no reason for Mom to keep her relationship with Kevin a big secret. Or is there?

> **HollywoodQT:** I don't think anybody understands me except u
>
> **NiceGuy16:** ur friend's right. Parents r aliens
>
> **HollywoodQT:** lol. U read Rhyann's blog.
>
> **NiceGuy16:** I really like u and ur friends r my friends 2.
>
> **HollywoodQT:** I really like u 2
>
> **NiceGuy16:** I want 2 meet u f2f.
>
> **HollywoodQT:** I carry ur photo with me all the time
>
> **NiceGuy16:** since we live so close 2 each other—why don't we arrange 2 meet?

> **HollywoodQT:** I don't know how 2 make that happen
>
> **NiceGuy16:** If ur open 2 meeting me, I can think about making it happen. Think about it and let me know. The thing is that I think I'm falling n luv with u. I know it's crazy since we have never met f2f but it's true. I'm really feeling u. I think about holding u n my arms, kissing u
>
> **HollywoodQT:** I feel the same way

Before I can finish typing my message to Sean, Aunt Phoebe blows into my bedroom like a tornado, nearly scaring me to death. I know she's going to freak because it's so late and we just had a conversation about this a couple of days ago.

"Divine, it's almost two in the morning," she declares. "What are you doing on that computer?"

I fold down the laptop cover, careful not to shut it completely. "I was just about to get off."

She glares at me with burning, reproachful eyes. "You're not gon' want to get up tomorrow morning for school. This is getting ridiculous."

"Aunt Phoebe, I'm not doing anything wrong. I was just online talking to one of my friends." I chew on my bottom lip, hoping she'll just turn around and leave.

No such luck.

"Well you can just stop talking to that friend of yours," she snaps angrily. "Now cut that thing off and get yourself in bed."

She's yelling at me. My shock quickly yields to fury and my tone changes. "Aunt Phoebe, I don't know why you're talking to me like this. I'm not a child."

A sudden thin chill hangs in the air.

Aunt Phoebe folds her arms across her chest, looking me up and down. "You could've fooled me by the way you acting lately."

Uncle Reed joins us.

I sigh in frustration as I shut down my computer.

"Divine, why are you still up?" he inquires.

"Ask Aunt Phoebe," I answer. "She has all the answers. You'd think she was perfect when she was my age."

"Okay, I've had enough of this. Unplug the laptop."

I look from Aunt Phoebe to Uncle Reed. "For what?" I can't believe they're being so unfair about this. I didn't do anything except stay on the computer a little past my curfew.

"I'm taking the computer out of your room. You can only use it when your aunt and I are around. And only for schoolwork—no email right now. Not until you learn the rules around here, Divine. We've had to speak to you about this a couple of times already. You are not allowed on the phone or the computer after eleven o'clock."

"You can't do this to me, Uncle Reed."

"I can and I will, young lady."

"This is not fair." Tears roll down my cheeks. "I can't believe you're treating me like this. I haven't done anything but maybe stay on the computer a little late."

"You're making a habit out of it, Divine," Uncle Reed replied. "Don't think we don't know what's going on inside our own house."

"You didn't know Chance was having sex," I say flippantly.

Aunt Phoebe stiffens. "My son didn't get no babies in this house, Miss Mouth Almighty. Now I suggest you take your little self to bed before we tangle."

Tangle? Is she talking about fighting? I shake my head in disgust. Aunt Phoebe is seriously tripping.

"Aunt Phoebe, if you'd just listen to me—"

"Divine, I don't need any more of your backtalk. Now your uncle and I told you over and over again about hiding out in your room and staying up late messing around with this computer. You just don't listen. You're hardheaded."

"Please don't take my computer."

"We're not taking it away," Uncle Reed explains. "You can use it—just not in your room."

Angry, I swipe at the tears streaming down my face. I hate Uncle Reed and Aunt Phoebe so much right now.

chapter 15

Frustrated, I toss a pillow at the door of my bedroom. One week has passed since they took my computer and I'm going nuts without it. I miss talking to Sean and I know he must think that I've abandoned him. Mom betrays me by siding with Aunt Phoebe and Uncle Reed on this.

I can't believe her sometimes. She could've insisted that they return my laptop to me. After all, she's the one who bought it for me. I'm so mad with her that I'm debating whether or not to go home for the Thanksgiving break three weeks from now.

I venture out into the family room, but there's nothing on television to hold my interest, so out of desperation, I seek out Alyssa. "I really need you to do me a big favor," I say as I enter her bedroom.

"What?"

"Can you send Sean an email for me? Aunt Phoebe is buggin'. I want him to know that the reason he hasn't heard from me is because of your mom."

Shaking her head no, Alyssa says, "Divine, I'm not getting in that. I think what you're doing is wrong. You do spend way too much time on the internet chatting with that boy. You acting like you addicted to it."

"I would do it for you. I've covered for you so many times."

"And I've covered for you too."

"I need to send Sean an email just to let him know what's going on."

"I don't want to lose my computer too."

"Alyssa, that's not going to happen, I just want to send *one* email. That's it."

"You promise?"

I nod. "Just one short email. You stand by the door to see if Aunt Phoebe or Uncle Reed's coming down the hall."

Alyssa walks over to the door, peering out while I take a seat at her desk. She glances over at me and whispers, "Hurry up."

I log on to my email account and type as quickly as I can. I don't want Sean thinking that I'm ignoring him. I see several emails in my account from him but I don't have time to read them. I glance over my shoulder at Alyssa. She's getting nervous.

"Hurry," she urges.

I type out my email message:

Sean:
Just wanted to let you know that the reason you haven't heard from me is because my computer has been taken from me and I'm only allowed to use it for homework. Got in trouble for being up so late the last time we were IMing. Will try to email you again soon.

"Aren't you done yet?"

I send the email. "Yeah. I'm finished."

I get up from the desk and my timing is perfect because we hear Aunt Phoebe's voice. I rush over and sit on Alyssa's bed, picking up one of the magazines on her nightstand.

"What are you two doing?" Aunt Phoebe questions. She glances from me to Alyssa. "Your dad rented some movies—why don't y'all come join us? I'm making popcorn."

I'm not in the mood to be around Aunt Phoebe and Uncle Reed. I'm still upset with them. "I think I'll pass," I say.

"Divine, your attitude isn't helping matters."

I give her a blank look. "What attitude? I don't have an attitude. I'm just not in the mood to watch a movie. I'm going to my room to do some reading." I can't resist adding, "If that's okay with you."

Aunt Phoebe glares at me.

"Mama, I'll help you make the popcorn," Alyssa offers.

She's just feeling guilty and trying to stay on her mom's good side. I don't really care myself. Right now, I'm mad at the world. Nothing is going my way and I hate it. Life sucks.

"You sure you don't want to join us?" Aunt Phoebe asks.

"Not this time," I say. "I just want to be alone." I get off Alyssa's bed and make my way to the door. "Have fun," I murmur on my way out. I run into Chance in the hallway, but ignore him. This is really all his fault. Aunt Phoebe and Uncle Reed wouldn't be tripping so hard if it weren't for him.

I LEAVE FOR Los Angeles the Wednesday before Thanksgiving. Right after my plane lands, Mom whisks me straight to The Cheesecake Factory in Marino Del Rey for dinner.

The place is busy and crowded as usual, but it's one of my favorite places to eat. I don't even have to look at the menu to know what I'm going to order.

Mom lays down her menu. "I bet I know what you're planning to order."

I smile. "The jambalaya. I haven't had it in a long time."

The waiter arrives to take our drink orders.

Mom eyes me. "So you still mad at me?"

"I'm not mad at anybody." I settle back against the cushions of the booth we're in.

She removes her sunglasses. "You broke your curfew. From what I hear, it's been more than one occasion. That's why they took your computer."

Our waiter returns with a strawberry lemonade for me and a bottle of mineral water for Mom. He pulls out a pad to write down our order.

Mom orders Cajun chicken littles and I order my favorite entrée—the jambalaya.

We discuss my flight and our plans for the holiday while waiting for our food to arrive.

My mouth waters at the sight of the waiter carrying the tray containing our orders. After saying grace, I quickly dive into my food.

"I'm so glad to be home." I stick a shrimp into my mouth. "I love this restaurant."

Mom wipes her mouth with a napkin. "Wow. You must really be upset with my brother and Phoebe. I haven't heard you say that for a while."

"I just wish they weren't tripping right now."

"Hon, you're still able to use it, but only in their presence. Phoebe said that you were staying up all night, talking online. She thinks it was a boy."

"That's her assumption."

"I doubt that you were up that late with Rhyann and Mimi, sweetheart. Remember, we were young once." She gestures with her hand. "You can tell me your side of this but make sure it's the truth."

I give Mom a wounded look.

"I'm listening."

She's in Mom mode. I hope she doesn't stay this way during the entire Thanksgiving holiday. I need a break.

"Okay. I did meet this boy online. He posted some comments on my blog."

"You have a blog?"

"Yes ma'am. Mom, a lot of kids have them."

"Then you shouldn't have a problem with me reading yours."

"Mom . . . it's like a journal. It's private."

"And you posted it on the internet? Not to mention, you just told me that this boy read it. It can't be too private."

"It's for other kids to read. Not adults."

This time Mom looks hurt.

"I thought you trusted me."

"Mom, I do. I just don't want to share every inch of my life with you. You don't share your entire life with me."

Mom takes a sip of her mineral water. "That's fine. I'm going to respect your privacy for now. But if I feel changes need to be made—all bets are off. Understand?"

"Yes ma'am."

"Tell me more about this boy."

"There's not much to tell," I say. "He's sixteen and he lives in Atlanta . . . the Buckhead area. He has four brothers. His father is a chemist and his mom is a lawyer."

"So what do y'all talk about that keeps you on the computer all night long?"

"We just be talking, Mom. About all kinds of stuff."

"If you plan on getting your computer back in your room, you need to respect the rules of my brother's house."

"I just didn't think it was a big deal."

"Breaking rules *are* a big deal, sweetheart."

"I'll do better." I promise Mom.

We spend the rest of our evening talking about a new store opening a couple of blocks away from the restaurant.

"I think you're gonna love their clothes," Mom is saying. I'm only half listening because my mind is on Sean and whether or not I'll ever get to talk to him again.

When we get home, Mom and I get comfortable and settle in the media room to watch a movie together.

Taking my hand in hers, she tells me, "I'm so glad you're home, baby girl. I miss you so much when we're not together."

"I miss you too."

"Outside of this little drama . . . are you still happy living with Reed? I want you to tell me the truth."

I think over Mom's question.

"I am," I say finally. "I love living there at the house. Uncle Reed and Aunt Phoebe just be tripping hard sometimes over nothing."

"They just want to protect you. We all just love our children so much—we try to keep you from getting hurt . . . from making mistakes, I guess."

"Y'all just need to lighten up some. Give us room to breathe."

"I'll take that under advisement."

Our conversation dies when the movie begins.

Two hours later, Mom and I leave the media room hand in hand. Mom is going to her room to study a script, so I ask, "Can I use the computer here at home? Or does Uncle Reed's punishment extend all the way out here too?" I have to ask because there are times that Mom seems to let Uncle Reed rule both houses.

"Up until eleven o'clock, Divine. I mean it. Don't let me down. If you do, then yes, your uncle's punishment will go into effect here as well."

I give her a hug. "Thanks so much, Mom. I really appreciate it." Before I head into Mom's office, I ask, "Are we having guests for Thanksgiving dinner?"

"Stella and her husband are coming over. Miss Eula will be here."

"So Kevin won't be eating with us, then?"

Mom meets my gaze straight on. "He may stop by for dessert, actually. His parents live in Marina Del Rey. He's in town to spend the holiday with them."

"I guess I better start getting to know him since he's becoming your best friend."

Mom points a finger toward me. "I'ma let you have that one, baby girl. *This time.*"

"I'm just saying that if Kevin plans on hanging around, then I need to get to know him."

The telephone rings. Mom sprints across the room to answer it.

Must be Kevin.

Since she's on the phone talking in a low whisper, I pull out my cell to check in with first Rhyann and then Mimi.

"We're in Jamaica," Mimi announces. "Mother wanted to spend the holiday in our villa down here."

"Cool. Wish I was there with you."

"Like why don't you join us? You could probably book a flight first thing tomorrow morning."

I glance over my shoulder at Mom, who's still in deep conversation, grinning from ear to ear.

"I need to stay here. Mom and I need to spend some quality time together. You know how that goes."

We talk a few minutes more until Mom gets off the phone and heads upstairs. As soon as I'm sure she's gone for good, I log on to the internet. I have about ten messages from Sean. At least six of them are wondering what happened to make me stop writing him. The seventh one confirms that he received my email and the last three are basically his checking in on me and to let me know that he's going to be in Michigan for Thanksgiving.

> Sean
>   I hope you're okay. I miss talking to you so much and I hope you check your email while you're in Michigan for Thanksgiving. If you do—Happy Thanksgiving. I really miss talking to you online.
>
> Love,
> Dee

THANKSGIVING MORNING, I wake up to an array of delicious smells. Mom is already in the kitchen with Miss Eula. I can hear them talking and laughing as I come down the stairs.

"Morning sleepyhead," Miss Eula greets me.

"Morning, hon," Mom says.

I hug them both. "Happy Thanksgiving."

Miss Eula looks me up and down. "Girl, you need to come home so I can put some meat on those little bones of yours. You so thin, I can hardly see you with my one good eye."

I laugh. "Miss Eula hasn't changed a bit."

After breakfast, I offer to help out in the kitchen.

"I don't think I cleaned out my ears this morning. Did I just hear you say something about cooking?"

Mom and I crack up.

"Miss Eula, I can cook a little. I can make the muffins. I'm good at that."

"Lawd have mercy. I never thought I'd see the day. My baby in the kitchen talking about she cooking." Miss Eula places a hand to her chest. "What done got into you?" Eyeing me with her one good eye, she says, "It ain't one of them smooth-talking boys, I hope."

"Miss Eula," Mom and I cry out in unison.

"Well," she pushes. "You better not let some old boy work his mojo on you. You got plenty of time for that foolishness."

"Miss Eula, you'd be proud to know that I'm still a member of the big V club."

Frowning, she questions, "The big what club?"

"The big V," I repeat.

"She means she's still a virgin, Miss Eula," Mom explains.

"Divine, I'm almost eighty. You need to tell it to me straight. I don't know nothing about all that slang talk. A bunch of mess if you ask me. Just tell it to me straight." She looks over at me. "So whatcha' calling it today? The big V club? Y'all got a club now? How many members? Two or three? The way kids sexing up these days—can't be too many in that club." She laughs.

I love Miss Eula because the lady is crazy. She keeps me laughing, but not only that. The woman can cook. Miss Eula and Jerome's grandmother, who raised him, used to work together for some rich family down in Tennessee. When his grandmother died, she took Jerome in, treating him like family. Jerome didn't remember his mother and father because they both died within weeks of each other when he was around two or three.

When Miss Eula's house burned down and Jerome heard about it, he offered to build her a new one. Instead, she said she wanted to never look back. Miss Eula asked if she could move to California and cook for our family. She didn't want any handouts.

Although she's not related by blood, Miss Eula's still family to us. She's the only one who visits Jerome almost every weekend.

Stella and her husband arrive with their little girl around two o'clock. The baby is so cute. I try to form an image of how Chance and Trina's baby will look. Hopefully, the baby will take after Trina. She's a pretty girl.

I surprise everyone when I offer to give the blessing when we gather around the dinner table.

"Most Heavenly Father, I just want to thank You for bringing me safely home to spend this holiday with my mom, and Miss Eula and with Stella and her family. I thank You . . . Father, thank You for the food and the love of cooking that You've given Miss Eula. Thank You, God, for everything You've done for me and for my family. Amen."

"A-A-Amen," Miss Eula bellows. "That sho' was a beautiful prayer."

"Thank you," I murmur. I don't know why I volunteered to do that, but in a way I'm glad I did. If I wasn't so mad with Uncle Reed and Aunt Phoebe, I'll call them and tell them.

Kevin Nash arrives around four.

He is fine but I'm still not sure I want him in my mom's life. It's not like I think she and Jerome should get back together—that's definitely not the answer. Besides, he and Ava are supposedly happily married.

Kevin tries to include me in every conversation. He's really working on me. My question is, why? If he and Mom are just friends it shouldn't matter how I feel about him.

"Are you enjoying yourself in Georgia?"

"Yes. I love it down there."

"My parents are both from this place not too far from you. It's a town called Warner Robbins."

"I've never heard of it."

"It's on the other side of Atlanta," Mom interjects. "Near Macon."

"Oh," I reply dryly. Like I really care where he's from. And to show him just how uninterested I am, I ask, "Miss Eula, could you please pass the iced tea?"

"Sure, honey."

The sudden quiet is deafening.

Stella ends the silence by saying, "Miss Eula, you outdid yourself with this red velvet cake."

"It's delicious," Kevin complimented. "Kara's told me what a good cook you are."

"Did Kara tell you that she's a pretty good cook herself?"

I glance over at Miss Eula, wondering whose side she's on.

I can feel Kevin's eyes on me. I pretend to be totally devoted to the slice of cake on my plate. I love red velvet cake but since Kevin's arrival, I don't feel hungry anymore.

Mom points at my plate with her fork. "I can't believe you haven't touched your cake yet."

"I think I ate too much at dinner. I'll eat it later."

I excuse myself from the table and venture off to my bedroom. Mom joins me a few minutes later.

"You wanna tell me what's going on with you?"

"Nothing," I respond. "Why do you think there's a problem?" Must be feeling guilty about something, I decide.

"Does Kevin being here bother you, Divine?"

I meet her gaze. "I hope you won't get mad when I say this but it's hard to believe that there's nothing going on between you and Kevin. I can look at him and tell that he really likes you."

"Kevin's interested in me," Mom confesses. "I like him too, but I told you the truth. He and I are only friends. We've been studying the Bible together."

My eyes widen in my shock. "Bible study?"

Mom nods. "Yeah. I told you it's not like the media has tried to portray. Kevin and his ex-wife had a very amicable divorce eight months ago. We knew each other but didn't become close until September."

"I know you said you like him. Is it a strong like—one of those I want him to be my boo kind of likes?"

Mom laughs. "I care for him, Divine. I really do, but I'm not acting on those feelings. God has to come first in my life. Once I get myself straight with Him . . . maybe then I can think about a relationship. Kevin is a nice man, hon. He's a good man and he respects my feelings on this."

"Are you sure you don't want a boyfriend?"

"Not right now, hon. God is all I need right now. He's my everything."

"It sounds strange hearing you talk like this."

A flash of sadness shows in her eyes. It doesn't last long, just enough for me to glimpse.

"I'm sure it does—when I was married to your daddy, I didn't have time for God."

"Mom, I'm so proud of you. I want you to know that."

She smiles. "I'm pretty proud of me too."

"Everybody must be wondering what we're doing," I say. "Maybe you should go join them."

"What are you getting ready to do?"

"I'll probably go down to your office and check my email."

Wrapping her arms around me, Mom says, "I love you, baby girl, and I want you to know that I'm proud of you as well."

We walk out of the room together. Mom takes the main staircase while I exit down the back stairway.

I call Alyssa and Chance to wish them a happy Thanksgiving, then check email. I try to contain my joy when I see that I have one from Sean. I sign onto instant messenger and nearly fall out of my chair when I see that he's still signed on.

Thank you, Jesus.

HollywoodQT: I'm so glad ur on

NiceGuy16: I took a chance 2 c if I might hear from u. I'm glad u sent the email. I didn't know what 2 think when u signed off like that. I was worried that I scared u off but also figured it could b a p911.

HollywoodQT: my stupid aunt and uncle are really tripping. They r so strict and they make me sick.

NiceGuy16: where r u now?

HollywoodQT: I'm home with my mother

NiceGuy16: In CA

HollywoodQT: yes

NiceGuy16: 4 good?

HollywoodQT: No. Just 4 the holidays. I'll be going home on Sunday

NiceGuy16: So tell me, r u the daughter of a famous actress? Is that why ur so secretive?

HollywoodQT: I have some ties 2 Hollywood. But u know that not everyone who lives n HW r celebrities

NiceGuy16: I thought u trusted me

HollywoodQT: I do

NiceGuy16: It's ok. I'm not tripping over it. I think ur cool no matter who ur parents may r may not be

HollywoodQT: Thx 4 understanding

We IM back and forth over the next ten minutes, then he tells me he's got to go. Another P911, I assume, and sign off.

Thinking back over our conversation, I smile. He's such a nice guy. I really like him. I really appreciate the fact that he doesn't press me for a lot of information. In a way, I'm a little surprised that he hasn't recognized me. Maybe he's one of those guys who don't keep up with celebrities.

Mimi calls me on my cell and we spend the next hour or so talking about her holiday, my day and about all the after–Thanksgiving Day sales she's going to miss while in Jamaica.

"You're going to have so much fun, hanging out on the beach; you won't miss the mad rush of people trying to find good buys, I tell her."

"Do you plan on doing any shopping?"

"Mom and I did all of our shopping on Wednesday. Tomorrow, I, like, have to totally do the daughter thing and visit Jerome."

"Bummer."

"Totally. But I haven't seen him in a while, so it's all good."

"Dee, why don't you move back home since your aunt and uncle are so uncool?"

"I thought about it, but I really like my school and I like hanging out with Alyssa. She's like my sister."

"What about me and Rhyann? Do you like your cousin better than us?"

"She's family. She's my blood. I love Alyssa—I love you and Rhyann too, but in a different way."

I can tell she's a little turned off by what I said, but it's the truth. Mimi makes up an excuse to end the conversation. I'm not offended. I was getting tired of talking to her anyway.

chapter 16

The next morning, I have to make the trip out to the prison with Miss Eula to see Jerome. Mom's decided that since Jerome is now married to another woman, her presence would be unwelcome.

Ava is already there with Jerome by the time we arrive.

She stands up and embraces me. "Divine, how are you, sweetie."

I look at her like she's crazy. She's never been like this with me before. But then, this is the first time I've ever been here without Mom.

"You gon' say hello to your stepmother?" Jerome asks.

"Hello," I manage.

We sit down at a table across from Jerome. He's pulled his dreads into a ponytail. He actually looks happy. Marriage must agree with him—especially since he's behind bars.

I steal a glance at Ava. Strangely, she looks happy too. She's practically glowing.

Whatever.

Jerome's eyes never leave my face. "What's going on with you, baby girl?"

"School," I respond. "That's pretty much it."

"Send me a copy of your report card. I wanna see how you doing."

I give him a puzzled look. "I already told you that my grades are good. Why do you need proof all of a sudden?"

Miss Eula elbows me. "Don't talk to your daddy like that."

"I don't need proof. It's just my seeing a copy of your report card in my cell will keep me motivated. Sometimes it gets hard in here. I miss you, baby girl. Can you understand that?"

I nod. "I'll send you a copy."

"Good girl," Miss Eula utters.

He smiles in gratitude. "I'm real proud of how you're turning out. You growing up to be a real fine young lady. Just keep them boys out your head. You hear me?"

"Amen to that," Miss Eula comments, sparking a laugh from everyone but me.

"You know, if I listen to you and everybody else I'll never get married."

"I can live with that," Jerome says. "Then I won't have to worry about some knucklehead breaking your heart."

Already done, I declare in my mind.

"How's my lil' man doing?"

I smile. "Jason's so cute, Jerome. And he's getting so big."

"I pray one day I'll get to see my son. He needs to know his old man."

Mrs. Campbell is never going to let that happen. She never

mentions Jerome but I don't think she's forgiven him yet for Shelly's death.

Ava tries to strike up a conversation with me. When she mentions loving shoes, I'm convinced that Jerome has schooled her on my likes and dislikes.

Still, I'm a slave to fashion and just the mere mention of shoes is enough to draw me into a conversation.

"The next time you come to California, we'll have to go shopping."

I'm down for spending money, so I say, "Okay." I'm never going to turn down a shopping spree. Besides, it's like I'm taking some of the money back that Mom had to pay her in the settlement. If I have my way, I'm going to drain off as much of the million dollars she received when Mom knocked her out. Ava's had plastic surgery but her nose still looks funny in my opinion.

"I know it's still a bit awkward for you, baby girl, but I want you to give Ava a chance. Can you do that for me?"

I can't believe he's putting me on the spot like this. "I already said I'd go shopping with her."

"When you come back home, I'd like for you to spend some time with her."

"Shopping isn't spending time together?" I ask.

Ava speaks up. "What he's saying is that you don't have to wait for your father to get out of prison before you visit. I'd like for you to maybe come to the house and spend the night. The more time we spend together, the quicker we'll get to know each other. I want you to see for yourself that I'm not the demon I was made out to be. I don't know what your mother has told you—"

She stops short when Miss Eula begins clearing her throat noisily.

"I just want you to get to know me for yourself, Divine. I hope that's not too much to ask."

"That's fine," I mutter.

My words spark smiles on both Miss Eula and Jerome's faces. Whatever.

THINGS ARE STILL tense between me and Aunt Phoebe and Uncle Reed when I return to Georgia on Sunday afternoon. Outside of responses to their questions, I'm not sure I'll ever talk to them again after they took my laptop out of my room. I hate that they're treating me like some little baby. I'll be sixteen in one month and two days.

Uncle Reed inquires, "How was your holiday?"

"Fine," I respond. Normally, I'd give them a rundown of everything I did, but not this time. I close my eyes and pretend to be asleep.

The ride from the airport to Temple is a quiet one except for Aunt Phoebe trying to sing along with the Yolanda Adams CD playing. Someone needs to tell her that she can't carry a note in a purse.

I'm glad to see Alyssa and Chance. I missed hanging out with them. Hopefully Alyssa and I are past all of our issues now. I don't like fighting with her.

"Are you still mad at my parents?" she asks when we're alone in my room.

"Yeah. What they did wasn't cool, Alyssa."

"Well, you were getting carried away. You know how they feel about us getting our sleep."

"They can't control when I sleep or when I don't. What if I had been in my room reading? What would they do? Take all of my books away?"

"Mama fusses at me sometimes for reading all time of night."

"Look, I know that she's your mom. I still think she and Uncle Reed are wrong for what they did. I'm never going to change my feelings on that. No matter how much you try to clean it up."

Alyssa eyes me hard.

"What?" I demand. "Why are you looking at me like that?"

"You're changing, Divine."

I shake my head in denial. "No, I'm not."

"Yes, you are," Alyssa insists. "Don't let this boy come between us. We're your family and we're gonna be here no matter what. You can't say the same about him."

"I can't say the same for you," I snap. "You put me down for Stephen a lot."

"I don—"

I hold up my hand, cutting her off. "Don't even say it. 'Cause you lying. Girl, you let that boy call here and you forget we even supposed to do things together. Half the time you got to ask his permission just to go to a stupid movie."

Alyssa heads to the door. "I can't stand when you start acting like this. I'll talk to you later."

I walk over and close my door, locking it. Leaning against it, I whisper, "Welcome home . . ."

My HOLIDAY VACATION ended way too soon, I decide when we have to go to school Monday morning. I feel worn-out but it's probably due to jet lag or something. Maybe my body is still on California time.

I finish off my email to Sean and send it while in the computer lab, pretending to work on my report for English Literature. I'm so sick and tired of everyone trying to tell me what to do. Nobody really cares about me or my happiness—no one but Sean.

He's right. We need to see each other face-to-face.

I know Sean's in class right now, so it surprises me when I hear back from him a short time later.

Hey Baby
I hadn't heard from you in a couple of days so I thought maybe

you weren't interested in me anymore. You're right about parents being such a trip.

I understand what you're going through because I deal with it on a daily basis. I've told you how my parents are. On the outside, we are the perfect family, but behind closed doors, my dad is a tyrant.

Look, let's meet up at this place called Maxwell's in Atlanta. My family owns the restaurant. Send me email if you can set something up. Can't wait to see you.

Love,
Sean

"I can't wait to see you too," I whisper.

"Divine, what are you doing in here?"

I quickly close the window before Chance can see the email. "I'm working on my report for English literature. Why?"

"I'm just making sure you're not trying to skip class."

"Like I'd skip my class to sit here in the computer lab—not my idea of a fun time."

"Well, I'll see you later."

I wave him away.

My friend, Deonne Massey, drops down beside me. She's fast becoming one of my new best friends. Alyssa's gone down a few degrees.

"Did you get it done?" she whispers.

I nod. "I called a car service and pretended to be my mom, so it's all set. I'm going to have a car pick me up from your house on Saturday around five o' clock to drive me to Atlanta."

"You're gonna have such a good time. Talk about romantic."

"I know. I'm so excited."

"Have you said anything to Alyssa about seeing Sean?"

I shake my head no. "Deonne, I don't want anybody to know. This is our secret. Okay?"

"Yeah. Sure."

"Are you sure your sister isn't going to have a problem with this? I don't want her calling my aunt and telling her that I left." Deonne lives with her sister since the death of their mother a couple of years ago.

"Lisa is cool, Divine. She real cool. She used to do stuff like this herself, so she understands. I told you, she said she'll do your hair for you."

We go back over our plan one more time because I don't want any room for failure.

As soon as I arrive home from school, I immediately get all of my chores out of the way. By dinnertime, my homework is completed as well.

While Alyssa is studying and Chance is working, I corner Aunt Phoebe in the kitchen. "A friend of mine wants me to spend the night at her house on Saturday."

"Who is this friend?"

"Her name is Deonne Massey and she's in my English and history classes. They live over on Morris Street."

Aunt Phoebe searches her memory. "I don't believe I know her people."

"She lives with her sister and her brother-in-law. They raised her after her mother died a couple of years ago. She was killed in a plane crash."

"Oh, I know who you're talking about now. She was on a flight heading to New York or somewhere. I remember hearing about that. She was a lawyer, I believe."

"Yes ma'am."

"That was so sad," Aunt Phoebe murmurs. "How is she doing? The girl?"

"Deonne seems fine most of the time but there's been a couple of times when I caught her getting emotional. She doesn't have many friends but she's a really nice girl."

"I'd like to meet her."

"You can meet Deonne and her sister when you drop me off."

Aunt Phoebe nods.

I return to my bedroom. Closing my door, I make sure it's locked before retrieving a package from my backpack.

Grinning to myself, I finger the tiny gift-wrapped present I bought Sean for Christmas.

Since we're planning to celebrate the holiday at Mom's house in Atlanta, I'm thinking about inviting him to come by for dessert or something. Mom won't have a problem with that.

Once everybody sees what a nice guy he is they'll all stop tripping.

"You're looking pretty happy around here. Where are you off to?" Uncle Reed inquired.

"I'm spending the night with my friend Deonne. She lives over on Morris Street."

"What's her last name?"

"Massey." I hope he's not going to ask me another question because I don't like lying to him or Aunt Phoebe. Besides, I'm ready to get out of here.

"Aunt Phoebe's going to meet Deonne and her sister when she drops me off."

"Okay. Good."

I'm relieved that Uncle Reed is fine with my spending the night out—especially with a girl he's never met. But I know the only reason he's okay with it is because he knows that if Aunt Phoebe doesn't like what she sees she'll turn around and bring me right back home.

I check the clock.

I need to get over to Deonne's house so I can change my clothes and be ready by the time the car arrives to take me to Atlanta.

I stroll back to my room to pack up my overnight bag; I pur-
posely waited until now so I wouldn't appear overly anxious.

"Since when did you and Deonne become such good friends?"
Alyssa questions. "Y'all don't hang that much at school."

"We do hang out together. I don't have the same lunch as she
does, so we talk mostly when we're in class, and before and after
school. You'd know that if you weren't always in Stephen's face."

Lowering her voice, Alyssa says, "I think you up to something,
Divine. You might as well tell me."

"Tell you what?"

"Are you and Deonne meeting some boys somewhere?"

I laugh. "No."

She isn't buying it. "Yes, you are. Either that or y'all got some
boys coming over to the house. Y'all doing something."

"Alyssa, stop trying to play detective," I tell her. "I'm just hanging out with my girl."

"Divine, you know what Mama always says . . . what's done in
the dark always comes to light."

I dismiss her words with a slight wave of my hands. "Whatever . . .
I need to be going."

"You're going to meet up with Sean, aren't you?"

I turn around, facing her. "What I do is my business, Alyssa.
What you need to do is just tend to your own business and stay out
of mine."

"Whatever you're about to do—you better make sure Mama
and Daddy don't find out. I'm going to Stacy's house and Penny's
spending the night there too. See you on Sunday."

We hug.

I'm surprised to find Trina sitting in the family room when I
walk out of my room. "I didn't know you were here."

She's six months' pregnant now and showing. I still can't get
used to seeing her with a belly.

"Chance and I are going to the mall to price some cribs." She gives me a tiny smile. "This is really happening. I'm having a baby."

I note a flash of fear in her eyes. "It's going to be okay, Trina. You have all of us to help you. Although you know I don't do diaper duty. I'm too much of a diva for that."

She laughs. "You so crazy."

"I'll see you later. I'm spending the night with Deonne."

"Have fun."

I give her a big grin. "I intend to."

Aunt Phoebe walks out of her room wearing a loud orange sweatsuit. She even found a matching baseball hat and tennis shoes. My hands on my hips, I say, "Aunt Phoebe, what in the world are you wearing?"

"You want a ride to your friend's house don't you?"

Laughing, I nod. "Yes ma'am."

"Then keep your comments to yourself, Miss Diva."

chapter 17

$\mathcal{D}$eonne's house is not too far from ours, so it doesn't take us long to get there. Aunt Phoebe and Lisa talk for a few minutes while Deonne and I stand by, listening. Lisa's pretty good at soothing my aunt's concerns.

Everything goes according to plan and I couldn't be happier. Seated in the back of a shiny black Town Car an hour later, I release a sigh of relief when my driver, Mitch Wallace, pulls off from Deonne's house.

I place a quick call to the phone number Sean gave me. My heart skips a beat when I hear a male voice. I'm a bit surprised how mature his voice sounds—it's not squeaky, doesn't sound like a boy my age.

"Sean?"

"Hey baby. You on your way?"

"Yeah. I should be there in about an hour or so."

"I can't wait to see you face-to-face."

I can't get over how deep Sean's voice is. He sounds so much older. Probably trying to impress me, I decide.

Alyssa's words haunt me but I force them out of my mind. She is getting more and more like Aunt Phoebe. She just needs to chill.

I run my fingers through my hair, fluffing up my curls. My outfit is fierce, and I know my hair is on point; I pull out my compact to check my makeup. I have to look perfect for my new boo.

I'm on my way to Atlanta; I have a great cover story, but my heart is racing and I can't shake the disturbing quakes of anxiety I feel.

Uncle Reed would tell me that it's my spirit convicting me.

I don't like sneaking around like this, but I didn't have any other choice this time. It's not like I'm going to do anything wrong like having sex. I'm just going to meet Sean face to face. Before he's officially my boo, I need to see if he's as cute as he looks in his picture.

MY DRIVER PULLS into the parking lot of Maxwell's an hour later. The place is packed. Sean's family must do very well with the restaurant. I just hope the food is as good as he says. "I'll call you when I'm ready to leave," I tell the driver, before stepping out of the car.

I can't believe I'm here. In a few minutes, I'll be meeting Sean face-to-face.

As soon as I walk in, this tall guy comes toward me. "Dee?"

I'm too surprised to do more than nod. Instead of a sixteen-year-old boy standing in front of me, I'm looking at a tall, slender guy with a bald head and a neatly trimmed mustache wearing all black. He looks like the guy in the picture Sean sent to me but older. "*Sean?*"

The hostess comes over. "I'll take you to your table now."

I'm still checking out this guy while we walk down the narrow aisle. "You're not sixteen."

He shakes his head no. "I'll explain as soon as we're seated."

As soon as we sit down, I say, "Okay—explain. Is this some kind of joke?"

"Dee, this is not a joke. I really wanted to meet you."

"Why?" I demand. "You're like what? Twenty-five?"

He laughs. "Actually I'm only twenty-two."

I stare wordlessly across at him, my heart pounding. What have I gotten myself into? After a moment, I ask, "Why are you pretending to be sixteen years old on the internet?"

He smiles at me. "It's pretty simple. I'm a reporter and I'm doing a story on TeenSpot and other sites like it. I wanted to get to know some of the members and I met you."

My body stiffens in shock. "So I was just a story?" I'm feeling really betrayed right now.

"No. Dee, it started off that way, but then I found myself wanting to get to know you better. I really like you."

I don't respond. I don't know what I'm feeling outside of betrayal at this point. I came here expecting a boy my age and I have this . . . this *man* sitting in front of me. He's cute and all, but he's kind of old.

"I'm sorry for not telling you the truth sooner, but . . . I just didn't want to risk losing you."

I meet his gaze straight on. "Lose me? It's not like we were dating or anything." I glance down at my watch. "I'm flattered that you wanted to meet me, Sean. I really wish you'd been honest with me from the beginning. I think I should head home. I just need some time to wrap my mind around this."

"You want to leave?"

"Yeah. I think I should."

He sighs in resignation. "I don't want you to leave but if you have to—okay."

Like I need his permission. I can't believe I did all this for some old guy. I pull my cell phone out of my purse.

"I can take you home," Sean tells me.

Internal alarm bells go off in my head. "You don't have to—I'm calling my driver."

"Please, I'd really like to do this. We can talk on the way."

The waiter comes over to take our drink orders.

"I'm fine. Thank you," I say.

Sean leans back in his seat, watching me. "You're angry. I'm really sorry about this. I never meant to hurt you."

"I'm not hurt. What I feel is that I shared some really private things with a person I thought I was getting to know."

"What can I do to make it up to you?"

"I just need to go home and think about some things."

"Are you saying you don't want to talk to me anymore?"

"I don't know, Sean. Right now, I just want to leave." I pull out a card and dial the number for my driver. "Hi. I'm ready to be picked up. I'll be waiting in front of the restaurant." I hang up, then get up from the table. "I need to go."

"I'll walk you out." Sean rises as well. When I pause, he adds, "Don't be scared, baby. I'm not going to hurt you."

I don't respond.

Sean follows me out of the restaurant. He places a finger to my cheek. "You're so beautiful."

I take a step backward. "Don't do that. I'm still mad at you."

"See, this is why I couldn't tell you the truth. I didn't want you to run off like this."

"You never should've lied to me."

"Don't you think you're being a little hypocritical?"

"What are you talking about?"

"You lied to me too. Didn't you?"

Folding my arms across my chest, I give him a hard stare. "Excuse me?"

"You and I, we understand each other, my precious Divine. I know what Jerome Hardison and Kara Matthews put you through. I've known for a while that they're your parents."

"H-how?" I manage between stiff lips.

Giving a slight shrug, he responds, "It wasn't that hard. Your photos are everywhere. You're definitely not camera-shy, and you shouldn't be. You're a beautiful girl. I have to tell you, your mama is a wonderful singer." He grabs my arm, holding tightly. "You know, I've never had a celebrity before. Yeah, we gon' have ourselves a real good time. I'ma show you the house where I grew up in LaGrange—that's where all my family secrets are buried. Don't worry, you're gon' like the place. Real fine house on the outside." His smile disappears. "Inside the house . . . lots of secrets." Putting a finger to his lips, Sean gives me a hard look. "Ssssh. Soon our secrets will be buried there too."

I don't want to consider the meaning behind his words.

He starts leading me to the parking lot. "C'mon, let's go someplace quiet so we can get to know each other better. Don't even consider screaming," he warns. "I have a gun."

I feel something poking in my side. In the back of my mind, I try to think of the self-defense techniques I've been taught. I don't know if he really has a gun, but before I let this man rape me, I intend to fight to the death.

Stubbornly, I position my body into a fighting stance, something I learned in my tae kwon do class. One arm bent, with my fist facing outward at about chin level; the elbow placed to protect my ribs. I bend my other arm with my fist facing upward in front of my abdomen.

"Oh, I got me an aggressive little—"

He's momentarily distracted by bright lights as a shiny black Town Car swings into the parking lot. The driver jumps out of the car, asking, "Are you all right?"

"We're just fine," Sean answers. He tries to pull me toward a black, broken-down van with out-of-state license plates.

"I'm talking to the lady. Miss?"

I try to pull away from Sean.

"Get away from her." The driver takes a step forward. "Let the girl go."

A couple emerges from the restaurant, looking from the driver to Sean, then to me. The man takes a step forward, asking, "What's going on here?"

Sean roughly shoves me down to the ground, and then takes off to the driver's side of the van. I get up, quickly running over to where the driver is standing, while Sean makes his getaway.

"Thank you, Jesus, thank you, Jesus," I mutter over and over again.

Fear and anger knotting inside me, I suddenly give way to my tears. The couple comes over to check on me, seeking answers. The woman tries comforting me while her husband calls the police.

I try to keep my fragile control while panic is rioting within me. Minutes later I hear police sirens in the distance.

Tears fill my eyes and run down my cheeks. "Thank you for saving me," I tell the driver.

He nods. "I thank God for being in the right place at the right time."

The reality of my situation brings on another round of tears.

"Where are you staying?" the woman asks. "We need to call someone to come get you."

Lowering my gaze, I confess, "My uncle and aunt are going to be so angry when they find out about this—they didn't know what I'd planned to do."

A policewoman joins us. The driver gives her a summary of what happened. When he's done, she tells me, "We're going to have to go to the police station, miss, there's no way around this. We'll call your parents and have them meet us there."

Right now, I don't care how mad my aunt and uncle get—I just want to be with them.

Down at the police precinct, a Detective Browning grills me about Sean and how we met. "He told me his name is Sean Tyler. That's all I really know. I thought he was sixteen and he's not—he's twenty-two. At least that's what he told me. He said he was a reporter doing research on TeenSpot."

"And you met him on the internet?" she asks.

"Yes ma'am."

"Do you have a photo of this young man?"

I nod. "It's in my Yahoo account."

They allow me to use one of the computers and log on to my account to retrieve the photo. The detective prints it out.

She leaves me alone for a few minutes.

When Detective Browning returns, she says, "The guy you know as Sean Tyler is really Theopolis Mack. He's been arrested before for online solicitation of a minor and sexual assault. He's also the main suspect in the death of a young girl in Atlanta, and we think he kidnapped and killed another."

"The g-girl . . . t-the one f-from S-Savannah?" I ask, my body trembling so much that I have trouble forming the words.

She nods. "You heard about it, then?"

"Yes ma'am."

"You are a very lucky lady. God was definitely watching over you."

Her words unnerve me. "Are you going to try and find him?" I ask, my voice barely above a whisper.

"We're going to do the best we can. We have a good description of the van and the license plate number. Once we catch him, he's not going to be able to bother you again. He's going to go to prison not only for murder—two murders if we can find the other body—but also for your attempted kidnapping and attempted sexual assault."

"I want to go home."

"Would you like for me to call your aunt and uncle?"

I nod and give her the phone number.

She walks a few feet away from me to make the call. When she returns, I ask, "Are they really mad with me?"

"They told me to tell you that they love you and they're on their way."

"I can't believe I was so stupid," I mumble.

"Don't beat yourself up over it. Just learn from this experience," the detective says sternly.

One thing I know for sure; this is not something I'll soon forget.

I COLLAPSE IN Uncle Reed's arms as soon as he and Aunt Phoebe arrive at the police station. "Uncle Reed, I know you're going to kill me, but please . . . can it wait until tomorrow? I-I j-just can't handle anything else right now."

When he puts his arms around me, I hug him tight and sob loudly. The shock has worn off and the reality of everything that's happened confronts me. If that Theopolis Mack had been successful, I would've been raped and killed. The man is a serial rapist. A murderer.

Aunt Phoebe pats my back, murmuring, "I'm so glad you're okay, sugar."

She's hugging me right now, but I'm sure when she gets me home, Aunt Phoebe is going to strangle me. The thing is that I can't be mad at her because it's exactly what I deserve.

I lied to her and Uncle Reed. I came all the way to Atlanta to meet a boy I'd been chatting with online. Everybody is always warning you to never do that.

Why didn't I listen?

I take a step back, leaving the warmth of her arms. "I'm so sorry, Aunt Phoebe. Please believe me. I learned my lesson. I really did."

"I know sugar. I know."

"And please don't be mad at Deonne or Lisa. I planned everything. It's really not their fault."

"Divine, you've been through enough tonight. We'll talk about all that stuff later. Right now, I just want to focus on you. Everything else can wait."

Tears roll down my cheeks. "If you don't want me to stay with you anymore, I'll totally understand, but I hope you won't send me away. I'm sorry I'm such a screwup lately. I can be better. If you give me another chance, I promise I won't blow it."

Aunt Phoebe places her hand under my chin, forcing me to look her in the face. "Sugar, our love for you is unconditional. We have never been the type of people to just give up on anything—we are not about to give up on you. Divine, you are family. You're ours—for the good and the not-so-good times. We love you like we love our own children."

Her voice is soothing and it makes me feel safe. I don't think I ever realized it until now. When I look at my aunt and uncle, they represent a safe haven.

Uncle Reed joins us and embraces me. "I just spoke to Detective Browning and she says we can take you home now, Divine."

"I'm so glad to hear that. All I want right now is to go home," I say quietly.

"You're going to be all right, sugar. You're safe now. Your uncle and I aren't gon' let anything happen to you."

I take Uncle Reed by the hand. "Thank you for loving me

unconditionally. I never realized just how safe you and Aunt Phoebe make me feel until tonight."

"We love you, Divine. All we've ever tried to do is protect you."

"I realize that now."

Squeezing my hand, Uncle Reed says, "Okay, let's get you home."

chapter 18

At home, Alyssa is in my room waiting on me. She hugs me. "You okay?"

I nod.

The room grows silent.

"Where's Chance?" I ask.

"He's in his room talking to Trina. At least that's what he was doing not too long ago." She pauses a moment before saying, "I thought you'd like to have someone in here with you for a while." Holding up her pillow, she says, "I even brought my own because I know how stingy you are about your pillows."

"Thanks," I whisper.

We stare at each other in silence until Alyssa blurts, "I feel like this is all my fault. Divine, I'm so sorry."

I look at her, puzzled. "Why do you feel this way? How is this your fault?"

"Because I abandoned you. Maybe I should break up with Stephen."

I shake my head. "No, you can't do that. Alyssa, you love that boy."

"But I love you too. Blood *is* thicker than water."

"This isn't your fault," I try to reassure her. "Alyssa, I was the stupid one. Not you. You kept trying to warn me, but I didn't want to hear it."

"I just had a bad feeling about that guy. I can't explain it."

"I still can't believe I was so stupid. The things he would say— he sounded like, so mature. They think he's the same one who killed that girl. They also think he's responsible for the girl from Savannah."

"They still haven't found her."

"He was so close to me, Alyssa. I could feel his breath on me." Frowning, I add, "He touched my face. He knew all about my mom . . ."

"God was looking out for you, Divine. I hope you can see that."

I agree. "Looking back, I see that God was trying to give me clues that something wasn't right about tonight, but I didn't want to see it."

"Divine, let's make a promise right now to never lie to each other about anything. I want us to be able to talk about anything— even though we may not always agree. I'll do better by making myself available if you ever need me. I promise, Divine."

"I promise too. Alyssa, I also want you to promise that you'll keep your plans with me when we make them. I'm not asking for all of your time. You need to remember how it felt when Penny was all wrapped up into James. That's how you made me feel."

"I won't do that again. I didn't like Penny choosing James over me at all."

"All I could think about when that murderer tried to kidnap me was how I just wanted to be back home with you, Chance, Aunt Phoebe and Uncle Reed. I didn't know if I would ever see you all again." Tears roll down my cheeks. "I've never been so scared. It was awful."

Aunt Phoebe enters the room with two mugs of hot chocolate. "Detective Wallace told us that our Miss Diva was getting ready to take down that old pervert."

Alyssa looks over at me. "Huh?"

"I wasn't about to just let him take me somewhere. I was going to go down fighting." I accept the mug from Aunt Phoebe. "Thanks," I murmur.

Aunt Phoebe gives the other one to Alyssa, who says, "Thanks, Mama." Looking over at me, she tells me, "Girl, you crazy. You was gonna try and fight that man?"

"I was going to try and run away—I just had to find the perfect opening. Once I started running, I didn't want to be cornered somewhere."

"I don't think I could've been so brave," Alyssa admits. "I'd be too scared."

Chance joins us, smelling like burgers and fries in his Wendy's uniform. "Hey girl. You okay?"

"What about me and Mama?" Alyssa teases.

"I know y'all all right. I wanna make sure Divine's okay. I got you a bat from Wal-Mart. You can keep it under your bed. Mama says it'll help you feel safe."

I stand up and give him a hug. "I love you, Chance. Even if you do smell like a grease monkey."

Aunt Phoebe and Chance stay in my room for another thirty minutes before calling it a night.

I take a long, hot bath to wash away the touch of that horrible Theopolis Mack. I pray that I will never have to lay eyes on that monster again.

IT TAKES ME a moment to realize that the screaming I hear is coming from me. I wake up drenched in perspiration.

Alyssa is holding me. "It's okay. It's just a bad dream. You had a nightmare."

Uncle Reed and Aunt Phoebe rush into the room with Chance on their heels.

"I'm okay," I tell them. "I just had a horrible dream about that man."

"I called Kara," Uncle Reed announces. "She'll be here tomorrow."

I nod. I don't care if Mom fusses me out—I just want to see her face. I miss her and I need her so much right now.

They don't linger long in my room once they see that I'm okay.

Alyssa and I lay back down.

"I hope I didn't scare you," I say.

"You didn't," Alyssa responds sleepily. She stretches and yawns, then falls asleep fast, leaving me to listen to the night sounds— sounds that were never frightening until now. Suddenly, every little branch that hits the bedroom window disturbs my serenity.

I don't know when I fell asleep but I wake up to the sound of my mother's voice.

When did she get here? I wonder. I glance over at the clock and am shocked to see that it's almost noon. I jump out of bed just as there's a knock on my door.

"Wake up sleepyhead," my mom says, opening the door.

"I'm up," I state. "I didn't sleep well last night. Where is everybody?"

"Reed and the kids are at church. Phoebe stayed here with you."

"Are you mad at me?" I question.

"No, baby. I will admit that I'm a little disappointed in the choices you made, but I'm not mad—I'm so grateful that you're okay and I hope you learned something from this ordeal."

"Oh, I have. I'm never going to talk to another person online unless I know them well. No strangers."

"You're one of the lucky ones, honey. Praise the Lord for watching over my baby girl."

A FEW DAYS later, at school, I feel a hand on my shoulder and whirl around ready to fight. "Boy, you almost got slapped. Don't do that again."

"Hey, I heard about what happened. Are you—"

"Don't even act like you care, Madison. Just get out of my face." I don't want to be around anything male right now.

Madison's not hearing me. He steps around me, blocking my path. "Divine, I still care about you."

I shake my head. "I really can't deal with this right now. Leave me alone."

"Why can't we be friends?"

Looking him square in the face, I state, "Because friends don't treat friends the way you treated me. Madison, you have your girlfriend. *Be happy.*"

"So this is how it is?"

I nod. "Only way it can be."

He eyes me intently before finally moving out of my way.

I blamed Madison for what happened, I realize after a moment. If he hadn't dumped me the way he did, then maybe I wouldn't have gone looking for love somewhere else. Maybe I would've been able to think more clearly.

I could've been killed and it's all Madison's fault.

"Was that Madison I saw over here talking to you?" Alyssa inquires just as she's walking up.

"Yeah."

"So what did he have to say?"

"How he's sorry about what happened to me. Like I'm really believing that."

"Maybe he means it."

"Alyssa, I just want to feel like me again. I want to feel normal."

She hugs me. "I'm sorry, Divine. I wish I could make this all better for you."

"I'm so stupid."

"You're not stupid. Stop saying that," Alyssa counters. "We all make mistakes."

"But this one could've cost me my life."

"You were able to walk away, Divine. Those other girls couldn't. You've been given a second chance. Take it. Handle your business."

When Alyssa walks away, I run into Nicholas. Without saying a word, he wraps an arm around me, holding me tight. I can't explain it, but I feel a sense of security for the moment. I feel safe.

He walks me to my next class.

I make it through the rest of my school day without too many people knowing what happened over the weekend. Deonne comes to me after class, saying, "I am so sorry."

I give her a smile. "You didn't do anything. I wanted to meet him, Deonne. I have to take responsibility for my own decisions."

Alyssa joins us a few minutes later. "Y'all ready to go?"

"I'm so ready to go home. I didn't sleep well and I'm tired." I switch my backpack from my left side to my right. "I'm going to bed early tonight."

"This card came for you," Aunt Phoebe announces when we get home from school. "Somebody just stuck it in the door."

I open it. "It's from Madison," I announce.

Dear Divine:

I know you don't want to hear from me but I can't forget the look of fear on your face today when I came up behind you. It bothered me because I didn't like seeing you so scared.

I want you to know that even though you might not ever talk to me again—I'm sorry for what I did to you. You are a very nice girl and I guess I didn't appreciate that about you before.

When we broke up, my mom said I was stupid to let such a nice girl like you go. She can't stand Brittany because she knows about her reputation.

I do still care about you and always will and it bothered me to see you all hugged up with Nicholas. I know he likes you and he's an okay dude. I guess I'm just jealous.

Madison

I hand the card to Alyssa. "Read it and tell me what you think."

"He still cares a lot about you. I've always told you that he did."

"So he says," I murmur. "But it doesn't matter anymore. Did you tell him or Stephen what I said earlier?"

She shakes her head no. "I didn't mention it to anybody."

"Then how could he have known?"

"I don't think he did," Alyssa responds. "Did you ever consider that maybe this is from his heart, Divine? You know he's not seeing Brittany anymore. They broke up a couple of weeks ago."

"I didn't know." I run my fingers through my hair. "But then I really didn't need to know. It's got nothing to do with me."

"What if he wants you back?"

"I don't want to even think about that. Alyssa, my life is so jacked-up right now—I can barely focus on school."

"You're not fooling me, I hope you know. I know you're still crazy about Madison."

I pretend I don't hear her.

"Divine, you know I'm right."

"So not listening to you," I murmur. "I have to study, so if you'll excuse me . . ."

"All right . . . don't mess around and let your pride get in the way."

Alyssa stays with me for the rest of the evening.

chapter 19

Mom is in Atlanta preparing for the big family Christmas. Since I'm on break from school, I'm at the house, helping her and Miss Eula in the kitchen. She wants to get most of the cooking out of the way today so that tomorrow, we can sit down and actually enjoy Christmas Day.

"Guess what?"

I look over at Mom. "What?"

"Miss Eula is gonna stay here in Atlanta with me. Jerome and Ava want her to live with Ava, but she refused."

I hug Miss Eula. "I'm so glad. I want you to stay with us."

"I was getting tired of California," she responds. "Wanted to return to my Southern roots."

I wash my hands before pouring the cooked macaroni noodles into a baking dish.

"Will you look at that," Miss Eula utters. "Our baby girl over there cooking . . . bless her heart." Putting her hands on her ample hips, she adds, "And she act like she know what she doing too."

I laugh. "Miss Eula, I told you—I can cook a little bit."

"God is a good God. Praise Him."

Mom hands me a cup of shredded cheddar cheese. "I'm going to need another cup of cheese," I tell her. "I can tell this isn't going to be enough."

"All right now," Mom responds with a smile. "Do your thing, baby."

"Mom, stop it. You're losing cool points."

She laughs.

"What time is Kevin getting here?" I ask.

"In another hour or so. He's going to call me when he checks into his hotel room."

"Alyssa is already freaking out that he's going to be here with us for Christmas. I think she has a mad crush on him."

"They should be pulling in at any time now." Mom checks on the ham baking in the oven. "When I spoke to Reed a few minutes ago, they were about fifteen, twenty minutes away then."

Ten minutes later, we hear the doorbell. Mom checks the security monitor in the kitchen. "It's Reed."

Stella's voice comes across the intercom. "I'll get the door. I'm on my way out anyway. Merry Christmas. I'll see y'all in the New Year." Stella and her family are spending a few days with her family in Temple and then they're flying to Seattle to spend the rest of the time with Rob's family.

I go out to meet Stella in the foyer. We greet the rest of my family and welcome them inside the house.

Mom and Stella have already exchanged gifts but I wanted to wait until now to give her mine. And the one for her daughter, Jasmine.

"Wait, I have something for Jasmine." I pull a present from under the Christmas tree. "And this one is for you and Rob."

Stella hugs me. "Thanks, sweetie."

When I head back to the kitchen, I find Aunt Phoebe already pitching in. Uncle Reed is in the family room with Chance and Alyssa. I finish my macaroni and cheese dish, then stick it inside the oven.

Mom also invited Trina and her parents to have Christmas dinner with us. I thought they would turn down the invitation, but they didn't. They'll be arriving tomorrow.

It's been two weeks since the incident and because of Theopolis Mack, I don't enjoy coming to Atlanta as much as I used to—I don't feel safe here.

That evening after everyone is settled in their rooms, I go to Mom's bedroom, knocking lightly on the door.

"Come in."

I step inside the room. "Mom, can I sleep in here with you?"

She moves a stack of scripts out of my way. "Sure. Climb right on in."

"I know you think I'm a big baby right now."

Mom wraps an arm around me. "It's understandable, Divine. You've been through something very traumatic."

"This one almost cost me my life."

"God had you covered, hon. I think maybe He allowed this to happen in order to teach you a very important lesson. You weren't honest about where you were going that night, Divine, you lied to everyone."

"I know and I'm so sorry. I've apologized to Uncle Reed and Aunt Phoebe. Mom, I definitely learned an important lesson and I won't forget it anytime soon. I just hope Uncle Reed and Aunt Phoebe really know how sorry I am."

"Divine, your aunt and uncle love you so much. They only want the best for you—they want the same for you as their own flesh and blood children."

"I know."

"You once accused me of just letting them take over."

"I'm sorry."

"No, you were right. Divine, I made a mess of my life and I just didn't want to mess up yours too. I figured Reed and Phoebe were so much better at parenting—I knew they would get it right."

"I don't think you were that bad."

"That's because you trusted me. Parents betray the trust of our children when we just let them run around like maniacs. Run around without rules or regulations—no accountability."

"I understand that now. I didn't back then, but I do now."

The clock strikes midnight.

"Merry Christmas, Mom."

"Merry Christmas to you too."

"Thanks for loving me and never turning your back on me. I know sometimes I'm difficult, but I am working on being better."

"I was actually just telling God that very same thing when you knocked on my door. God is our heavenly Daddy and He loves us no matter what we do. He allows things to happen to us sometimes so that we'll learn from our mistakes."

"I guess that's what Uncle Reed is talking about when he goes around saying, grace and mercy."

Mom nods.

"Life is so hard."

She nods again.

"Well, one thing is still the same and that's that I'm still cute."

Laughing, Mom adds, "And humble."

I RUN INTO Madison outside of the cafeteria the first day back from Christmas vacation.

"I know you said you didn't want to talk to me," he begins. "But I just need to know that you're doing okay."

"I'm better," I tell him. "I don't have nightmares as much—only when I read or hear something on television about him. People have been wanting to interview me, but I can't deal with that right now. Testifying in court is going to be hard enough when the time comes. They're really trying to keep this out of the press, so please, Madison, don't tell anyone."

"I won't. I don't even think Stephen knows. The only reason Alyssa told me is because she knows how much I care about you."

"Madison, I'm sorry for all the attitude I've been giving you."

"I guess I deserved it. I didn't handle things well with you and for that I'm sorry, Divine."

"I guess this is where we start over."

He smiles. "I'd like that."

"As friends," I clarify. Right now I only want to focus on my relationship with the Lord. He saved me and He did it for a reason: to show me why teens need parents and guardians to give them guidance. I have a much better understanding why Aunt Phoebe and Uncle Reed are so protective.

"I learned from what you went through myself. I'm a dude, but we ain't even safe out there . . . you know. I was trying to hook up with some girl I met online one time, but when I talked to her on the phone—I got this weird vibe. Man, she sounded like a dude. She was trying to sound like a girl, but I wasn't feeling that. I hung up."

"You never told me about this."

"Divine, I was too embarrassed. It was stupid. But see, if I'd told you about it—maybe you wouldn't have gone off and tried to meet that dude."

"I don't know, Madison. I can be hardheaded when I want. None of this is your fault. I want you to know that. But I do think you have a point about talking about it. Maybe if I speak up I can help other girls—boys too. Maybe I can keep them from making the same mistakes I did."

"Whatever you decide to do, Divine, I got your back."

I hug him. "Thanks so much, Madison."

"I know you not ready to hear this, but I'ma say it anyway. I love you, Divine. Whenever you ready to be more than friends, I'm here. I'm here for you, boo."

Those words nearly bring me to my knees, but I fight to keep those old feelings from swaying my decision.

Be cool, I tell myself. I can't just take him back like that. Right now, it could just be the thought that I could've died that's got him being so emotional.

I vow to give myself and Madison some time to really decide what it is we want to do. In my heart I already know. My feelings for Madison are strong and never really went away.

But do I trust him with my heart a second time?

JEROME CALLS UNCLE Reed's house the following evening. His phone call is totally unexpected so I can only assume that Mom's told him what happened.

"Why you so quiet, baby girl?" he asks.

"Have you talked to Mom?"

"No. It's been a while. Since me and Ava got married, your mom don't have too much to say to me anymore."

It's going to be worse if he hears this from someone else, so I might as well get it over with and tell him what happened.

I take a deep breath, exhaling slowly before saying, "Jerome, there's something I need to tell you. I hope you won't get mad, but I'd rather you hear it from me."

"What is it?"

"I met this guy . . ." I pause and clear my throat. "I met this guy on the internet. Anyway I went to Atlanta to meet him—only it wasn't a sixteen-year-old boy like I thought. It was a man."

"A what?" he growls. "You went somewhere with a man? Girl, what were you thinking?"

"Jerome, please listen," I plead. "I really need you to listen to me."

"Okay, baby girl. I'm listening."

"I didn't go anywhere with him. He tried to kidnap me but he wasn't able to. There was another couple as witnesses, plus my driver—and I wasn't going anywhere without a fight So he just took off."

"Divine, are you all right?"

"I'm getting better. I . . . I really thought he was a nice boy, Jerome. I really did."

Jerome is silent.

"Are you there?"

"I'm here."

"Will you please say something? Yell at me—whatever. I deserve it."

"Honey, I thank the Lord that you're safe."

I hear him sniffling.

"Jerome?"

"I don't ever want anything to happen to you. I love you, Divine. I love you more than I love my own life. I don't think I realized just how much until . . ."

"I love you too."

It occurs to me that if Mom didn't tell Jerome what happened—why did he just call out of the blue like that? He usually just writes me letters.

"Did you call me for a reason, Jerome? You usually write letters."

"Yeah, I did. I wanted to tell you that you're going to have another little brother or sister."

"How?" I ask.

"Ava's pregnant."

I gasp in my surprise. "By who?"

"Divine, girl, I'm the father."

Puzzled, I mutter, "But you're in prison. You two can't . . ." I gasp. "Did you two do it in front of everybody?"

He laughs. "Silly, there are rooms for married people. Ava and I can have conjugal visits."

"Like ugh."

"You asked."

"Are you going to try and populate the world now?"

"No. I always wanted more children. Your mom and I . . . we tried but she kept losing the babies."

"Ava's going to be alone for her pregnancy," I state.

"I'm hoping you'll try and be there for her. She really loves me, Divine. Always has. She wants to be a part of your life too. Ava knows she'll never replace your mom, but she just wants to be a friend to you."

"She wants to be my second mom."

"Is anything wrong with that?" he asks me.

"Not really. I guess I can spend some time with her this summer. When's the baby due?"

"July."

"Mom's spending most of her time in Atlanta now, but I wanted to come out to Los Angeles for the summer. I guess I can stay with Ava if she doesn't mind. Can Alyssa come with me?"

"I don't think that'll be a problem. Let me clear it with Ava. Okay?"

"Wow. I'm impressed."

"What?"

"You're changing, Jerome."

"Prison will do that to a man. I never meant to take a life and even though it was an accident—I'm still in here. Mostly because I didn't trust that a jury would find me innocent. My bad boy image would've done me in. Baby girl, I can't be living that way no more. I got you and I got Jason and now this new baby on the way . . . I got to stand up and be a real man. You know what I'm saying?"

"Yes sir."

"I meant what I told you. I'ma do right by you and the other kids."

"I believe you, Jerome."

"My time's up, baby girl. I love you."

We say our good-byes and hang up.

Uncle Reed comes into the family room, where I'm sitting.

"How is your father doing?"

"He's great. In fact, he and Ava are going to have a baby."

"They are?"

I nod. "How gross is that?"

He laughs.

"Uncle Reed, it sounds like he's really starting to make some changes in his life for the better. Maybe marrying Ava was the best thing for him."

"Maybe," Uncle Reed agrees.

He sits down in his favorite recliner. "So what are we watching this evening?"

"You want to watch a movie with me?"

"Sure, if you don't mind."

He spends a lot of time at the church, and we rarely get much one-on-one time, so I jump on this opportunity. Aunt Phoebe and Alyssa are over at Trina's house with Chance. They're going shopping for baby stuff. Smiling, I say, "I'd love it, Uncle Reed."

chapter 20

"*Ava's* pregnant," I announce while Alyssa, Mom and me are having dinner at the Cheesecake Factory in Atlanta. We're having a girls' weekend, which included facials, manicures, pedicures and lots of shoe-shopping.

Mom is clearly surprised. "She is?"

"That's what Jerome told me. The baby is due in July."

"That's great. I'm so happy for them."

I survey her face to see if she's truly as happy for them as she says. Mom looks peaceful, I decide. I guess she and Jerome are really and truly over. She doesn't look like she has any regrets. She's clearly moved on with her life.

"I didn't know you could do stuff like that while you're locked up," Alyssa comments. She reaches for her soda and takes a long sip.

Mom cuts up her chicken into tiny bite-sized pieces. "Some prisons . . . allow conjugal visits for married couples."

"That's just so gross to me," I say. "I don't even want to think about it. Jerome and Ava . . . ugh."

Mom shakes her head and laughs.

"So what do you girls want to do for spring break? Have you been thinking about it?"

Alyssa shrugs. "I don't care what we do. I wish we could go somewhere now—it's cold here. Can you believe they were talking about snow? Last month it wasn't so bad, but now it's really freezing."

"It's January. I think it's one of the coldest months in the year." Mom takes a sip of her drink.

"How about we go to the Bahamas?" I suggest. "I love Nassau."

"Well, I was thinking of taking you ladies to Puerto Rico or maybe Mexico."

Alyssa can barely contain her joy. "I don't care where we go. I like all of them. I've never been outside of Temple so any place is cool with me."

"You're stupid," I say with a laugh. "I wouldn't mind going back to Martinique. I love it there."

"Can we go there?" Alyssa asks. "Divine talked so much about it—I'd like to see some of it for myself."

Mom laughs. "She told you about all the cute boys she saw on the island, didn't she?"

Alyssa nods with a grin.

"Are y'all sure about this? Martinique?"

"Yes ma'am," we say in unison.

"What about Chance? I feel bad about not asking him to come along with us."

"Mama says Chance needs to stay here in case Trina goes into labor. She's due around the time we're out for spring break."

"That's something I'm hoping to miss," I say. "Trina is a big whiner anyway. Just think—when she goes into labor she's never going to shut up."

"That's so mean," Mom says to me.

"But it's true. She whines about everything, doesn't she, Alyssa?"

"She does."

"Hon, you can be a bit of a whiner too."

I pretend to be offended. "Who? Me?" Shaking my head in denial, I add, "Not me. I'm way too cute to whine."

"And humble," Alyssa and Mom respond in unison.

"DID WE DO something wrong?" I ask when Alyssa and I are called to the family room. I run through a laundry list of things in my mind, trying to figure out what I might be in trouble for. I haven't done all of my chores, but that couldn't be it. I haven't missed curfew . . .

"Y'all feeling guilty about something?" Uncle Reed inquires.

My aunt and uncle chuckle at the expressions on our faces.

Aunt Phoebe gestures for us to sit down.

"We just wanted to talk to y'all for a moment. We've been talking and we feel we owe you and Alyssa an apology."

"For what?"

"We were wrong to assume that you two would go out and make the same choices Chance made. We were so focused on protecting you that we stopped listening to you."

"Mama, we understand that you're just trying to be a parent."

"A good parent," I contribute. "I know it can't be easy being a parent. It's definitely not easy being a teenager." I inhale and exhale slowly. "And since we're doing all this confessing, I have to say that I was wrong for lying to you and Uncle Reed. Even to you, Alyssa. I just wanted my freedom so bad. I guess I'm not really ready to start dating. For one thing, I have terrible taste in boyfriends."

"I wouldn't say that, Aunt Phoebe says. "That Madison is a really nice boy, I think."

"Great." I sigh. "Now you say that. He and I are so over. I'm like Mama right now—I'm trying to get my life right with God."

Alyssa laughs. "She says that now. In a couple of weeks, I bet it'll be a different story."

"I'm serious. I want to get right with the Lord. Until then, no boyfriends."

MADISON WALKS BESIDE me while Stephen and Alyssa trail behind us. School just let out and we're on our way home. I was surprised when Madison came running up behind us.

"Have you thought about us?" he asks.

"I have. I've thought a lot about us, but before we can get back together, there are a few things we need to get clear."

"I'm listening."

"I'm not sneaking around to see you, Madison. It just doesn't work. If you can't handle just seeing me at school . . ."

"I can live with that. Besides, I think your auntie's coming around. She's letting Stephen come over for Sunday dinner and all."

I laugh. "Yeah. She said I could invite you over for dinner too on Sunday."

"Stephen and I talked. We gon' be coming to church on Sunday."

"Our church?"

Madison nods. "I want to change my life too."

"That brings me to another thing. I am happy to be in the big V club, Madison. In case you don't know, I'm talking about being a virgin. I know you're not one but I—"

"Whoa. Girl what you talking about?"

"Didn't you do it with Brittany?"

"*No.* No, I didn't do nothing with her. Did she say something like that to you?"

I shake my head no. "I overheard some boys talking about it. They were saying you did."

"They was probably trying to mess with you."

"Madison, you don't have to lie. Everyone knows you were in a relationship with Brittany. I mean, some people do have sex."

"I didn't do nothing with Brittany. I ain't gon' lie. She wanted to have sex, but I couldn't do that. For one thing I wasn't feeling her like that. My heart still belonged to you."

"Really?"

"Yeah. I started talking to her because I wanted to make you jealous."

"Why? *You* broke up with *me*."

"But as soon as I did, I realized it was a big mistake and I tried to get you back. You turned so cold on me . . . I just wanted to get even."

"Well, it hurt me. I can't lie about that."

"The last thing I ever want to do is hurt you, Divine. Believe that."

We arrive at the corner where Stephen and Madison go one way and Alyssa and I head in another direction.

Madison leans down to kiss me but I take a step backward. "Not yet. I'm not quite ready for that part of the relationship."

Stephen and Alyssa suck face.

I give in to the urge to shout, "Aunt Phoebe's driving this way."

Both Stephen and Alyssa nearly drop to the ground, while Madison and I fall against a nearby fence laughing.

"Divine, you are not funny," Alyssa screams. "You almost gave me a heart attack."

"I couldn't help it," I manage between chuckles, tears rolling down my cheeks.

When Stephen and Madison are out of hearing distance, Alyssa utters, "I'm going to focus on my relationship with the Lord. No boyfriends for me. Yeah right."

"I feel I'm at a good place with God. I've got my priorities straight. Besides, I'm not rushing into anything with Madison. We're taking our time."

"That's good. I noticed you didn't let him kiss you just now."

"Nope. He's going to have to wait." Winking at Alyssa, I say, "I think he knows that I'm worth waiting for."

Later that evening, I'm in the middle of studying for a chemistry exam when Aunt Phoebe shouts, "Divine, sugar, come here."

I walk up to the family room. "Yes ma'am?"

"Detective Browning is here to see you."

"How are you, Miss Hardison?"

My hand clutching my shirt, I start chewing on my bottom lip. "Please tell me that you caught that murderer."

"Theopolis Mack killed himself this morning. I just got the call about twenty minutes ago. I was in Villa Rica visiting my aunt, so I came right over here to tell you myself. It's probably all over the news right now."

"He's dead?"

"You won't have to worry about him ever coming after you. He's gone. He died without ever telling us where the other girl is buried. However, he left a note confessing to killing her. Can you think of anything else he may have said to you in passing? It may have seemed unimportant to you at the time. Something you didn't tell us the last time we talked."

Tears fill my eyes and run down my face. "There was this one time he mentioned something about taking a trip to a house in LaGrange. I think he said it was where he grew up. He says all the family secrets are buried there. I was so scared at the time that it didn't really make any sense to me."

"Did he happen to mention exactly where it's located?"

Shaking my head no, I say, "Just that the house is in LaGrange. I guess he was planning to take me there after he killed me." With that sudden realization, the contents of my stomach rise to my throat.

I run off to the nearest bathroom and vomit.

After brushing my teeth and washing my face, I go back to the family room. Detective Browning is still there.

Aunt Phoebe embraces me. "You okay, sugar?"

"Yes ma'am. I'm fine."

Detective Browning asks me a few more questions before she leaves.

"I wish I could've done something more," I say to Aunt Phoebe. "I feel so bad for that girl's parents."

Pressing a hand to my stomach, I say, "It just makes me feel so sick that I can't help the police."

"Sugar, you may have helped more than you know."

I can't help but consider just how blessed I am to have gotten away from Theopolis Mack.

chapter 21

"*So* you think you ready to do this?" Madison questions.

Sitting in front of my laptop, I switch my cell phone to my other ear. "Yeah. It's time. I don't want another person getting hurt this way. If there's something I can do to keep that from happening—I'm going to do it."

"You're doing the right thing, Divine. Girl, you got a lot of courage. I'm really feeling that."

His words make me smile.

"Thanks so much, boo. I really needed to hear those words."

His sister picks up the telephone. "I need to use the phone, Madison. Hey, Divine."

"Hello, Marcia," I respond back. At least she's trying to be a little friendlier these days. I'm still wishing Madison's parents would allow him to get a cell phone. He's planning on getting a real job this summer so that he can buy his own.

"I'll be off in a minute," he tells her, with barely concealed irritation.

We talk for a few minutes more. When Marcia interrupts our conversation a second time, I say, "I need to get started, so I'll let you go for now," I say. "I'll call you later."

"Okay. But call me when you finish so that I can check it out."

"I will. I'll let you, Alyssa and probably Mimi and Rhyann read it."

I sit in front of my computer staring at the empty text box. Initially, when I sat down, I knew exactly what I wanted to say, but now I'm not so sure I can go through with it.

To write out my experience with that pervert, Theopolis Mack, means reliving every second of that fear. I know that if someone reads about my experience it might prevent them from making the same mistake—but having the courage to reveal everything is another story.

Mostly, I think I'm afraid that people will look at me as being stupid. But Madison and Alyssa both tell me that even if they do I should still share my story. Then again, it's not like I'm planning on using my real name or anything.

I don't want to preach to anybody, but I want to make other kids aware of the dangers lurking around on the internet.

I wanted a fresh start, so Alyssa deleted all of the previous entries, leaving no trace of the lies NiceGuy16 wrote.

In fact I've created a brand-new blog under a very generic name: Me02814.

I actually followed Aunt Phoebe and Uncle Reed's advice and didn't post photos of myself. I don't have any information relating to me under the profile section. In fact, I even signed up for yet another free web-based email address for use exclusively with this blog.

I take a deep breath, exhaling slowly. Gathering my thoughts together, I begin typing.

The words come slowly at first, and then gradually my fingers start to race across the keyboard.

I came across this slogan on a safe surfer website linked to the National Center for Missing and Exploited Children that says: Don't Believe the Type. I can truly identify with this message because I was a victim. I actually fell for the words this murderer typed to me. I believed every word and today I am very blessed to be alive.

My experience has not only opened my eyes to the evil that exists in the world, but it's opened my family's eyes as well.

I now have the full support of my aunt and uncle to use this blog for sharing my testimony and hopefully educate others on the importance of internet safety. I don't want another boy or girl to go through what I experienced. Even though I survived the ordeal and the man is dead, I still wake up sometimes in the middle of the night totally freaked. I'm more jumpy now. I hope by other kids reading this, they will spread the word to their friends and family members.

Do not share private information or exchange pictures with someone you don't know. Always think before you respond to any questions. Perverts are experts in getting information from you before you even realize you've told them anything. The main thing is to never ever meet someone in person, especially when you're alone.

Out of all of this, one of the most important lessons that I've learned is one that I know will stay with me forever.

It's tough being a parent, it's tough being a teen and it's really tough being a follower of Jesus, but in all things and in all situations, the question we should always ask ourselves is, what would Jesus do?

Me

author's note

I hope you have enjoyed reading *Divine Confidential*. While the story is a fictional one, the issues portrayed are not. According to the Cyber Tip Line, one in five kids are sexually solicited over the internet—and chat rooms are probably the most dangerous places.

There are thousands of chat rooms, websites and other places online containing things that may make you feel scared, uncomfortable or confused, whether sexual and/or violent in nature. Just remember that you hold the power to leave any area you feel you shouldn't be in.

When surfing the internet, please remember Divine's advice:

- Never share your personal information with a stranger or post information such as pictures, your home address or phone number in profiles.
- Never ever meet someone in person that you don't know.
- Keep the lines of communication open with your parents and/or guardians.

You can help delete online predators by reporting them to: www.cybertipline.com.

Readers' Group Guide for
divine confidential

Summary

Divine Matthews-Hardison is back! After spending the summer in the glamorous world of Hollywood, Divine returns in the sequel to *Simply Divine*, to live with her aunt, uncle and cousins in the small town of Temple, Georgia. She can't wait to get back to her family . . . and her boyfriend, Madison.

But tenth grade holds some surprises. Her aunt and uncle won't allow her to see boys outside of school, her cousin Alyssa doesn't seem to have time for her anymore, and the kids around her are getting into trouble—serious trouble. When Divine turns to internet chat rooms for support, she finds an internet predator instead. Once again, Divine finds that she must turn to her family, and to her faith, for answers and support.

A Conversation with Jacquelin Thomas

Q. **Why did you choose to continue Divine's story in *Divine Confidential*?**

A. I fell in love with the character and just wanted to explore her teen years further.

Q. How do you see Divine's evolution from the beginning of *Simply Divine* to the end of *Divine Confidential*?

A. I think she's matured some—she's definitely learned what it means to have the love of family, and she's growing in her faith.

Q. Teenagers face many difficult issues. Why did you choose to focus on the physical, emotional, and spiritual dangers of sex?

A. Because teens are dealing with this on a daily basis. Not only are they struggling to deal with their own feelings, but they are being pressured by others to have sex. It's on television, the radio—everywhere. To them, being sexual has become the norm, but I want to remind them of the importance of abstinence.

Q. In spite of being "Hollywood royalty," Divine Matthews-Hardison faces many of the same difficulties dealt with by teens everywhere. What do you hope your teenage readers will learn from her story?

A. That it doesn't matter how much money you have, how you look, or where you live—our experiences are universal.

Q. In both *Simply Divine* and *Divine Confidential* you stress the importance of family, especially parents, in the lives of teenagers. What do you think constitutes a healthy relationship between teens and their parents? What is the best advice you can offer parents and their teens?

A. Communication is key. Parents should not only talk to their children, they have to listen as well. Teens should feel comfortable enough with a parent to share what's really going on without fear of judgment. Also, while it's good to be a friend to your teen, it's more important to be the parent. Teens need guidance.

Q. **Divine's parents, Jerome and Kara, have made some pretty major mistakes in their lives. Jerome, in particular, has made the same mistake as Chance—having a baby out of wedlock. Why do you include Jerome and Kara's stories in a novel focused on the choices teenagers make?**

A. Because I want to remind teens that parents are not perfect—they're human and they make mistakes. Mostly I wanted to show that teens should hold their parents accountable and vice versa.

Q. **Is it difficult to write from the perspective of a fifteen-year-old girl? How did you keep your own, adult sensibility from creeping into Divine's voice?**

A. It's challenging in that it's been a looong time since my teen years. But having raised teenage daughters and now a son who will soon be entering his preteen years, it's getting easier. Also I've had some help from the teens at church.

Q. **Did anything in your own experience help shape *Divine Confidential*?**

A. I'm very passionate about the plight of missing and exploited children. I wanted to bring awareness to the dangers of the internet in this book because so many readers identify with Divine and her friends. Most often, we aren't affected by a situation until it happens to us or someone we know. By living Divine's experience with her, I hope readers will walk away with a better awareness of the situation.

Q. One of the things that seems to drive Divine to the internet chat rooms is the loneliness and insecurity she feels after being dumped by her boyfriend, Madison. What advice would you give teenagers dealing with similar feelings?

A. Meeting someone on the internet is not the answer. Try reading a book or journaling your feelings. Talk to friends or a family member. The Cyber Tip Line has a wonderful tag line: Don't Believe the Type. Internet predators are looking for teens who are hurting and feeling lonely—they are skilled in drawing you out and getting inside your head. You can't trust emails, photos, or even the voices. Be smart and be safe.

Q. What role does faith play in Divine's story? How can religion help other teens?

A. God is the answer to all of the problems in the world. He really is. Divine had a lesson to learn, and while the temptation to sneak off to meet Sean was great—God had provided several opportunities for her to change her mind. I want readers to remember: God always gives you an escape. You only have to make the right choice. Daily prayer and reading your Bible will help you make the right decisions. Don't know how to pray? Email me at: prayer@simplydivinebooks.com.

Questions for Discussion

1. Describe Divine's arrival in Atlanta in the opening scene of the book. What do you gather about Divine's relationship to her aunt, uncle, and cousin Alyssa from the way she greets them in the first few pages?

2. "Blood is thicker than water," Kara says when she learns that Divine and Alyssa have been fighting. Family ties are tested

and strained many times in this novel. What are some of the things that threaten to pull Divine's family apart? How does the family overcome these problems?

3. Trust is an important theme in *Divine Confidential*. Discuss the ways that trust is gained, lost and restored in the relationships portrayed in the novel.

4. At the end of chapter one, Divine says, "I feel like I've changed a lot since becoming a Christian a few months ago, but then there are days when I think I'm the same Divine I've always been." How has Divine changed? How is she the same?

5. How does Trina's pregnancy affect the lives of the other characters in the book? What type of mother would Trina be?

6. Is Divine's anger over Alyssa and Madison's friendship justified? How should Divine have handled the situation?

7. Do you think Aunt Phoebe and Uncle Reed are overprotective? Are their rules about dating fair?

8. What compels Divine to get involved in internet chat rooms? Is this behavior in character, or do other factors contribute to this activity?

9. How does sex affect Divine and the other teenagers in the book? Do you think their experiences are typical of most teenagers?

10. Why do predators like Theopolis Mack use the internet to connect to their victims? What are some of the dangers of the internet, especially for teenagers, and how can people avoid them?

Activities to Enhance Your Book Club

1. Do some research on internet safety. How do internet predators gain access to their victims? What can teenagers do to stay safe on the internet? Find a way to spread the word about what you've learned. Write an email message and forward it to friends, or design posters to display at your school.

2. Fashion is very important to Divine. For your next meeting, everyone should come dressed as their favorite character from *Divine Confidential*.

3. Hold your discussion over a dinner of homemade Southern foods. Find recipes at www.soulfoodcookbook.com.

"*Mimi,* I'm dying for you to see my dress," I say into the purple-rhinestone-studded cell phone. "It's this deep purple color with hand-painted scroll designs in gold on it. I have to be honest. I—Divine Matthews-Hardison—will be in *all* the magazines. I'll probably be listed in the top-ten best-dressed category."

Mimi laughs. "Me too. My dress is tight. It's silver and strapless and Lana Maxwell designed it."

"Oh, she's that new designer. Nobody really knows her yet." I'm hatin' on her because she's allowed to wear a strapless gown and I had to beg Mom for days to get her to let me wear a halter-style dress.

I make sure to keep my voice low so that the nosy man Mom claims is my dad can't hear my conversation. It's a wonder Jerome actually has a life of his own—he's always trying to meddle in mine.

I can tell our limo is nearing the entrance of the Los Angeles Convention Center because I hear people screaming, and see the rapid flashing of cameras as diehard fans try to snap pictures of their favorite celebrities while others hold up signs. I'm glued to the window, checking out the growing sea of bystanders standing on both sides of the red carpet.

The annual Grammy Awards celebration is music's biggest night and the one major event I look forward to attending every year. Singers, actors and anyone really important will be present. Media coverage is heavy and I know as soon as I step out of the limo, the press is going to be all over me.

Settling back in the seat, I tell Mimi, "I'll talk to you when you get here. I need to make sure my hair is together. You know how these photographers are—they're like always trying to snap an ugly picture of celebrities to send all over the world. That's the last thing I need—some whack photo of me splashed all over the tabloids. See you in a minute. Bye."

Cameras flash and whirl as limo after stretch limo roll to a stop. I put away my phone and take out the small compact mirror I can't live without, making sure every strand of my hair is in place. A girl's gotta look her best, so I touch up my lips with Dior Addict Plastic Gloss in Euphoric Beige. I like this particular lip gloss because the color doesn't make my lips look shiny or too big in photographs.

I pull the folds of my gold-colored silk wrap together and blow a kiss to myself before slipping the mirror back into my matching gold clutch. I'm looking *fierce*, as my idol Tyra Banks loves to say on *America's Next Top Model*. To relieve some of the nervous energy I'm feeling, I begin tracing the pattern of my designer gown. This is my first time wearing what I consider a grown-up gown. I've never been able to wear backless before, but thankfully, my mom has a clue that I'm not a baby anymore. I'll be fifteen soon.

"Divine, honey, you look beautiful," Mom compliments. "Anya did a wonderful job designing this gown for you. It's absolutely perfect. Doesn't make you look too grown up."

My smile disappears. She just had to go there.

"Thanks." As an afterthought, I add, "You do too."

My mom, renowned singer and actress Kara Matthews, is up for several Grammys. On top of that, she's scored starring roles in three blockbuster movies, one of which will have her leaving in a couple of weeks to film the sequel in Canada. She can be pretty cool at times but then she goes and ruins it by going into Mom mode. To get even, I say and do things to wreck her nerves. Like . . .

"I hope I see Bow Wow tonight. He's so hot . . ." I can't even finish my sentence because the look on Mom's face throws me into giggles. My dad, Jerome, comes out of an alcohol-induced daze long enough to grumble something unintelligible.

He's never allowed me to call him daddy. Says it makes him feel old, so he insists that I call him Jerome.

Hellooo . . . get a clue. *You are old.*

It used to bother me that Jerome didn't want me calling him Dad when I was little. But after all the crazy stuff he's done, I'd rather not tell anyone he's related to me. Although I've never actually seen him drink or whatever, I've watched enough TV to know what an addict looks like. If I could sell him on eBay, I'd do it in a heartbeat. I can just picture the ad in my head.

Hollywood actor for sale. Okay-looking. Used to be real popular until he started drinking and doing drugs. By the way, he really needs a family because he's on his way out of this one. Bidding starts at one dollar.

Mom interrupts my plans to auction Jerome by saying, "Divine, I don't want you sniffing around those rap artists. You stay with me or Stella. *I mean it.* Don't go trying to sneak off like you usually do. I don't care if Dean Reuben lets Mimi run around loose. You better not!"

Mom and Jerome make a big deal for nothing over me talking to boys. Period. I'm fourteen and in the eighth grade. I'm not even allowed to date yet, so I don't know why they're always bugging whenever I mention meeting guys. I will admit I get a thrill out of the drama, so I figure giving them a scare every now and then can't hurt.

"You stay away from that Bow Wow," Jerome orders. "He's a

nice kid, but you don't need to be up in his face. Don't let that fast tail Mimi get you in trouble."

This subject has so come and gone. All his drinking must be making him forgetful or something. Rolling my eyes heavenward, I pull out my cell phone, flip it open and call my best friend just to irritate him.

"Mimi, we're about to get out and stroll down the red carpet," I say loud enough for him to hear. "Where's your car now?" Mimi's dad is an actor too. He's always out of town working, which Mimi loves because then she can run all over her entertainment-lawyer mom. Her dad is the strict one in her family. For me, it's Mom. She's the only grown-up in my family.

Our limo stops moving. The driver gets out and walks around to the passenger door.

"We're here, Mimi. I'll see you in a few minutes." I hang up and slip the phone into my gold evening bag.

Cameras flashing, the media are practically climbing all over the limo. As usual, my mom starts complaining. But if the media isn't dogging her, her publicist comes up with something to get their attention, which isn't hard to do with my dad's constant legal battles. I just don't get Mom sometimes.

Mom claims she doesn't really like being in the spotlight and the center of attention, but me, I love it. I'm a Black American Princess and I'm not ashamed to admit it. I take pleasure in being pampered and waited on. Mostly, I love to shop and be able to purchase anything I want without ever looking at a price tag.

"I wish I had a cigarette," Mom blurts. "I'm so nervous."

I reach over, taking her hand in mine. "Don't worry about it. I hope you win, but even if you don't, it's still okay. At least you were nominated."

She smiles. "I know what you're saying, sweetie. And you're right, but I *do* want to win, Divine. I want this so badly."

"I know." Deep down, I want it just as bad as she does. I want

Mom to win because then I'll have something to hold over that stupid Natalia Moon's head. Her mother is singer Tyler Winters. As far as I'm concerned, the woman couldn't sing a note even if she bought and paid for it. And I'm pretty sure I'm not the only one who thinks so, because she's never been nominated for a Grammy.

The door to the limo opens.

Leo, our bodyguard, steps out first. He goes everywhere with us to protect us from our public. There are people out there who'll take it to the extreme to meet celebrities.

Mom's assistant Stella gets out of the car next. All around us, I hear people chanting, "Kara . . . Kara . . . Kara."

A few bystanders push forward, but are held back by thick, black velvet ropes and uniformed cops.

"They love you, Mom."

Smiling, my mom responds, "Yeah . . . they sure do, baby."

I'm so proud to have *the* Kara Matthews as my mom. She's thin and beautiful. Although she's only five feet five inches tall, she looks just like a model. I have her high cheekbones and smooth tawny complexion, but unfortunately, I'm also saddled with Jerome's full lips, bushy eyebrows and slanted eyes. Thankfully, I'm still cute.

"Hey, what about me? I got some fans out there. They didn't just come to see yo' mama. She wouldn't be where she is if it wasn't for me."

I glance over my shoulder at Jerome, but don't respond. He's such a loser.

I have a feeling that he's going to find a way to ruin this night for Mom. Then she'll get mad at him and they'll be arguing for the rest of the night.

I've overheard Mom talk about divorcing Jerome a few times, but when he gets ready to leave, she begs him to stay. I wish they'd just break up because Jerome brings out the worst in Mom, according to Stella.

Stella turns and gestures for me to get out of the limo. It's time to meet my public.

Okay . . . my mom's fans. But in a way, I'm famous too. I'm Hollywood royalty. Kara Matthews's beloved daughter.

I exit the limo with Leo's assistance. Jerome will follow me, getting out before Mom. She is always last. Her way of making an entrance, I suppose.

I spot a camera aimed in my direction. I smile and toss my dark, shoulder-length hair across my shoulders the very same way I've seen Mom do millions of times.

Mom makes her grand appearance on the red carpet amid cheers, handclapping and whistles. We pose for pictures.

Here we are, pretending to be this close and loving family.

What a joke!

I keep my practiced smile in place despite the blinding, flashing darts of light stabbing at my eyes. It's my duty to play up to the cameras, the fans and the media.

I can't imagine my life any other way. . . .